DARK WHISPERS

HELEN HARPER

CHAPTER ONE

THE FOURTH PLINTH AT TRAFALGAR SQUARE IN THE CENTRE OF London is a wonderful thing. Usually. Instead of a rigid stone statue, temporary artworks and sculptures take pride of place, ranging from an enormous bright blue cockerel to the marble torso of a disabled female artist.

I'd always appreciated the showcasing of different artists' work; they added unusual dimensions and a less traditional air to the large square. I did *not* appreciate a supposed vampire drenched in blood dancing around on top of the plinth with a lethal-looking knife in one hand. A vampire whose naked body I'd been tasked with removing.

'How long has he been up there?' I enquired to nobody in particular.

One of the uniformed bobbies drafted in from the nearest station shrugged. 'About ninety minutes, I'd say. Apparently he came prepared. He stripped off, climbed up and poured a bucket of blood over his head.' The policeman paused. 'He must have brought the bucket of blood with him,' he added unnecessarily.

'Uh-huh.' I squinted up at the plinth. It was cold and there was a steady drizzle that was doing nothing for my mood. It didn't seem to bother the guy, however, or the late-night tourists and passers-by who were pretending to be shocked but whom I suspected were feeling titillated delight rather than genuine revulsion.

'I will suck your blood!' the man yelled, hopping from foot to foot. 'I am a creature of the night and I will sink my fangs into your throat and drink you all dry! Don't get too close or you'll all end up dead.' There was a note of fearful hysteria to his words despite the threat.

I noted the empty bucket lying a few feet away from the plinth. Thick, half-congealed blood stained the steel interior. I hoped it wasn't human in origin. That would be all we needed.

I peered more closely at the man. The parts of his face that weren't covered in the sticky red stuff displayed signs of acne, and his dark hair was receding. His cheeks were sunken and he didn't appear particularly healthy. There also seemed to be some shallow cuts across his thin arms, bony chest and upper thighs. I winced. He'd probably self-harmed.

'We've tried to get him down, but every time we get close he either slashes himself or threatens to slash us,' the policeman explained. 'Sooner or later someone will get hurt.'

Someone was *already* hurt. I sighed. Mental health still isn't taken nearly seriously enough in this country.

A well-dressed woman pushed her way towards us, her nose raised imperiously. 'I hope you'll do something about this soon. It's disgusting that this sort of thing is allowed to happen. That monster should be locked up. Look at him waving his bits about like that! It's a disgrace! There are children present!'

I found it curious that she was more concerned about his lack of clothes than the fact that he was covered in blood, waving a long-bladed knife in the air and self-harming. It was eleven o'clock at night and I couldn't see any children around. I believe we make too much of an issue about nudity, but maybe I've become immune to such things after all the time I've spent around werewolves. Given their shapeshifting natures, they are frequently in a state of undress.

'We are dealing with it, ma'am,' I said politely. 'I suggest you move along.'

She bared her teeth at me in a manner strangely reminiscent of the supes. 'Dratted vampires. They think they own this city. We should get rid of the lot of them.' She whirled away and marched off with her heels clicking. I didn't watch her leave.

'Should we call DS Grace?' the young policeman asked.

'He has the night off. I'm on call.' I gazed at the man on the plinth. Blood was dripped down his pale body, mingling with the raindrops and pooling at his feet. It was hard to judge how much of his own blood he'd lost from his cuts, but he had to be feeling light-headed.

'What about Lord Horvath? Can't you call him?' The policeman was well-trained enough not to wring his hands and display his anxiety, but it was obvious from the slight tremor in his voice.

'There's no point,' I said.

The focus of our interest spun round on his toes, wobbled and nearly lost his balance. The watching crowd gasped. 'Don't worry about me!' he shouted. 'I am supernatural! I could fall from the top of the Shard and I would recover.' He thumped his chest. 'I. Am. Immortal.'

No, he wasn't. I sighed again.

'Why not? Why can't you call him?' the policeman demanded.

'Because that man up there is not a vampire,' I said. 'He's not even a supe. He's human, which means he is not Lord Horvath's responsibility.' I wasn't yet sure whether the plinth's occupant was delusional and genuinely believed he was a vampire, or whether there was more to this.

'How – how – how do you know that?'

I pursed my lips. 'Without wishing to denigrate his appearance, the simple truth is that vampires are more physically attractive and less clumsy than him. And they're not immortal, no matter what people believe.'

I shook my head. Vampire or not, the man had to be dealt with before matters got out of hand. I straightened my shoulders. The faster I got him down and into the hands of a competent medical professional the better.

Marching up to the base of the plinth, I angled my head upwards. 'Hey,' I said. 'How's it going?'

'Step back! Step back, puny human! I could kill you so easily! You don't know what I'm capable of!'

I probably had a better idea than he did. And I'm not human – not technically.

'Sir,' I said, watching him carefully. The cuts across his skin were numerous but didn't appear life-threatening, and he wasn't shivering. Given the chill in the air and the ongoing drizzle, plus his unnaturally thin body, that was strange. 'My name is Emma Bellamy. I'm a detective constable with Supernatural Squad and I can help you. Why don't I help you down and get you a blanket and a hot mug of tea, then we can talk about your situation?'

The man spread his arms wide. 'I don't drink tea! I drink blood!' He threw his head back and laughed uproariously. 'I *only* drink blood!'

I didn't blink. 'Then we'll get you some blood, if that's what you'd prefer.' I reached down, picked up the bucket and gave it a sniff. I'm not a vamp and I don't have the skills of a werewolf, so I couldn't tell if the gloopy remnants were human or not. Either way, it was gruesome.

I held the bucket towards the man. Perhaps he would tell me. 'There's a bit of blood left in here,' I suggested. 'If you're thirsty.'

'Pah.' He turned his head away in disgust. 'It doesn't work. It's pig's blood. The Chief told me it wouldn't work, and he was right. I need human blood.'

Interesting. 'The Chief?' I asked. 'Who's that?'

He didn't seem to hear me – or he didn't want to.

I tried a different tack. 'What's your name?'

He looked at me suspiciously, as if he believed I was trying to catch him out. Close up, his pupils were dilated and his skin appeared pale and clammy beneath the streaks of blood. Drugs. Perhaps that was why he wasn't feeling the cold and was convinced he was a supe. But that was an easy explanation for all this drama, and in my experience easy explanations were often not true.

I pushed up onto my tiptoes and lowered my voice, forcing the man to crouch to hear me. I could have grabbed him and hauled him down, but that would only have heightened his anxiety and probably caused even more problems. 'I'm a supe like you,' I murmured. 'We don't usually give out our real names, but I gave you mine so now it's okay for you to give me yours.' I gestured between us. 'It makes us equals, you see.'

He frowned at me and scratched his head. His hair and fingers were sticky with blood. 'You're a vampire?'

'I'm something else.'

The crease between his eyebrows deepened. 'I didn't hear you before,' he said in an overly loud whisper. 'What's your name?'

'Emma,' I said. 'You can call me Emma.'

His brown eyes shifted from left to right. 'I am the Night Stalker.'

Er…

'But you can call me Jim.'

I smiled. That was better. 'Nice to meet you, Jim.'

He started to shake his head. 'Oh no. It's not nice at all. *I'm* not nice. I'm evil and dangerous. You don't want to know me. I'm not cured, you see. I'm a vampire. And I *will* hurt you.'

I nodded. 'Okay.' Sometimes it's better to play along. 'How long have you been a vampire, Jim?'

'Nine months,' he whispered.

I let out a low whistle. 'Not long. We all know that young vampires are the most dangerous.'

'I am *very* dangerous. If you get too close, I'll rip out your throat with my teeth.' He opened his mouth, showing me his normal incisors in all their human glory. 'See?'

'I do see.' I held up my hands as if in submission so that he'd believe that I agreed with him. I was beginning to get an idea how I could bring this stand-off to an end. 'Why don't you give me the knife, Jim?' I suggested. 'Then I can use it to defend myself against you.'

He looked confused, then glanced at the weapon he was holding tightly in his right hand as if he'd forgotten it was there. 'This isn't for you,' he said. 'It's for me. I need it to stop myself from hurting you.' His eyes widened and he looked around. 'Or anyone else. There are a lot of people here.'

I made a gesture behind my back, indicating to the uniformed police officers waiting behind me that they should move the watching crowd further away. Then I reached up, keeping my movements very slow so that Jim could see what I was doing, and placed my hand gently on his wrist.

'I told you already,' I said. 'I'm a supe. You can't hurt me like you might hurt other people. Give me the knife and I'll take care of it for you.' I looked into his eyes. 'You know my real name, so you can compel me to return it to you whenever you want.' That wasn't true, of course. Even if Jim were a supe, it was highly unlikely he could achieve such a feat – but he didn't know that.

'Really?' he asked.

'Really.'

He sucked on his bottom lip for a moment. 'Okay, then. Okay.' He released his grip on the knife and I reached out carefully to take it from him – but unfortunately that was the very moment a motorbike roared down the road behind us, its engine backfiring loudly.

Jim panicked and I saw the power of reason leave his eyes, to be replaced with pure fear and zero logic. He tightened his grip on the knife once more and lunged forward. I turned my head but the blade's tip still sliced into the soft flesh of my cheek, followed a moment later by throbbing pain and the gush of my own hot blood. Shit.

There were screams from some of the people behind me but I paid them no attention. All my focus had to be on Jim.

'No,' he muttered. 'Oh no.' He turned the blade towards himself.

I had no choice – I had to act. I leapt up, my body colliding with his as I reached for the knife to make him drop it. He clutched at me, shock and horror mingling in his expression, as momentum carried us backwards onto the ground below.

I managed to half-twist in mid-air so that my body took more of the impact than his. It was an instinctive move – and an incredibly stupid one. My movements not only caused Jim's body to spin but also his hand, and when we landed I felt the knife blade slice deep into my side. Fuck. That hurt. That really hurt.

Jim realised what had happened a few seconds after I did. He sprang away and finally let go of the weapon. 'I didn't mean to do that! I didn't mean to do that!'

The uniforms were already moving towards us, tasers and batons raised. I gritted my teeth and hauled myself up to a sitting position. 'Wait,' I called. 'Let me…'

It was too late. They ran at Jim – and he ran away. I hissed and reached for the knife, squeezing my eyes shut before yanking it out of my body and letting it clatter to the ground. Involuntary tears of pain sprang to my eyes but I couldn't waste time feeling sorry for myself. I scrambled up and, clutching my leaking wound, ran after the lot of them.

The pain shattered my body. Every step made me want to scream in agony but nevertheless I ploughed ahead. Even at my worst, I'm faster than any human at their best. I've died enough times, and gained enough strength and power as a result, to push my body to inhuman limits.

I blocked out as much of the hurt as I could, locking it away into a corner of my mind. The blood pouring from my side didn't matter, neither did the fact that I was almost certain the tip of the blade had nicked one of my kidneys. I crossed Trafalgar Square and darted across the road towards the Mall. I could see the running shapes in front of me and hear the police officers yelling at Jim to stop. He ignored them as he sprinted towards St James's Park.

At least it wasn't full moon, I thought. At least the park wasn't full of bloodthirsty werewolves unable to control their baser urges. Then his fleeing form was swallowed by the line of trees. Shit. He'd be a lot harder to find now.

I overtook the first police officer as he burst into the park, then passed the second one before the trees gave way to the silent paths beyond. Within moments I'd drawn level with the other two, who were thundering towards the small lake. I passed them too, feeling their uncomprehending stares at my back. I ignored them in the same way that I ignored the pain, and continued searching for Jim. I couldn't see him. Where had he gone? Which direction had he taken now?

There was a splash to my left, followed by a series of surprised and unhappy quacks from some slumbering ducks that had been disturbed. There. Down that way.

I sucked in a breath and turned towards the noise but it was too damned dark and, despite my best efforts, I hurt too damned much. I searched the trees and scanned the empty grass and quiet lake.

Jim had gone.

* * *

DAWN WAS SLIDING its way across the horizon when DSI Barnes appeared. She passed me a cup of coffee and sat down beside me on the pavement. 'You wouldn't think it's that hard to find a naked man in the centre of London,' she said. 'And yet it appears to be.'

I grunted and took a sip. The coffee was lukewarm but it still tasted like nectar on my dry tongue. Little dots kept appearing in front of my eyes and my legs felt weak. I knew I was in a bad way.

'You look like shit,' Barnes observed.

I didn't bother responding.

'Are you sure that this man is human?' she asked.

'Yep.'

'He's obviously very dangerous.'

'Only to himself.'

Barnes didn't miss a beat. 'He stabbed you.'

'That was my fault, not his.'

'All the same,' she said, 'not everyone can recover like you can. It would be prudent to find him as quickly as possible before he attacks someone else.'

Suddenly I felt very, very tired. 'We've been looking. We called in reinforcements. Unless you know something that I don't, he's in the wind.' I took another gulp of the coffee. 'I'll sort out this wound in my side and then I'll look some more. He can't have gone far – he'll have found somewhere to hole up. If I can get a lead on his identity, that will help. Night Stalker Jim will show up sooner or later.'

Barnes watched me silently.

'What?' I asked.

She still didn't say anything. Frustration flared, momentarily overtaking the throbbing pain of my knife wound. Bloody hell. 'I was called out,' I muttered. 'I didn't volunteer.'

'You were called out because he was believed to be a vampire, Emma. He's human and therefore no longer your concern.'

I hated starting something and not finishing it. 'Whoever he is, he needs help not handcuffs.'

'I'm not arguing with that,' she said calmly. 'All I'm saying is that he doesn't fall under Supe Squad's remit. I've already spoken to DS Grace. He agrees with me.'

'I know those are the rules,' I said stiffly. 'And I know I didn't speak to him for long. But I established a connection with him and I honestly think...'

She shook her head. 'Your part is over. Everyone at the Met appreciates the effort you put in. Everyone also knows that you have other concerns right now, with the supe summit due to start. Your priorities lie elsewhere.' She tilted her head and gazed at me. 'You don't need me to tell you that. The case has already been passed on.'

'Fine.' I sighed. I knew she was right. I didn't really have the inclination – and I certainly didn't have the time – to go searching for a human. Let's face it, my resistance was more out of habit than desire. 'Did you bring it?' I asked, changing the subject.

She nodded. 'I also took the liberty of calling Horvath, who has sent a car. I'd prefer it if you did it in there rather than out in the open. Anti-supe sentiment is on the rise. The last thing we need is a public display of supernatural abilities.'

'You realise that sooner or later the supes will fight back if things continue as they are,' I said quietly

'I'm more than aware of that.'

'They might not have much in the way of numbers, but they do have strength. And wealth. And generations of oppression to stir them up.'

She cocked her finger at me. 'I recruited you for Supe Squad, remember? I don't need reminding that we're sitting on a tinder keg that could blow at any moment. The summit will go a long way towards defusing tensions. It's a good idea.'

I was glad she thought so. Sometimes it was hard to know what Barnes was thinking. 'Have you heard anything from the minister yet?' I asked.

Barnes's expression was studiously blank. 'The Minister for

Supernatural Affairs has informed me that he has a minor operation scheduled and unfortunately will be unable to attend the summit.'

Damn it. 'Is that the truth? Or is he looking for an excuse to stay away because he thinks the summit will crash and burn?'

'Well,' she murmured, 'when I suggested that the Home Secretary take his place, I received little more than howls of laughter.'

My stomach tightened in a brief spasm of anger. Supes are citizens of this country as much as humans are. I knew that Lukas and some of the more powerful supes had lines of communication with various members of the government, and that often discreet favours were exchanged. But the supe summit wasn't going to be discreet. That was the entire point.

'If the summit is a success, it won't matter,' Barnes said. 'The government will backtrack quickly enough and offer its support.'

Yeah, yeah. At this late stage it wasn't worth getting my knickers in a twist, but it was still annoying.

DSI Barnes stood up and held out a hand to help me. I was more than happy to accept it. I flashed her a smile then we hobbled over to a sleek black limousine. I didn't need to peer inside to know that Lukas was in there waiting for me. My heart warmed instantly. This would be easier with him next to me.

'You're not quite at death's door, you know,' Barnes said. 'You can still go to hospital and get patched up properly.'

'The recovery time will take too long, and I don't have the weeks or months to spare. My way is faster.'

'Hmmm.' She passed me a small black bag. 'I can't say I like this, Emma.'

'I can't say I like it either.' I managed a smile and opened the bag to check the contents. 'Thank you.'

DSI Barnes was too discomfited to tell me I was welcome.

'Don't worry,' I said. 'This way I'll be back at work before evening.' I winked at her, opened the car door and got into the back seat. I waved at Barnes before the door closed and turned to Lukas. 'Thanks for picking me up.'

He leaned across, gave me a brief kiss and glared at the bag. 'This is not a good idea.'

'It's a great idea.'

'D'Artagnan…'

'My body, Lord Horvath. My rules.' I looked at the plastic sheeting covering the seats. 'Besides, you've clearly come prepared.'

He looked away, pain flashing across his face.

'Will you hold me?' I asked. 'While I do it?'

'If that's what you want.' His voice was stiff.

I reached up and touched his face. 'You don't have to.'

He growled. 'Yes, I do.'

I kissed him again, more deeply this time. Then I reached into the bag, pulled out the small handgun and prepared to shoot myself in the head.

It really was better this way.

CHAPTER TWO

I NEEDED TO PEE.

The thought pushed insistently into my consciousness. I grunted and shoved it away. I was warm and snug and far too comfortable to heave myself from bed. It was three nights since I'd encountered Jim and killed myself to avoid weeks of painful recovery, and I was still enjoying the luxury of sleeping at night. It certainly beat searching through a dark park while slowly bleeding out. Duvets over death any time. I kept my eyes resolutely closed. I'd drift back to sleep in a moment … any moment now, in fact.

Unfortunately my bladder had definitely decided against the joy of unbroken sleep. I could pretend all I wanted, but it wasn't going to work; I definitely – *urgently* – needed to pee. I opened one eye and peered at the clock. Twenty-two minutes past four. I had to get up at six; the least my damned body could have done was hang on for another hour and a half. Alas, it wasn't to be.

Sighing, I slid my leg out from where it was hooked round Lukas and abandoned the gorgeous warmth of both his body and the silken duvet. The faster I did this, the less chance there would be that I'd wake up fully. If I was quick, I might slide back into sleep again. I heaved myself to my feet, taking care not to disturb Lukas, and padded to the bathroom. Bah: phoenix or not, able to resurrect myself or not, I still possessed plenty of physical frailties. Make this quick, Emma, I told myself. In and out.

I wasn't foolish enough to turn on the light. This was a high-speed mission and the warm bed was beckoning me. I flushed, fumbled for the tap to wash my hands and started to stumble back to the bedroom. I'd have made it in record time if I hadn't stubbed my toe on a protruding table leg along the way.

Hissing in pain, I bent down to rub the offended digit. Ouch. Fucking ouch. I gritted my teeth. If I hadn't been fully awake before, I certainly was now. Lukas had far too much priceless antique furniture with pretty but pointy flourishes lying around his house. Beautiful to look at during the day, potentially lethal in the dead of night. I smiled. Much like vampires themselves.

I straightened up and glanced out of the window to my left. I looked away – then my thoughts caught up with my sleep-addled brain and I looked again. Why, in the name of all that was holy, was someone standing stock till across the street and staring up at me at this hour of the night?

I took an involuntary step backwards, although logic told me that the shadowed stranger couldn't see me through the slatted blinds and dark night shadows. My eyes narrowed. From the way they were standing and their body shape, they looked male. Male werewolf, in fact: squat body, broad shoulders … yeah, I was almost sure he was a naturally born wolf. But this was Soho and we were in the middle of vampire territory. Few werewolves loitered around here at any time of day, and they certainly wouldn't attempt it before dawn unless they had a very good reason.

I scratched my cheek. The four werewolf clans and the vampires maintained an uneasy peace and generally respected each other enough to avoid confrontation. However, I wouldn't put it past any of the werewolf alphas to test the boundaries of supernatural decency. Normally I'd leave them to such pointless shenanigans. The wolf out there was creepy, but technically he wasn't breaking any laws. Except this wasn't the time for daft supernatural political manoeuvres, not with the supe summit merely a day away.

I frowned. I'd have to find the time to pay all four alphas a visit and remind them to toe the line, at least for the next week or so. Too much was at stake for this idiocy.

Annoyed, I started to turn away again. That was when the other approaching shadows caught my eye. The mysterious male stiffened and raised his hands, apparently indicating surrender. The other figures didn't seem to care about that. The hairs on the back of my neck prickled. God*damnit*. Something was definitely about to go down.

By now, sleep couldn't have been further from my mind. I sprang into action, whirled towards the bedroom and grabbed my dressing gown. I shrugged it on, belting it round my waist as I ran downstairs to the front door. Shoes of some description would have been a great idea but I didn't have time to find any.

I hastily unbolted the door, grabbed my trusty crossbow that was propped against the wall, and darted out just in time to see the sharp kick aimed at the stranger's midriff. He doubled over with a pained grunt. 'Hey!' I yelled.

There were five people, and not one of them looked in my direction. Detective Constable Emma Bellamy, authority figure and respected member of the supernatural community, that was me.

I tried again, raising my voice. 'Stop!'

Another person clenched their hands into fists and punched the man on the side of the face. His head snapped to the right with the force. He wasn't trying to defend himself and his attackers, who were definitely also werewolves, certainly weren't pulling their punches.

Barefoot, I ran across the road, grabbed the nearest bloke and yanked him back before leaping in front of the now-bleeding stranger and putting my hands on my hips. 'Back up twenty paces,' I commanded, this time allowing my voice to thrum with compulsion. 'Now.'

Three of the four attackers did as I ordered, unable to deny or ignore my words. But supernatural compulsion isn't foolproof, and it doesn't work on everyone. It doesn't even work on all werewolves, despite the hierarchical nature of their existence. The stronger ones could withstand my commands, more's the pity.

'DC Bellamy!' Buffy simpered and flicked her hair. 'Nice outfit!' She waved a hand at my dressing gown. 'Terrycloth really is under-rated as a fabric.'

I rolled my eyes. Of course *she* was here. And, of course, she was the one who could ignore my commands despite being ranked an epsilon towards the bottom of the complex werewolf pyramid of authority.

I could have pressed my point and used her real name, Patricia, to amplify my compulsion, but if I failed again I'd lose face. I wasn't prepared to dispense with all my advantages against her just yet. Despite – or perhaps because of – her rather vexing wiles, I liked Buffy but that didn't mean I wouldn't arrest her if she deserved it. I liked her in the way I also liked sharks: from a considerable distance. Unfortunately Buffy's lupine teeth were probably sharper than a Great White's.

I adjusted my grip on the crossbow to make sure she knew it was there. 'Two Sullivan werewolves and two Fairfax werewolves,' I said. 'Working together to assault...' I glanced at the male and frowned. Up close, there was not a smidgen of doubt that he was a wolf, but I didn't recognise him and he wasn't wearing any identifying tags. That was unusual. 'Another wolf,' I finished.

I looked him over again. Blood was streaming from his nose but it wasn't a mortal wound, despite the swelling that was already appearing. He looked to be in his thirties with glossy chestnut-brown hair and a smooth tan that seemed too natural to be from a bottle. Beyond the wounds he'd just received, I couldn't see any visible marks or scars marring his skin. That was also unusual for a werewolf of his age; they were prone to injury because of their often violent lifestyles during the full moon.

Buffy examined her manicured fingernails as if she were bored. 'Our alphas have become friendly. We have a lot of shared interests these days.'

Yeah, yeah. When Lord Fairfax was around, relations between the two clans were frostily cordial and little more. Since Toffee had been ordained as the new Fairfax alpha, Lady Sullivan had sought to take her under her wing. Nobody doubted that this was because Lady Sullivan thought she could control the new Lady Fairfax and manipulate the rest of her clan. Whether that would be true or not remained to be seen.

Buffy continued, 'In any case, detective, this is a werewolf matter. It doesn't concern you.' Her tone was light but there was no mistaking the hard look in her eyes. She enjoyed playing the part of the girlish ingenue, but the reality couldn't have been further from that. 'I suggest,' she said, 'that you go back to cuddles with your Lord and your own sweet dreams.'

'I'm a Supe Squad detective. I won't let you attack a man in the middle of the street.'

Something flashed in Buffy's yellow-tinged gaze. 'It's a werewolf matter,' she repeated. 'You know the law.'

I folded my arms. I wasn't going anywhere. She was perfectly correct: unless her hapless wolfie victim had committed a crime against a human, anything he did was a matter for the clans. But there was an edge of manic terror in the eyes of the silent werewolf standing behind me, and I wasn't in the habit of permitting vicious assaults while I watched. I was bored with sticking to those sorts of rules, especially when it meant that people ended up getting hurt. It had upset me to leave the hunt for non-vampire Jim to others; I wasn't leaving this man.

I turned to him. 'Who are you?' I asked softly. 'Which clan are you in?'

He licked his lips nervously. 'My name is—'

'Don't say another word,' Buffy ordered.

His shoulders immediately hunched and his head dropped. He was prepared to totally submit to her, which meant he was probably unranked and without much power or strength. But he didn't look weak, and unranked werewolves rarely caused this amount of bother. I wondered if he'd come here because he wanted to find me and ask for my help. That would be unusual – but nothing about this situation was remotely normal.

Buffy wasn't backing down. 'Leave, DC Bellamy. This is none of your business.'

The man flinched but he needn't have worried. There was absolutely zero chance that I'd walk away. From the way Buffy altered her stance, she knew it too.

'I'm not looking for a fight with you, Buffy.' I kept my voice calm. 'That's not what I do. But I'm not leaving either.'

She gazed at me for a long moment. 'We'll see about that, detective.' She raised her head and called across the street. 'Lord Horvath! You are looking mighty fine.'

I stiffened. I'd been so focused on the wolves that I'd not realised Lukas had woken up and come outside. I glanced across and saw him standing in the doorway, leaning against the doorframe and wearing nothing more than a pair of tight black boxers.

Buffy giggled. 'He's so sexy, right? I can see how he managed to wrap you round his little finger. How often does he drink your blood, DC Bellamy?'

I gritted my teeth. Never. Almost never. Not unless he absolutely had to. And I wasn't wrapped around his finger. I loved him – but I was my own person. So was he, for that matter.

Buffy giggled again and sauntered over to Lukas. She placed a hand on his arm and batted her eyelashes at him before gently caressing his skin. She wasn't doing it because of Lukas, she was doing it because of me. She shouldn't have bothered. I was still learning to trust Lukas fully but I had no worries whatsoever about this sort of crap.

Lukas gazed at her with his black eyes. In a barely audible voice he said, 'Take your hands off me.' Every word was cloaked in steel and laced with menace. Tease the Lord of all vampires at your peril.

Buffy snatched her hand away and took a step back, immediately realising she had overstepped the mark. 'My apologies.' She dipped her head. 'I meant no disrespect.'

'Not to me, perhaps.' Lukas regarded her coolly. 'But you certainly did to DC Bellamy.'

Buffy curtsied to Lukas without any melodrama or suggestion of humour. She turned her back to me and started murmuring, her voice so quiet that I could only make out an odd word or two. 'Lord Horvath … werewolf … ours … law…'

I squared my shoulders and prepared to march over to join the conversation.

'Detective Constable Bellamy.'

My head whipped round. It was the strange male werewolf. The other three wolves all glared at me but didn't dare move towards us.

'You have to listen to me.' He spoke nasally and I suspected that Buffy had broken his nose when she'd punched him. At least the bleeding had stopped; small mercies, I supposed. 'There's a man coming to your summit. He's very dangerous. You have to—'

'Oi!' Buffy whirled away from Lukas and strode towards us. 'I didn't give you permission to speak!'

I sighed. 'Shut up, Buffy.'

'DC Bellamy,' she snarled, dropping all girlish pretence. 'We've been through this. You need to step away.'

I shook my head. 'Not gonna happen.'

'Emma.' It was Lukas.

I stared at him. His expression was unreadable, but I knew what he was thinking and what silent message he was trying to convey. He was telling me not to get involved. Neither the law nor public opinion would be on my side if I did, and apparently neither would Lukas. He wouldn't say anything else in front of other supes, plus we had an unwritten rule about keeping our professional and personal lives wholly separate. Not interfering in each other's professional affairs was the only way we could manage our relationship and maintain our integrity. However, it rankled that he'd allow Buffy and her wolves to drag this poor bloke away and beat him up. Or worse.

'As I've already said, this wolf and what happens to him doesn't concern Supe Squad,' Buffy interjected. She'd returned to her default facade of bright yet vacuous, even though we all knew she was anything but. Buffy had worked out that Lukas wasn't going to get in her way, and she probably thought that I'd step down too.

I looked from Lukas to Buffy to the mysterious wolf. The terror in his eyes hadn't dissipated, but there was dull resignation too. I came to a decision. 'You're under arrest,' I said to him.

Lukas muttered something under his breath.

'You do not have to say anything, but it may harm your defence if you do not mention when questioned something which you later rely on in court. Anything you do say may be given in evidence.'

'You can't arrest him!' Buffy started forward. 'For fuck's sake!'

'Except I just did arrest him.' I offered her a smile.

She started to splutter. 'On what charge?'

I shrugged. 'He was loitering in this area in the middle of the night and he matches the description of a burglar recently spotted operating in London.' This was a big city; there had to be a thief somewhere with brown hair and a decent tan who'd been reported to the police.

Yes, I was abusing my position, but no, I wasn't going to apologise for it. Not until I found out more about who this guy was, what his muttered warning had been about and why he was so scared. I'd done enough walking away this week. 'Burglary is a serious crime, Buffy.'

She drew in a breath. 'Lady Sullivan will not be pleased.'

Was Lady Sullivan ever pleased? 'Pleasing her is not my responsibility.' As I took hold of the man's elbow and steered him towards Tallulah, I wondered if he was the first bloke ever to be arrested by a barefoot police officer wearing a bath robe. Oh well; in this job it was important to think on your feet and be adaptable.

'With this stupid conference coming up,' Buffy began, 'Supe Squad ought to be more careful where they stick their noses. If all the werewolves pull out, you'll end up looking pretty stupid. All your big ideas to bring peace and happiness to the world will come to nothing without us.'

I stopped and looked at her. 'Is that a threat? From you?' She met my eyes. 'Well?' I demanded.

Buffy pulled a face. 'No,' she said. 'But Lady Sullivan—'

I rolled my eyes. Enough already. 'It's a summit, not a conference.'

'What's the difference?'

Summit sounded grander. I sniffed and opened Tallulah's passenger door. I never bother to lock the lurid purple Mini because everyone knows who she belongs to and nobody would dare to try and steal her. Hell, nobody in their right mind would *want* to steal her. She is a temperamental rust-bucket with more personality than any sane driver would want in a car. And she smells funny.

I reached in and pulled the front seat forward before directing the mysterious wolf to the cramped backseat. He didn't resist and neither did he complain about the smell, which was a point in his favour.

'Leave,' Lukas said to Buffy.

'But—'

He gave her a warning look and she scowled but did as she was told. 'C'mon, boys,' she muttered. 'I've had enough of this place.'

The other werewolves looked at me.

'Go on,' I said. 'Get out of here.' I folded my arms and watched as Buffy and her little entourage stalked away. It was only when I was certain they were out of earshot that I turned to glare at Lukas.

He splayed out his hands in an irritated gesture. 'That wasn't a good idea,' he stated.

'I won't stand idly by and allow a man to be assaulted right in front of me, Lukas.'

His expression didn't change. 'He's a werewolf. Human laws don't apply.' He paused. 'As you know.'

'Do you know who he is? Did Buffy tell you?'

'All she said is that he's an omega wolf who's more dangerous than he looks and who's been AWOL for years. He's returned to London unexpectedly and the clans have to assert their authority over him. I'm not saying it's right, I'm saying it's what they do.'

Huh. I wasn't sure I'd met any omega werewolves other than Devereau Webb – and I wasn't convinced the ex-crime boss counted as omega because no classification suited Devereau Webb's status. He'd turned himself into a werewolf deliberately, then openly snubbed all four clans. He rarely seemed to be in the city and I had no idea what he was up to these days, but there was no denying that he possessed as much power and strength as any of the four alpha leaders.

In any case, omegas were wolves who were outside the usual clan system. Sometimes it was because they didn't fit in; sometimes it was because they'd been exiled as a result of their unsavoury deeds. The latter either ended up in the Clink, the supernatural equivalent of Belmarsh Prison, or were summarily put down by their own kind. Nothing about this particular were-wolf suggested he was dangerous enough to warrant either action.

I gazed curiously at the huddled shape inside Tallulah. Until I knew more about him, I'd withhold my judgment.

Lukas watched me for a moment then sighed. 'I suppose,' he said finally, 'that this means you're not coming back to bed. Will you at least put on some shoes and clothes?'

I gave his bare muscled chest and legs a pointed look. As if he could talk. 'Will you keep an eye on that fellow while I do?'

A muscle twitched in his cheek. 'Only because I'm concerned about your welfare. Watching him for a few minutes doesn't mean that I agree with what you're doing.'

'You've already made your feelings clear,' I said softly. 'I'll be five minutes.'

Lukas nodded. I muttered thanks and pretended not to see the dark, forbidding expression on his face.

CHAPTER THREE

I DIDN'T SPEAK TO THE WEREWOLF, OTHER THAN TO CHECK THAT HE was alright and to tell him we were heading to the Supe Squad building. Thanks to Tallulah's cramped rear, he was hunched uncomfortably and could only nod at me. I pushed away my many burning questions; they could wait until he was in an interview room and I could record what he had to say. I knew I'd overstepped a line by arresting him for a non-existent crime, and I knew I'd be castigated for it, but I refused to feel guilty. There was a story here – and I wanted to find out what it was.

I parked right outside the front door. A figure wearing a top hat stepped forward from beneath the awning of the smart hotel next door. It was too early for Max, the friendly bellman who worked there; this was his belligerent counterpart, Stubman, and I already had a pretty good idea about what he was about to say. Maybe, I thought hopefully, I could slide inside quickly to avoid him engaging me in conversation.

On the slim chance that it might discourage him from speaking, I avoided eye contact as I extricated myself from Tallulah. I pulled the front seat forward so that the werewolf could get out.

Unfortunately, the fact that my back was turned and I was obviously busy did nothing to stop Stubman from complaining.

'You!' he spat. 'This summit thing is your idea, isn't it? Do you have any idea how disruptive it's going to be? The world doesn't revolve around you and your damned supes. The rest of us are still trying to earn a living and enjoy a quiet life. But you...' his voice quivered with anger '...you're putting a stop to all that!'

Good morning to you, too. I put my hand on the werewolf's elbow and turned to face Stubman. 'We've been through this, sir,' I said, as politely as I could manage. 'The supernatural summit is an excellent opportunity for supes to learn how to understand other communities better.' I paused. 'And vice versa. All any of us want is a quiet life, no matter who we are.'

'That's not true and you know it! There's not a damned bloodsucker in the world who wants a quiet life. And as for those bloody wolves...'

Next to me, the werewolf opened his mouth and snarled, revealing sharp teeth. He jerked as if to lunge at the bellman and Stubman leapt a foot backwards. I tightened my grip on the werewolf's elbow although it wasn't necessary. If he'd wanted to escape or attack Stubman, he'd already have done so.

'Monsters!' Stubman hissed. He glared at us both before stepping inside to the dubious safety of the hotel lobby.

I shook my head and glanced at the wolf. 'That wasn't very helpful, you know.'

He raised his heavy shoulders dismissively. 'Maybe not,' he rumbled. 'But that idiot deserved it.'

Perhaps. But it would add fuel to Stubman's fire and encourage his fear of supes. It was fear that sparked his hatred – fear together with entrenched prejudice.

I tutted softly then directed the wolf inside. I'd find a way to smooth Stubman's ruffled feathers later, together with managing everything else on my ridiculous to-do list.

* * *

IT WAS FAR TOO EARLY for the others to be in, so I deposited the wolf in the cleanest interview room and went to the office to make us both a coffee. When I returned with two steaming mugs, his head was in his hands. 'Chin up,' I said, not unkindly. 'I'm here to help, and a hot drink is a good enough start.'

The wolf looked up, a spasm of gratitude crossing his face. 'Thanks,' he grunted. He met my eyes. 'You didn't have to come to my aid like you did. In fact,' he added, 'you probably shouldn't have.'

'Probably not,' I said cheerfully. I reached across and clicked on the ancient tape recorder. 'Would you like me to call someone? A solicitor, perhaps?'

'No, I'm good. Anyway, I don't know anyone in London any more.'

'I can call someone in to represent you.' Under the circumstances, it might be a good idea. Someone like the gremlin solicitor Phileas Carmichael would jump at the chance, regardless of the early hour.

He shook his head. 'No. I don't want anyone else here.'

It was his choice. 'Okay. If you change your mind, let me know. Why don't you tell me what all this is about and who you are?'

The brown-haired wolf took a gulp of coffee and savoured the taste for a moment, then inhaled deeply and met my eyes. 'My name is Nathan Fairfax. I'm thirty-four years old, and I was born into the Fairfax clan.'

Interesting. I leaned forward. 'But you're no longer part of that clan?'

A flicker of pain crossed his eyes. 'I rose to gamma rank by the time I was twenty-four.'

I blinked. Gamma wolves were subservient only to betas and,

of course, alphas. To reach such lofty heights at such a young age was almost unheard of.

He laughed humourlessly at my expression. 'Yeah,' he said. 'I was something of a prodigy. But I was up my own arse and had an ego the size of Everest. I didn't have much respect for my Lord Fairfax. The week before my twenty-fifth birthday, during the first full moon of the year, I challenged his leadership.' He fiddled with his shirt cuffs. 'I lost.'

Ah. 'Lord Fairfax was annoyed?'

Nathan smiled faintly. 'That would be an understatement. He immediately de-ranked me for daring to presume that, as a mere gamma, I could challenge him. I didn't take the demotion well, and in the end the insult was too much, I left the clan and turned omega.'

He shrugged awkwardly. 'It wasn't the smartest move in the world. I was arrogant enough to think that the Fairfax clan would realise what they'd missed, Lord Fairfax would beg me to come back and all would be forgiven. The truth is that as soon as I left, they stopped thinking about me. I was no longer a Fairfax wolf and therefore I no longer existed. What I should have done was swallow my pride, keep my head down and pay my dues. Instead I made a rash decision and ended up persona non grata.'

He gestured to indicate that it was now water under the bridge. 'Like I said, I was up my own arse.'

I gazed at him. Admittedly I was only hearing one side of the story, but complete de-ranking would have been an over-reaction on Fairfax's part. Hierarchy challenges were part and parcel of being a werewolf; usually any werewolf who challenged another and failed lost nothing more than a single rank. I suspected that Nathan Fairfax had almost got the better of the late Lord Fairfax and was severely punished as a result.

No wonder the new Lady Fairfax was concerned about him. It was still early days in her tenure and she had a lot of ground to make up to redeem her clan. It seemed likely that she'd dragged the Sullivan wolves in to help her get rid of Nathan, rather than the other way round. What was most interesting to me was that Nathan Fairfax was humble enough to blame himself for what had happened all those years ago – and that he didn't appear to hold any grudges.

'Did you stay in London once you became omega?' I asked. I already knew he couldn't have but I still wanted to hear his answer.

'It's illegal for a supe to live out of this area,' he replied quickly.

'I'm aware of what the law says. I'm not about to charge you with a petty misdemeanour like that, Nathan.' I met his eyes. 'I might be a police officer but I'm not that kind of person. I'm a supe, too. I get it. Besides, in order for the supe summit to be wholly inclusive and to encourage all supes to attend, the government's agreed a temporary amnesty for all supernatural creatures regardless of where they might secretly live. You're safe in that regard, I promise you.'

Nathan licked his lips and looked away. 'I moved up to the north,' he said. 'Cumbria.'

'And when you heard that Lord Fairfax had died, you decided to return to the capital?'

He shook his head. 'No. I burned my bridges with the Fairfax clan when I turned omega. I decided to come when I heard about the supe summit.' A flicker of optimism illuminated his face. 'I've watched the news and I know that your aims are to relax the laws surrounding the supernatural community and to improve the way humans see us.' His eyes shone. 'This is a real opportunity to change the status quo, to make all our lives better. Thank you for organising it.'

He was even more upbeat about the upcoming summit than I was, and I was thrilled that he could see its potential. As my recent brush with a bugbear had proved, there are all sorts of undocumented supes out there who remain hidden – and possibly highly dangerous. The more we could bring them out into the open while easing human concerns about our kind, the better things would be.

It was true the summit had been my idea initially, but I couldn't take credit for how it had come together. 'You're welcome,' I said. 'But I'm not the one you should be thanking. There's a committee of supes and humans who've done all the heavy lifting. Supe Squad's involvement is mostly centred around security and legal discussions.'

Nathan smiled. 'It wouldn't be happening without your input. Even I'm aware of that, and I've been living in the middle of nowhere for years.'

I didn't argue; at that point, I was just glad that the summit was taking place. 'You said there was a dangerous man planning to attend. Who were you talking about?'

Nathan Fairfax stopped smiling. His fingers twitched and the look of fear returned to his face. 'The Chief,' he whispered.

I stiffened. Night Stalker Jim had mentioned someone called the Chief as well. I wasn't a fan of coincidences, and this particular one didn't bode well.

'He's coming. He's not a good person, detective. I don't know what he's planning but I know it'll be bad. You need to stop him from attending and keep well away from him. He'll suck you in, make you trust him and then he'll stab you in the back when you least expect it.' He grimaced. 'Worse. He'll make you stab all your friends in the back, too. He has a silver tongue and a black heart. You don't know what he's like, but I promise you he's evil. He's so very, very evil.'

I frowned. As much as a second mention of this mysterious Chief concerned me, I wasn't a fan of over-blown melodrama. I find it hard to believe that anyone is wholly evil or wholly good. 'He's a supe?' I asked, doing what I could to avoid doubt colouring my voice.

'Human,' Nathan whispered. 'Probably. He's bad, that's for

certain. That's why I came to find you. You weren't at your flat and I knew enough to suspect you'd be with Lord Horvath. I thought that if I waited until you left for work, I could speak to you and warn you.'

It wasn't the smartest way to talk to the police. If he'd wanted to avoid the Supe Squad office because he needed to keep away from other werewolves, he could have phoned. Or emailed. Or written a letter.

I left it for now because there were other matters to consider. 'Do you know this chief's real name?' I questioned.

Nathan's response was forestalled by the interview room door opening to reveal a thunderous-looking Detective Sergeant Owen Grace. Fuck. I'd thought I'd have longer.

'DC Bellamy,' Grace bit out. 'A word, please.'

I rose to my feet. 'I'll be back soon, Nathan.'

The werewolf nodded distractedly. 'Okay,' he said. 'Okay.'

I smiled at him and walked out, allowing the door to close and self-lock behind me. Then I followed Grace to the office to receive my bollocking.

* * *

I SAT down on the squashy sofa which was Fred's favourite spot for a nap. I suspected this was going to take some time, so I might as well make myself comfortable. DS Grace was barely my superior but, as the senior Supe Squad detective, he had overall responsibility for the office and how we worked.

He wasn't a bad guy, and he wasn't any more incompetent than the rest of us, but in the six months since he'd joined Supe Squad he'd struggled to understand the supe community. I also knew he hated the fact that *I* was a supe and had more of an insight into supernatural matters than he did. He'd never say anything, but he also mistrusted Lukas and my relationship with him. And he was convinced that almost every supe was out to get him. Sadly, that part was probably true. Grace could be … over-enthusiastic in his efforts to uphold the letter of the law. His zeal was one of many reasons I'd learned to relax my approach. Slavish adherence to archaic rules that sought to keep supes in their place didn't help any of us.

Grace paced up and down the room. His cheeks were suffused with red and his mouth was turned down at the corners. Yep, he was very unhappy. 'Do you have any reason to be holding that werewolf here, Emma?' he demanded. 'Any reason at all?'

'I arrested him on suspicion of burglary, so technically yes. That's the official reason.'

Grace's fingers curled into fists. 'And the unofficial reason?'

'He's here for his own protection.' I quickly outlined what had happened.

Grace stopped pacing and ran a frustrated hand through his hair. 'I received a call at five o'clock this morning from Robert, one of the Sullivan betas.'

I could imagine what he'd said. 'He was putting in a formal complaint?'

'Indeed he was.' Grace glared at me as if the Sullivan clan's inclination to be a pain in everyone's arse was my fault. 'Two minutes after I put the phone down, I had a call from Lady Fairfax herself.'

'Uh-huh.'

'And then, as I was leaving the house, I had yet another call. Can you guess who phoned me?'

I considered, wondering what move I'd have made if I were either Sullivan or Fairfax, then I snapped my fingers. 'Would that be Detective Superintendent Lucinda Barnes?' I asked.

'Got it in one,' Grace said darkly. 'As you might imagine, DSI Barnes was even less impressed than I was to be woken up at the crack of dawn.'

Wow, Lady Fairfax really was threatened by Nathan. She was pulling out all the stops to get to him. 'Clearly,' I said, thinking aloud, 'there must be something to this guy if the clans are working so hard in such a short space of time. They don't want us to talk to him.'

'Don't you think, Emma, that their energetic attempts to get this lone wolf released to them is because you humiliated them this morning by stepping in and interfering with their operation? They lost face because of your illegal actions—'

'Arresting someone, even a supe, is hardly illegal!' I protested.

Grace gave me a long look. 'We all know what you did.' He sighed. 'Not that I can blame you. However, it's possible they were only going to rough him up. Now that you're involved, they'll end up doing much more simply to make a point. You likely made matters ten times worse for that man.'

'I—' Damnit, Grace could be right. That was galling. I reminded myself that I didn't know everything and I certainly wasn't infallible. Nobody was.

'Why was he outside Lord Horvath's home?' Grace asked. 'Was it because of you or because of Horvath?'

'Me, I think. He's made an allegation about someone called "the Chief" who's apparently highly dangerous and is planning to disrupt the summit.'

Grace's eyes snapped to mine. 'I see.' He nodded. 'We can use that. He's a potential witness to a future crime, a serious future crime. It'll buy us some time to fend off Sullivan and Fairfax and think about how best to proceed. Do you think it's a genuine threat,?'

'That's what I'm hoping to find out,' I said. 'I don't know who the Chief is, but the human at Trafalgar Square the other night also mentioned someone called the Chief.'

Grace's face darkened and he rubbed his chin. 'I see. Come on, then. Let's find out together.' He turned on his heel and marched out of the door.

I breathed out and reminded myself that just because DS Grace didn't always understand supe ways and he was a stickler for the rules didn't mean he couldn't offer helpful insights. I jumped up to my feet and followed him into the corridor. 'Thanks, sir,' I said. 'I appreciate I might have made an error this morning, and I appreciate that you understand why I made it.'

Grace didn't answer. He was standing beside the interview room door, gazing in without moving. My brow creased as I caught up to him. When I saw what he was looking at – or rather what he *wasn't* looking at – I stiffened. For fuck's sake.

'We've got to do something about the bloody security around here,' he muttered. 'I knew we should have made sure we had steel-reinforced doors installed instead of these shitty wooden ones.'

I gazed at the door. It looked as if Nathan Fairfax had broken out of the interview room with one carefully planted lupine kick. He had been irritatingly stealthy and swift, and I'd been so focused on persuading Grace that what I'd done was right that I hadn't heard a damned thing.

'Why the hell would he run away? He's in real danger out there, and I made it more than clear that I was on his side.'

'We're the police, Emma. The only side we're on is that of the law.'

I barely managed to avoid rolling my eyes. That wasn't remotely true, not when it came to me and supes. I pushed past Grace and stalked to the front door, flinging it open to look up and down the street. There was no sign of Nathan Fairfax. The only person outside was Stubman who was watching me with a mixture of malevolence and undisguised glee.

'Lost someone?' he asked with a snide smirk.

'Did you see where he went?'

Stubman met my eyes with a defiant glint. 'No. Didn't see a thing.' And then he turned away.

CHAPTER FOUR

PC Fᴿᴇᴅ Hᴀᴄᴋᴇʀᴛ's ᴇʏᴇs ᴡᴇʀᴇ ᴡɪᴅᴇ. 'Yᴏᴜ ᴀʀʀᴇsᴛᴇᴅ ᴀ ᴡᴇʀᴇᴡᴏʟғ and you didn't book them in properly or remove their belongings?'

I winced. 'It wasn't exactly a proper arrest.' DS Grace and I had watched the CCTV footage from the interview room once it was clear that Nathan Fairfax wasn't anywhere nearby. Less than a minute after I'd left the room, it looked like he'd received a text message. He'd gazed at his phone for a long moment then broken down the door with incredible speed.

Fred let out a low whistle. 'All the same...'

'I know, alright? I know.' My failings and mistakes as far as Nathan Fairfax were concerned were both obvious and grave.

'The supe summit begins tomorrow,' Fred continued. 'The champagne reception is tonight. It's not as if we have time to go searching for a single werewolf with a death wish.'

I gritted my teeth. 'I know.'

'Supes from abroad are already checking into the DeVane hotel. Final security sweeps still need to be made. We don't know who this Chief is, or if he poses a danger. And the clans—'

I held up my hands. Enough. 'I know, Fred. I fucked up.'

'Not as much as Nathan Fairfax has if he runs into any clan wolves again,' he stated baldly.

I pulled a face, then reached up and rang Lady Fairfax's front doorbell. For once, I wasn't stone-walled or left hanging around on the doorstep. One of Lady Fairfax's betas, a werewolf I recognised from Lord Fairfax's day, gave Fred and me a perfunctory smile and ushered us inside.

We were led into a drawing room lined with old books, full of expensive ornaments and reeking with the distinct odour of old money. Fred narrowly avoided knocking over a Ming vase; he gave a small squeak as he brushed past it and sent it rocking. The beta's eyes flashed but he merely put out a steadying hand to ensure the priceless object remained upright. He beckoned us forward.

When I saw that Lady Fairfax and Lady Sullivan were waiting for us, I wasn't sure whether to be pleased that I wouldn't have to make a trip to the Sullivan stronghold or dismayed that I'd have to deal with both alphas at the same time.

Neither woman smiled. There was at least thirty years separating them but they managed to gaze at me with exactly the same icy expression. Maybe there was some sort of lupine finishing school for alphas which taught werewolves how to look as disapproving and stern as possible.

I straightened my shoulders and raised my head. I wouldn't let them cow me into submission, despite their hard-eyed stares and my guilt at losing Nathan Fairfax. When faced with these alphas, attack was by far the best form of defence. 'Where is he?' I asked.

Lady Fairfax's brow creased slightly. It was a tiny movement and barely noticeable, but it still gave her away. 'Where is who?' she enquired.

'Nathan Fairfax.' I placed emphasis on his second name and sent a message silently: omega or not, he used to be one of yours.

Lady Fairfax sniffed. 'He ceased to be a Fairfax the day he became omega. He is unworthy of our name.'

Whatever. 'Where is he?' I repeated.

'You're the one who arrested him,' Lady Sullivan said. 'You should know where he is, Emma.'

'It's DC Bellamy to you,' I told her.

Sullivan shrugged as if she couldn't care less, but we both knew her use of my first name as if we were friends was pure power play. 'Did you drop the ridiculous burglary charges?'

'In the end, he wasn't officially charged,' I said smoothly. 'He was only helping us with our enquiries and it was a case of mistaken identity.'

'How very convenient,' Lady Fairfax sneered.

I sighed. Several months ago, when I'd known her as Toffee, she'd been much friendlier. Then again, given what had occurred only a few hours ago, I couldn't blame her for her antagonism.

I flicked my gaze from one alpha to the other. They clearly didn't know where Nathan Fairfax was and probably weren't responsible for the text message that had drawn him away from Supe Squad. I mulled over my options, glanced at Fred and made a decision. It was time to be candid.

'Nathan *Fairfax*,' I said, 'was loitering outside Lord Horvath's home early this morning because he wanted to discuss a potential threat to the supe summit. The summit is the only reason he returned to London, although,' I added pointedly, 'the law states that he should have remained here regardless of his clan status. I didn't know this when I intervened in the attack from your wolves. I did that because I couldn't stand by and watch someone beaten half to death. If you think I wouldn't do the same thing again, then you don't know how I work. I understand that he falls under supe jurisdiction, but that sort of assault doesn't help any of us.'

I softened my voice. 'You know why the summit is happening. You know it's because we need to find ways to encourage the humans to look more favourably upon *all* supes. A shift in attitude will benefit all of us. Attacking someone in the middle of the street, whether the victim is a supe or not or deserves it or not, is far from helpful. That sort of action benefits none of us.'

Lady Sullivan glanced at her counterpart. 'I disagree.' She gave a languid shrug. 'It would have benefited *me*. Omega wolves need to be kept in their place. Call it a pre-emptive strike, if you like.'

'That's ridiculous. You can't attack people because of what they might do!'

She folded her arms. 'Look at Devereau Webb. Look at what happens when we let wolves do what they want.'

'Devereau Webb hasn't done anything. You're afraid of Webb because he's stronger than any of you. You're worried that he'll create a fifth clan that will leave the rest of you for dust. I know him.' Kind of. 'I don't think anything could be further from his mind.'

Sullivan glared. 'Devereau Webb might not be thinking of such things now, but that doesn't mean he won't in the future. If he gets away with such idiocy, other peripheral werewolves will think they can do the same. Imagine what it would be like if every Devereau Webb and Nathan bloody Fairfax in the country decides they're strong enough to set up on their own. It would be chaos for British werewolves. The rest of the country already hates us. We don't need to give them more reason to despise us.'

She gave me a narrow-eyed look. 'I can assure you that none of us will benefit from such a scenario, DC Bellamy. Not even the humans. You know how the law limits our population numbers. Your summit won't change that, no matter how you might pretend to believe otherwise.'

I wasn't trying to alter that particular law; I wasn't sure I'd want to even if I could. 'We are getting off topic,' I said stiffly. 'I need to know that when Nathan resurfaces, he won't be in danger from any clan werewolves.'

'He needs to know his place.'

Irritation flashed through me. 'He does know his damned place.'

Lady Fairfax acted as if I hadn't spoken. 'This is the way of the wolf. You might be a supe, but you are not one of us. You sleep with a vampire, DC Bellamy, and you work with humans. You're not like us.'

Fred cleared his throat. 'What's the alternative, ma'am? You can complain about Detective Constable Bellamy to anyone who will listen. Who knows? You might succeed in getting her removed from Supe Squad. But you won't achieve anything in the long run. She's not a wolf but she *is* a supe, and she's a damned sight more concerned about the future of the supernatural community than anyone else in Supe Squad will ever be. And that community includes every single werewolf in the country. You'd do well to listen to her. Beating up lone wolves who present no real threat is nothing more than vain posturing. In my experience, people who have to flex their muscles to advertise their strength are the weakest of us all.'

I gazed at Fred with astonishment. Not that long ago he wouldn't have had the confidence – or the energy – to say boo to a goose; now he was scolding two Lady alphas. Five minutes earlier he'd been scolding me too. I was impressed – then I glanced down and realised his hands were shaking. He understood what he was doing by speaking up, which made his little speech even braver.

'So,' Lady Sullivan said, 'the little boy speaks after all. Bravo.' She sounded bored, though I supposed it was better than sounding offended. 'We're not the ones trying to pick a fight, we're only safeguarding our interests. And we're not the ones who broke the law this morning. That was you, not us.' She gestured at Lady Fairfax. 'In any case, what happens to the omega wolf isn't my call. As he is a former Fairfax clan member, it's entirely up to my esteemed colleague.'

Talk about passing the buck and avoiding responsibility. Lady

Sullivan's werewolf, Buffy, had been leading the assault on Nathan Fairfax and, from what I'd seen, the Fairfax fellows had been little more than obliging bystanders.

The new Lady Fairfax took her time answering. When she did speak, there was an edge of honesty in her voice that surprised me. 'Whether you believe it's posturing or not, as a new alpha I have to flex my muscles. I have a lot to make up for after what my predecessor did. The omega wolf has not been in London for ten years. That's a long time to harbour resentment and plan revenge against my clan.'

'I questioned him,' I interrupted. 'He's not remotely vengeful. He blames nobody but himself for what happened all those years ago.'

Lady Fairfax gave me a long look, clearly thinking I was naïve to take Nathan Fairfax at face value. 'If my wolves find him,' she continued, 'they will endeavour to make sure he understands his place and prevent him acting on any negative impulses he has towards us.'

In other words, they were still going to assault him. 'But—'

She held up a finger. 'But,' she said firmly, 'he will not be severely hurt. As long as he is willing to keep his head down while he is here, he will not suffer any more than is necessary for us to make our point and ensure he acknowledges our authority.' She raised her eyebrows. 'And you, DC Bellamy, need to adhere to your own laws and keep out of the way during Nathan's … re-education.'

'I have to speak to him again to find out about the man he thinks is a threat to the summit.'

'I'm not stopping you from doing that. You have your job to do, DC Bellamy, and I have mine.'

She sounded reasonable and I knew she'd made concessions that Lady Sullivan would never publicly agree to. I met her eyes, searching for any sign that she was fobbing me off with lies, but she appeared to be speaking truthfully. Anyway, even if she were not, I didn't have a leg to stand on legally. Nathan might not like it, and he might be cuffed around the head a few times so the Fairfax clan could make a heavy-handed point, but at least he wouldn't be seriously injured. It was more than I had a right to ask for.

'Okay,' I said finally. 'Okay.' And then, because I could now afford to say it, 'Thank you for listening to my concerns.'

'I'm not a monster, DC Bellamy.' Lady Fairfax's eyes were clear. 'None of us are.'

'I know. I'm trying to make the rest of the world realise that, too.'

She nodded. 'For what it's worth, I am looking forward to the summit. It's a good idea and I'm aware of the work you've put in to set it up.'

'Thank you. I believe it will be useful. We can come together as supes, share ideas and potentially make a real change. It's a chance to present a different, more positive image of supes to the British public. I'm very glad that you're coming.'

Lady Sullivan sighed audibly and clicked her tongue. 'For goodness' sake. This is getting ridiculous. I'm already bored hearing about the summit. You've got what you wanted, detective, and we will get what we wanted. Nobody will die in the process and we'll all live happily ever after. Can you piss off and leave us in peace now?'

I managed a smile. Just. 'As you wish. Have a good day.'

'Of that you can be sure.' Then she glanced at Fred. 'And you, PC Hackert,' she drawled, 'you have a very good day too.'

Fred's cheeks flamed red. 'Uh, thanks.'

'If you want to come round and see me on your own some time, my door is always open.'

He started blinking rapidly in alarm and Lady Sullivan laughed musically. Before matters descended into chaos, I grabbed his arm and steered him out to safety.

Another thought occurred to me and I turned my head. 'Out

of interest,' I called, 'how did you know that Nathan Fairfax was standing outside Lord Horvath's home?'

Lady Fairfax's cool eyes met mine. 'We received an anonymous phone call in the middle of the night. I don't know who it was from.'

I searched her face. As far as I could see, she was telling the truth. Hmm. I nodded my thanks and returned to Fred so that we could leave.

CHAPTER FIVE

I COULD DO NOTHING MORE FOR NATHAN FAIRFAX; UNLESS HE turned up in front of me for a second time, his future was out of my hands. I certainly didn't have the time to go searching aimlessly around the busy London streets for him, any more than I had time to search for Night Stalker Jim. Although technically I had arrested Nathan, he wasn't a wanted criminal and he wasn't under investigation. I'd have to hope that he could take care of himself. Omega or not, he was still a werewolf. He knew the score.

I called to update Grace on what had been agreed with Lady Fairfax, then Fred and I piled into Tallulah and headed for the DeVane Hotel.

'You did well back there,' I said. 'Your words tipped the balance. I owe you one.'

Still slightly flushed from the encounter, Fred managed a grin. 'You're welcome, boss. I only spoke the truth and the werewolves know it.'

'I hope so. If the Sullivan clan pulls out from the summit at the last minute because they want to make a point, the next few days will be a disaster.'

'They'll be there.' Fred sounded confident. 'Too many other supes have confirmed their attendance. None of the clans will dare to stay home – they'll look foolish if they do. The supe summit is the biggest thing that's happened in decades.'

In theory; I wasn't going to relax until this evening's champagne reception was underway and I could look around and see that everyone had actually showed up. The summit needed to be a success, and I was nervous that it would be more of a damp squib than a roaring firework. I sent out a silent prayer to whoever might be listening.

Tallulah groaned as we reached the next set of traffic lights and I frowned. She'd been in the garage for a full service only last week. There was no need for any strange noises.

'Do you think that Lady Fairfax was telling the truth?' Fred asked. 'Do you think she'll make sure that this Nathan guy isn't badly hurt?'

'Yeah, I do' I said. I was less convinced about Lady Sullivan because she could be a law unto herself, but I didn't say that aloud. I suspected I didn't need to.

I sighed. 'Lukas was pissed off that I got involved and so was DS Grace. I'm not supposed to sidestep supe law like that. When it's a question of morals versus laws, it's bloody hard to make the right decision.'

'You can only do your best and stick to what you think is right,' Fred said. 'It's all any of us can do.'

I couldn't disagree with that. I indicated to turn left and spun Tallulah's wheel. A moment later the imposing structure of the DeVane Hotel came into view. It wasn't the impressive old building that caused me to gape, however.

Fred let out a low whistle of dismay.

'Do you think those people are also doing their best and sticking to what they think is right?' I asked faintly, staring at the wall of protestors that had taken up position across the road from the hotel. Fred grimaced.

There were hundreds of them. The supe summit didn't officially start until the next day and yet there were already placards and chants and a sea of angry faces. *Vampires suck* read one sign being held aloft by a bald-headed man wearing a T-shirt at least two sizes too small for him. Yeah, yeah. That was hardly new. *Werewolves eat children.* Nope, they didn't. *Supes are evil.* I sighed. There was both a redundancy of imagination and of common sense.

'It's not all bad,' Fred said, pointing at a smaller group of humans who were being kept away from the others and who were dressed as supes.

I wasn't convinced I approved of their signs either. *Marry me, Lord Horvath!* I snorted and rolled my eyes. 'If this is what it's like today,' I grumbled, 'imagine how bad things will get tomorrow.'

'It proves how important the summit is,' Fred said. 'Sentiments like these are why we're doing this.'

'Yeah,' I agreed. 'It's just depressing to see them.' I changed gear and prepared to turn into the DeVane car park. Tallulah groaned again and started to splutter. Oh no, not now. The little car choked, then her engine cut out right in front of the protestors. There was an immediate chorus of loud cheers.

'Tallulah,' I said aloud, 'you're better than this.' I turned the ignition key. She spluttered but did nothing more. 'C'mon, girl.' Still nothing. I gritted my teeth and tried a different tack. 'Get moving now or I'll take you to the knacker's yard.'

I tried the key again, and this time she roared into life. Praise be.

The watching crowd jeered as we drove down the slope into the underground car park. 'I don't want to sound crazy,' Fred said, 'but it kinda seems like Tallulah did that on purpose.'

I grunted; where this daft purple car was concerned anything was possible. I was just glad that I hadn't had to get out and push. I shook my head and tutted. Surely my day could only get better from here on in.

* * *

THE GRAND INTERIOR of the DeVane Hotel was as busy and loud as the road outside, but here the buzz was positive and the people were upbeat. I looked round, impressed at how the hotel management had stepped up to the challenge. They could have politely declined the opportunity to host the first-ever supernatural summit and cited any number of excuses to avoid taking part but, not only had they agreed to host it, they'd pulled out all the stops.

The distinctive scent of verbena and wolfsbane was filtering through every corniced crevice and marbled corner, although only supes would be able to smell its potent mixture. There were signs and posters directing guests and exhibitors to the rooms where the panels and workshops would take place, and there was a gigantic banner stretching across the main lobby with the words *Supernatural Summit* emblazoned across it in bright blue. All the branding and colours had been carefully selected. We were avoiding red for its obvious connotations with blood, and black was deemed too funereal. Blue, however, projected calm and confidence.

There wasn't a cheesy wolf howling at the moon anywhere to be seen; neither were there any cartoon vampires with ridiculously large fangs. I'd had my doubts when the decisions were made, but I had to admit that the overall effect was well worth the effort. The supe summit was a serious undertaking with high expectations, and the branding reflected that.

Fred trotted away to talk to the hotel's security team and I took a moment to enjoy the sight of several months' hard work coming to fruition.

'Detective Constable Bellamy.'

I turned my head and saw the petite form of the hotel manager, Wilma Kennard. She was dressed as immaculately as ever, without a single stray hair or smudge of make-up. I doubted anything ever ruffled her.

When we'd first met, it had resulted in the discovery of DC Anthony Brown's dead body. Until I'd arrived at Supe Squad, Tony was its only detective. Kennard had been polite and professional throughout the investigation into Tony's death, and she'd displayed a lack of prejudice towards supes. Since those tumultuous events, she'd been promoted to overall manager and no longer had to work the night shift. It was a move I wholly applauded – especially now.

'Good morning.' I smiled and gestured at the lobby. 'It looks as if you have everything in hand.'

She blinked, as if the idea that the DeVane Hotel could be anything other than meticulously organised had never crossed her mind. 'It's hardly the first time we've hosted a conference, detective.'

No, but it was probably the first time they'd hosted a conference with protestors chanting outside. I doubted that the Annual Accountancy Convention or the International League of Knitting and Crafting attracted boos, jeers and angry placards. 'Well,' I said, 'your experience shows. Thank you for all your hard work.'

She inclined her head. 'You're welcome. Why don't I show you around so you can see how everything will work?'

'That'd be great.'

Kennard led me to a long table that was being set up to the right of the front doors. 'Participants will register here,' she told me. 'They will receive a lanyard, which they'll be expected to wear at all times, together with a printed schedule and map so they can find their way around the hotel.' She gave me a long look. 'I'm afraid we have to advise everyone to remain within the hotel and its grounds for the duration. It's not a rule we can enforce legally, but for the sake of safety and security—'

I nodded. 'I understand. I'll spread the word and encourage the delegates to stay put.'

A flicker of relief crossed her face. 'It's annoying, I know, but a necessary precaution. It helps that you made it a requirement for every delegate to book a hotel room and stay overnight.'

I'd received considerable resistance from the organising committee for asking it to implement that rule, but the last thing we needed were large numbers of supes wandering around between here and Soho and Lisson Grove. It would only encourage scuffles – or worse – with the humans who hated the idea that a bunch of supes could organise themselves in this fashion.

'What about hotel guests who aren't part of the summit?' I asked.

'There are only about thirty or so. Most people cancelled their bookings when the summit dates were published.'

I winced. 'Sorry about that.'

She shrugged. 'The number of supes attending the summit will more than make up for any lost bookings.' She leaned in and lowered her voice. 'And between you and me, we're already seeing a rise in numbers for after the summit is over. People want to say they slept in the same bed as a supe.'

I wrinkled my nose. Weird.

'We're also getting a lot of press inquiries.' Her tone was laced with disgust.

'You don't like the press?' I'd have thought for someone in her position courting the media was routine.

'It depends on which press,' she muttered. 'We've had trouble in the past with guests' privacy being invaded by certain journalists. It's astonishing the lengths some of them will go for their next story.'

I could imagine.

Kennard continued in a normal voice. 'The keynote speakers will address their audience in the ballroom. It's this way.' She led me away to the ballroom doors. I peered inside at the rows of chairs and nodded approval. 'The workshops,' she continued, 'will take place in the East Wing. We've grouped them according to general supernatural ethnicities. For example, "The Facts About Pixie Dust" and "How To Speak To Humans As A Lesser-Known Supe" will start at midday tomorrow next to each other in meeting rooms eighteen and nineteen. "Basics of Blood" and "Caring For Your Fangs", together with "Dispelling the Dracula Myth", will be further away in rooms forty-one, forty-two and forty-three.'

'And the steering committee on improving supe and human relationships?' I asked, focusing on the more important meetings that were scheduled to occur.

'They will be in the larger Rose Room.'

Excellent. For the first time in several weeks, I felt a glow of optimism. The supe summit had the potential to make a genuine difference to all our futures. As long as all the attendees behaved themselves, I reckoned we'd garner good enough press to start a shift in attitudes towards our existence.

I checked my watch. The champagne reception was due to begin in just under six hours' time. Despite the growing group of protestors outside, things were looking positive.

'The rest of Supe Squad are upstairs in a suite on the seventh floor,' Kennard told me. 'I'm told they're expecting you.' She pointed at the nearest lift. 'You can head up that way.'

I smiled my thanks and walked over. As I pressed the button to call the lift, someone stepped up to wait beside me. 'Hi, D'Artagnan,' Lukas drawled.

I gave him a slow smile. 'Hi.'

'I hear the wolf this morning escaped.'

I started. 'How did you—?' I began. No, there was no point in asking. Lukas had eyes and ears everywhere. 'Never mind.' I sighed. 'He vanished into thin air.'

'You shouldn't have got involved, you know.'

The lift doors slid open and we stepped inside. 'I did what I had to,' I said stiffly. 'It's not up for discussion.'

Lukas reached across me, pressed the button for the seventh floor and the lift doors closed smoothly. 'It messed with my morning routine.'

Feeling grouchy, I glared at him. 'What routine is that?'

He cupped my face in his hands and leaned in. 'The one where we do this.' His lips descended on mine.

Almost immediately, I went from spiky and annoyed to a puddle of lust. Lukas's body, hot and hard, pressed against mine. I pushed into him, my hands reaching for his hips. The lift jolted slightly as it started to rise but, with the taste of Lukas on my tongue, I barely noticed.

'You smell good, D'Artagnan,' he murmured in my ear. He dropped one hand and brushed the tips of his fingers against my breast. I gasped. Then the lift jerked and he stepped away, smoothing his black hair with one swift movement and leaving me flushed and bereft.

'Feeling better now?' I managed to ask, my gaze on Lukas as a couple stepped into the lift and stood in front of us facing the doors.

'I certainly am.' Lukas gave me an arch grin. His hand strayed to mine and our fingers entwined. I remembered to keep breathing and tried to slow my hammering heartbeat.

The couple, a tall thin man and a woman who was wearing flats but still matched his height, didn't turn around. 'Did you type up those notes I dictated?' the man asked his companion.

The lift stopped again and the doors opened to reveal a frowning Liza. 'You took your time getting here,' she said. 'Kennard called and said you were on your way. We're down the hallway.'

'Excuse me,' I murmured to the couple. They moved to the side to let Lukas and I exit.

'Yes,' the woman behind us said as the lift doors closed. 'I emailed them to you first thing, Chief.'

I stiffened and whipped round but it was already too late. The doors were firmly shut and the couple had gone.

CHAPTER SIX

I SPRANG FORWARD AND REPEATEDLY PRESSED THE LIFT BUTTON TO call it back. When that didn't work, I whirled for the emergency exit and the stairs, ignoring the confused expressions on Lukas's and Liza's faces.

The heavy exit door thudded against the wall as I threw it open. I barely noticed as I started sprinting upwards, taking the steps three at a time. It's a good thing that my phoenix abilities mean I'm fast. I needed some decent speed to catch up.

As soon as I reached the next floor, I lunged for the door and opened it. Nothing, just an empty corridor. I let the door close and ran upstairs again. Nothing. I pushed on upwards, aware that the DeVane Hotel was only twelve-storeys high and the odds were in my favour.

I reached for the door on the tenth floor. As soon as it opened, I heard them. They were out of sight somewhere down to my left. I held my breath, taking care to let the door close silently this time, then I darted on the balls of my feet towards the sound of the voices.

'You need to call down and get some fresh ice,' the man was

saying. 'There's a lot of work to be done today and I need to stay moist.'

Moist? Ick. I pulled a face as I stopped at the corner. I pressed my back against the wall and peeked round.

'I'll see to it, Chief,' the woman answered politely. She delved into her handbag, took out a keycard and swiped it against the door. I caught a glimpse of her youthful, freckled face but could only see the Chief in profile. He had a hawkish nose and pock-marked white skin. The door opened and their hotel room swallowed them up. I moved back and waited for a moment.

Further down the hall, the door to the stairs re-opened and Lukas popped his head out. When he saw me, he frowned and opened his mouth to speak. I put my finger to my lips and shook my head, then I scooted round the corner on tiptoe until I could see the number of the couple's hotel room: 1032.

I gazed at the closed door for a moment then moved in closer, cupped my ear against its smooth surface and listened. The DeVane Hotel took its guests' privacy seriously and I couldn't hear a damned word. My lips thinned and I stepped away.

It didn't matter that I couldn't eavesdrop. I've got you, Chief, I thought. Whoever the fuck you are.

* * *

'WE'VE GOT a list of all the guests staying in the hotel and their room numbers, right?' I asked, pacing around the confines of the suite commandeered for Supe Squad.

'Only the ones who are attending the summit,' Liza answered. 'We don't have access to any of the other guests, and I doubt the hotel would give us that kind of information without a warrant.'

'Look up room 1032. Is it one of ours? Who's in there?'

Liza sent me a long-suffering look. 'What exactly is this about?'

'Good question,' Lukas murmured.

'The werewolf this morning suggested that there was someone dangerous called the Chief who was here to disrupt the summit. And the bloke at Trafalgar Square a few days ago also spoke about someone called the Chief.' I paused for dramatic effect. 'That woman in the lift just now called her companion "Chief".'

'Uh…' He scratched his neck. 'That's it? That's what caused all this running around?'

'It's not paranoia if they're really out to get you,' I replied.

Liza cracked her knuckles and opened her laptop. 'The problem isn't being paranoid,' she declared. 'It's not being paranoid enough.'

I wasn't sure whether to be comforted by that statement or dismayed.

'Well,' Lukas said, 'if we're going down the jumping-at-shadows route, I'll get together a few of my vampires. We'll go up, knock on this Chief's door and find out what's going on. We'll know in an instant whether your worries are justified.'

I shook my head. Sometimes the direct approach worked, but not always. 'Not yet. Not until we know more about him. If he does pose a risk, I don't want him to know we're onto him. If he simply likes being called big names by younger women, I don't want to alarm him. Most of the humans in this hotel are already on edge and we don't need to add to that unnecessarily.'

'My way is much faster,' Lukas said. He raised his eyebrows, as if to remind me that I'd put a bullet in my own brain a few days earlier for that same reason.

'But my way is much better,' I answered, not allowing myself to get side-tracked. 'We need more evidence before we make a move. Remember that we're supposed to be promoting inclusivity. We can't turn this into a witch hunt until we know who this man is and what his intentions are.' I glanced up and we gazed at each other for a long moment. Something dark and filled with smoky promise glittered deep in Lukas's black eyes and I felt my cheeks heating up once more.

'There's a bedroom back there,' Liza said, without looking up from her screen.

I coughed. Lukas merely smiled.

'Okay,' Liza said, saving me from further embarrassment even though she'd caused it, 'I have your Chief. He's definitely here for the summit. He booked two spots less than a week after the dates were announced.'

I hadn't realised I'd been holding my breath. I exhaled loudly and went to look at the screen. 'Lance Emerson,' I read aloud. It didn't ring a bell. 'What do we know about him? What kind of supe is he? Where's he from?'

'I've never heard of him,' Lukas said, his smooth brow creasing.

'This is why we should have done proper background checks on everyone who's attending the summit,' Liza muttered

I folded my arms. 'One of the summit's goals is to encourage every supe to feel comfortable enough to live in the open, no matter who or what they are. Background checks wouldn't help with that in the slightest.'

She glared at me. 'Great, Emma. Except now we may have a psychotic anti-supe terrorist attending our own summit. Maybe he's planning to blow us all up. Or put arsenic in the drinking water. Or wave a magic wand and turn us all into frogs.'

I stared at her. I didn't have a good response to that. 'Uh ... ribbit?'

Liza rolled her eyes.

'Sorry.' I managed a quick grin. 'We need to find out who Lance Emerson is and why he's here, ideally without alerting him.'

'I'll put some feelers out and ask around,' Lukas said.

I nodded. 'I'll do the same. Someone is bound to have heard of him.'

Liza returned to her screen. 'I'll see what I can turn up on the internet and police databases.'

'That sounds like a good start.' I checked my watch. There was still plenty of time before the evening reception. 'We'll find out who this guy is. He might be nobody – he might enjoy being called Chief because it makes him feel like a big man. Nathan Fairfax might have been talking about someone else. Hell, for all I know he might have been spinning stories and making things up. But let's be cautious. We don't want anything to disrupt the summit and we can't afford any negative PR. We need it to work – *all* supes need this summit to work. It's a new beginning for everyone.'

Liza and Lukas stared at me. 'What?' I asked.

'Let's just say, D'Artagnan,' Lukas drawled, 'that it's not the first time you've made that sort of stirring little speech about the supe summit.'

I frowned. 'I want it to make a real difference. I won't apologise for that.'

He smiled at me, flashing his white fangs. 'Never apologise, D'Artagnan.' He licked his lips slowly. 'Never.'

Liza jerked her thumb backwards. 'The bedroom is still there if you need it.' She pretended to fan herself. 'But before you go, I have one other question.'

I tore my eyes away from Lukas and glanced at her. 'What is it?'

'Should I call DS Grace and tell him about your suspicions? The man's an idiot, but he is technically in charge.'

'He's not an idiot, Liza. He's just…'

'Anally retentive? A stickler for pointless details? A blond-haired pain in my arse with a stupid dimple in his cheek when he smiles?'

'What does his dimple have to do with anything?' I asked, baffled.

Liza looked away. 'Nothing.'

I nibbled my bottom lip. 'I'll speak to DS Grace.'

She shrugged. 'Suit yourself. Go on, then. First one to find out something useful about Lance Emerson wins a shiny gold star.'

* * *

LUKAS PLANTED a swift kiss on my mouth and headed into Soho to talk to his vampires. I wandered towards the hotel bar, hoping to find a few early birds whom I could question subtly.

I spotted a few giggling pixies sitting at a corner table. From the glasses in front of them, they were already doing some investigations of their own but their questions appeared to be focused on the best cocktails the DeVane Hotel offered rather than potential security risks. That didn't mean they couldn't help.

I pasted a smile on my face and joined them. 'Hey! You're here for the summit, right?'

All three pixie heads swivelled in my direction. 'Yes,' answered the blue-haired one, who appeared to be the oldest. 'And you're DC Bellamy.' She nudged her friends. 'She's the one I was telling you about. The one who can't die.'

Their eyes widened and they immediately straightened their backs. 'Hi, detective,' they squeaked in unison.

'I hope you're enjoying yourselves and having fun.'

'Losht of fun,' the pink-haired pixie said. Her friend elbowed her sharply in the ribs. 'I mean lots. Lots of fun.' She giggled.

I couldn't stop myself from smiling. 'Good. You're not too concerned about the protestors outside, are you?'

The first two pixies snorted derisively but the third one, whose blue hair shimmered in the sunlight streaming through the DeVane's large, impressive windows, looked away. I frowned. 'You have concerns?'

'No. They're out there, we're in here. I'm not worried,' she said in a tone that belied her words.

'Belly is a bit shaky after what happened last month,' the giggly pixie said hastily. 'Don't mind her.'

I pulled up a chair and sat down without waiting to be invited. 'What happened last month?'

Belly's eyes slid away. 'Nothing.'

'If she won't say it, then I will,' her pink-haired friend declared, a tad too loudly. 'She was jumped by three drunk human lads on her way home. They tried to drag her into an alley but she kicked one in the nuts and got away. Only just. The bruises are still fading.'

Shit. I stared at her. 'I didn't hear anything about this. Did you report it?'

Belly folded her arms defensively across her chest. 'No. There wasn't any point in reporting it. They'd never get caught and they'd never be charged. It's easier to forget it ever happened.'

'We're not werewolves or vampires.' Her friend's light tone and easy attitude were replaced by something far more bitter. 'We don't have power or strength or authority to fall back on if we need them.'

Belly sniffed. 'Indeed. You might mean well, detective, but you couldn't actually do anything about it. The humans would get off with a warning at best. We're fair game to them – we always have been. They're too smart to go after vamps or wolves, but we're pixies. We're not strong. It's harder for us to defend ourselves, so we're seen as victims no matter what we do. I won't fall into that category. I'm *not* a victim.' She glared at me. 'I refuse to be. It's the only reason I agreed to come to this summit.'

The bubbly green-haired pixie raised her glass, a flicker of desperation in her eyes as she tried to claw back the happy atmosphere. 'And the cocktails are good, so we're still going to enjoy ourselves,' she said firmly.

I kept my attention on Belly. 'I can take a statement from you now. We can find a quiet room nearby and—'

'No.'

'Or we can go down to the Supe Squad station—'

'No.'

I persisted. 'I want to help. You were attacked and I'm really sorry that happened. Let me do something to stop it happening again.'

Her eyes met mine. 'You won't stop it from happening again. You can't. Besides, it was weeks ago. I don't want to talk about it and I don't want to make a statement. I want to forget it ever happened and have a good time with my friends.' She scowled at me. 'Now piss off, detective.'

Damn it. That could have gone a lot better. 'I—'

The pink-haired pixie stared at me. 'Do as she says. Leave us in peace. We were having fun till you came along.'

I wasn't doing any good by staying. I cursed to myself and stood up. 'If you change your mind, I'm always available.'

The pixie screwed up her face and turned away. I grimaced. I could have handled this entire conversation differently. I *should* have handled it differently. And I still had to ask them about Emerson. 'Have any of you heard of a man called Lance—?'

This time even the green-haired pixie said it. 'Bye, detective!' she chirped before I could finish my sentence.

I clenched my jaw and then I walked away.

CHAPTER SEVEN

THE ANGER AND HURT IN BELLY'S EYES WOULDN'T LEAVE ME. THE supe summit was for people like her and situations like this; those pixies needed to know that if they reported a crime it would be taken seriously. The human fuckwits who'd attacked Belly also needed to know that sort of behaviour wasn't acceptable under any circumstances and they would be arrested and charged for it.

No matter how much I rationalised the aims of the summit, or promised myself that I'd seek out Belly once it was over and try again to persuade her to make a statement, I couldn't stop the rage flaring deep inside me. Supes were not fair fucking game. This had to stop.

Something – or rather someone – took hold of my elbow. I didn't pause to think but reached back, grabbed whoever it was and threw them over my shoulder. They landed badly, crashing into a chair and falling heavily onto the marble tiles.

All the seated customers and most of the hotel staff stopped to stare as I looked down at Kennedy. Oops. That was something of an over-reaction on my part. 'Sorry.' I extended a hand towards him.

Kennedy ignored it and heaved himself up to his feet with a grunt. 'Bloody hell, Bellamy.' He rubbed the back of his head. 'That was uncalled for.'

'Sorry,' I said again. I glanced at the drink in his hand. 'How is it that you're still holding onto that and haven't spilled a drop?'

He grinned slightly. 'Practice.' He peered at me. 'You've got stronger since the last time we spoke. And more jumpy.'

I grimaced. 'I've died a few times since then.'

Suddenly his eyes grew sharp. 'You ought to be careful. You don't know your own strength, and you don't know what the consequences of such strength might be.' He took a sip of his drink and smiled amiably. 'I saw you from across the room. You looked upset and I thought you might need a wee pick-me-up. I didn't think it would be me who'd end up needing to be picked up, but there we go.' He nodded at the bar. 'Now *you're* buying.'

I couldn't argue with that. While the guests and employees returned to whatever they'd been doing before, I walked across the room with Kennedy. He limped dramatically until I gave him an exasperated look, then he winked and offered me a mock salute.

We sat on two bar stools. I felt my heart sink when I saw two gremlins shuffle away from me at high speed. The last thing I wanted was to make the London supes afraid of me. I needed them to trust me, not fear me. Throwing a satyr over my shoulder because he'd dared to touch my elbow wasn't the best way to appear warm, cuddly and unthreatening.

'Chill out,' Kennedy told me, after I'd ordered a double whisky for him and a soda for myself. 'I know a lot is riding on this conference, but it's going better than you think and it's not even started yet. A large European supe contingent has arrived, and I'm certain I saw a few Yank vamps checking in earlier.'

'Thanks, Kennedy.' I gave him a sideways look. 'I have to admit, I didn't think I'd see you here.'

'Are you kidding?' His long golden ears twitching, he waved

an arm around. 'This is history in the making. I wouldn't miss it for the world. And the bar here is excellent.'

'Detective Constable Bellamy?' interrupted a smooth female voice.

I half-turned as a business card was thrust in my face. Taking it, as much to stop it from flapping in my eyes as for any other reason, I squinted at its owner. It was a woman with a slightly puffy face that suggested a tad too much Botox and light-brown hair tied in a bun. She looked to be in her early forties and was wearing a lot of make-up, but she was still attractive. She was wearing a tailored black business suit that looked expensive, albeit with black trainers on her feet instead of high-heeled shoes or smart pumps. If I wasn't mistaken, she was human.

I glanced at the card. Juliet Chambers-May, senior correspondent. Ah, a journalist. I noted the logo of the *Daily Filter* and felt my angry black gloom return. The *Daily Filter* was a right-wing rag with considerably more money than morals. 'Ms Chambers-May,' I said politely. 'What can I do for you?'

She trilled out a fake laugh. 'Oh please, darling, call me Juliet. I don't stand on ceremony. I'm much too down to earth for that.'

The string of cultured pearls round her neck, manicured talons instead of fingernails and excessive make-up suggested otherwise, but I played along. There wasn't much else I could do. 'How may I help, Juliet?'

She beamed widely. 'That was quite some move you pulled off there. Why did you attack this ... man?' She blinked innocently at Kennedy, giving his downy ears and large frame a pointed look. 'And what *is* he?'

Instead of taking offence at her obvious disdain, Kennedy smiled lazily and extended his large hand. 'Darling,' he drawled, 'I'm a satyr.'

The journalist didn't look remotely surprised; she was obviously aware of Kennedy's heritage and had only asked in a vain bid to establish her own superiority. 'Goodness. Does that mean wine, women and song?' She glanced down at his crotch. 'Is it only your ears that are covered in fur, or are other parts of your body equally animal?'

Juliet Chambers-May appeared determined to be as politely offensive as possible and her clipped accent only added to the effect. I noted from the dark looks she was receiving from two vampires nearby that we weren't the only people she'd been trying to upset.

She was going to have to try harder to get an angry reaction out of Kennedy or me. 'The two of us are old friends,' I said. 'In fact, Kennedy helped to train me with a crossbow. The physical greeting you witnessed was nothing more than an inside joke.' I displayed my teeth in a smile to match hers. 'Thank you for your questions and have a good day.' I turned away.

I should have known she wouldn't give up that easily. She tapped my shoulder insistently. 'I was hoping you could answer a few more questions.'

'Maybe later,' I said. 'I'm busy right now.'

Her eyes drifted to the drink in my hand. 'Mmm. Yes, I can see you're *very* busy. Are you on duty, detective? Is that vodka?'

She was doing her absolute best to piss me off. 'All interview requests need to go through the Supernatural Squad office.'

'I only have a couple of questions and then I'll get out of your hair.' Without pausing for breath, she continued. 'Do you genuinely believe it's a good idea to have so many supernatural creatures in the same place at the same time?'

I debated ignoring her, but I knew it would be better to answer her damned questions and get her out of my way as quickly as possible. 'It would be difficult to have a supernatural summit without them,' I said.

'But some of them are very dangerous. Has the hotel taken out extra insurance? Are they safeguarding their staff?'

'You'd have to talk to the DeVane Hotel management about that.'

'Oh, don't worry, detective, I'll definitely do that.' She fluttered her eyelashes at me for reasons I couldn't quite grasp. 'Your boyfriend, Lord Lukas Horvath, is in attendance.'

I waited.

'Detective?' she prompted.

'I didn't hear a question,' I said.

Juliet smiled tightly. 'He has quite a reputation. If he has sex with other vampires while he's here, will you attack them like you attacked Mr Kennedy?'

What. The. Actual. Fuck? I stared at her. Okay. She was upping her irritation game.

'I hear ghouls are attending the night sessions. Will you be providing dead human bodies for them to munch on?'

There was no longer any point trying to answer her questions because I suspected that she didn't want any answers. She certainly didn't look like she'd listen to anything that didn't fit her own agenda.

'I've been informed,' she continued, 'that there will be several druids. This is a God-fearing Christian country. Is it wise to promote dangerous religions that go against the beliefs of the great British public?'

I was starting to get a headache. Beside me, Kennedy folded his arms. He was the easiest-going person I knew but even he looked as if he wanted to punch Ms Chambers-May in the face.

'Speaking of dangerous religions,' she added. Bloody hell. She still wasn't finished. 'Why is the leader of a cult here at your conference?'

Huh?

'What are you trying to achieve by including those sorts of people, detective?'

I forced my expression into a blank mask. I wouldn't reveal any of my thoughts to her. 'The aims of the supernatural summit,' I said, quoting directly from the publicity material, 'are to foster greater openness, understanding and compassion. It is an inclusive event and both supes and humans are encouraged to attend. Goodbye, Ms Chambers-May.'

'But—'

Kennedy growled. 'It's time for you to go.'

I could see from her eyes that she was considering her options and debating whether to continue to push her luck, but Kennedy's brief snarl made up her mind. 'Thanks for your time,' she said brightly. She wheeled away and sauntered out of the bar in pursuit of her next hapless victim.

Kennedy rolled his eyes, an irritated golden sheen flitting across his irises to indicate his annoyance. 'I'm all for freedom of the press,' he muttered, 'but that woman is a vicious menace. At least once the summit starts, the likes of her will be limited to where they can go in the hotel. She probably considers herself a pillar of democracy.' He sniffed. 'Don't go making the mistake of thinking you can change her mind about supes. She's not the sort who listens to other viewpoints, no matter how valid they might be. You'd be wise to stay away from her – she's more dangerous than you'd think.'

'Uh-huh.' I tapped my fingernails against my glass. 'Who do you reckon she was talking about when she said there was a cult leader here?'

'I imagine she meant that Emerson bloke. I thought *he* was annoying until I met Juliet Chambers-May.' Kennedy exhaled heavily and downed his whisky. He raised a finger towards the bartender to order another without realising that I'd gone completely still and was staring at him.

I kept my tone very calm and very even. 'Kennedy,' I said. He glanced at me. 'What Emerson bloke?'

His clever eyes sharpened. 'He's from up north,' he said. 'He approached me when I arrived this morning with a leaflet about his organisation, The Perfect Path of Power or some other bull-shit. He has a vision for the future of all supes. As far as I can tell, it involves leaving London illegally and joining him up-country while handing over the details of all my bank accounts.' He tilted his head. 'Why?'

I jumped off my stool. 'I can't say yet. Do you still have the leaflet?'

'I binned it almost straight away.'

That was a shame but it wasn't the end of the world. I flashed him a bright smile. 'Gotta go, Kennedy. Sorry again about the throwdown.'

'You didn't finish your soda!'

I waved at him as I turned away. 'You have it.'

'I don't do soft drinks,' he grumbled.

I paid him little attention. I had other things to think about.

* * *

Liza was still in the Supe Squad suite. Fred had reappeared and was hovering by her shoulder, an anxious look on his face.

'I've got something,' I announced, without mentioning that the something had come from a chance question by a terrible journalist. I was well aware that the information I'd unearthed had been down to luck rather than my investigative powers.

'So have we,' Liza crowed.

Excellent. 'You first,' I said.

'Everything suggests that Lance Emerson is the chief that your werewolf mentioned this morning. He checked into the hotel three nights ago and is staying until the morning after the summit ends. He's down to attend several workshops. A few months ago he put in a request to host a presentation but his petition was denied.'

Okay. 'What kind of presentation?' I asked.

Fred read from a piece of paper. 'He called it "Meditation Techniques To Keep Our Inner Monsters At Bay".'

I raised an eyebrow. 'He wanted to use the M word at a supe conference? No wonder the planning committee shut him down.'

Fred snorted. 'Yeah, he clearly didn't get the memo about the summit's goal being to try and stop the rest of the country from thinking of supes as monsters.'

'Is he a supe?' I asked. Nathan Fairfax had seemed to think so, but I wanted to be sure.

Liza wrinkled her nose. 'I think he's human.'

'You're not certain?'

'He claims that he's descended from Merlin.'

Uh… 'Merlin the magician? King Arthur's Merlin?'

'Yep.'

'Was Merlin real?'

She shrugged. 'Your guess is as good as mine.'

'So Emerson is a druid?' They were humans, just … special humans.

'No. The druids are a tight community. They don't get out much and they don't advertise themselves very often, but they have publicly distanced themselves from Emerson. They think he's a crackpot.' She brought up a public Facebook page and showed me a post from several months earlier. 'It says here that Lance Emerson has been banned from all druid activities, all his social media posts have been removed from their pages, and contact with him is to be avoided.'

It was beginning to sound like Nathan Fairfax wasn't the only person who was concerned about the Chief. 'We've got druids attending the summit,' I mused.

'Only three,' Liza said. 'Most of them declined the invitation.'

'They still might know what this is about.' I looked at Fred. 'Can you find them and see if they're prepared to talk about him?' Fred was young and unthreatening. That made him the perfect person to approach the wary druids.

He straightened up. 'Absolutely.'

'Good. Do you have anything else?' I asked Liza.

'Emerson has a large property in Cumbria near the Scottish border. I found several police reports that indicate he has a rather heavy-handed approach towards any hikers and dog walkers who stray onto his land. Compared to Scotland, our Right To Roam laws are limited and weighted towards the landowners, but Lance Emerson has still fallen foul of the rules. Locals also say that they often hear chanting coming from the property, and a few farmers nearby seem to believe that Emerson has stolen several animals. Mostly sheep, I think. Despite the efforts of local police, the sheep haven't been recovered. Neither have their bodies.'

'Bodies?'

Liza drew in a breath. 'There was an allegation that animals were being sacrificed by Emerson's organisation.'

I felt ill. 'Sacrificed? Why? To whom?'

'That part's not clear. Emerson runs a group called The Perfect Path Of Power and Redemption but I haven't been able to find out if they worship any particular deity.'

Feeling distinctly uncomfortable, I rubbed the back of my neck. Sacrifice smacked of blind devotion, ancient uneducated traditions and a sprinkling of, dare I say it, evil. I was starting to think that Nathan Fairfax had been right to voice his concerns – and that Juliet Chambers-May had been spot on when she spoke about a cult. 'Where did the allegation come from?'

'This is where it gets more interesting,' Liza said.

More interesting? 'Go on.'

'Three years ago, a young woman presented herself at the local police station in Thursby in Cumbria. She said that she was a werewolf and she'd been manipulated into staying with Emerson for a number of months. Apparently he promised her that he could heal her and remove her … uh … animal.'

My mouth dropped open. 'You're kidding me.'

'Nope.'

'Why are we only hearing about this now? Her case should have been referred immediately to Supe Squad.' My eyes narrowed. If the clans knew about this and hadn't passed on the information, there would be hell to pay. I'd make sure of it.

'It would have been referred to us, and the clan alphas would have been included from the outset, if it hadn't been clear that the young lady was definitely not a werewolf,' Liza said.

A sudden chill zipped down my spine. First Night Stalker Jim, now this woman. 'She was lying?'

'From what I can gather, the Thursby police believed she was delusional rather than deliberately untruthful. They interviewed Emerson. He confirmed that she'd been staying with him and the Perfect Path because she was under the mistaken impression that she was a supe and couldn't be persuaded otherwise. He'd been counselling her in an effort to get her to recognise the truth.'

'They believed him?'

Liza shrugged. 'They had no reason not to. The woman wasn't a wolf. They did a blood test to check.'

'It's messed up,' Fred said. 'Unless she grew fur overnight and suddenly had overwhelming cravings for raw meat, why would she think she was a werewolf?'

'It wouldn't be the first time. There's a reason why we use wolfsbane and verbena to weed out non-supes,' Liza replied.

My unease was growing. There was far more to this than the usual confused humans who wandered into Supe Squad convinced they were supernatural. 'It's amazing what people will allow themselves to be persuaded of,' I said grimly. I glanced at Fred. 'Ever felt run down?'

'Sure.'

'Lost your appetite?'

'Yeah.'

'Received a few mysterious bruises that you can't quite explain?'

He folded his arms. 'Boss, I might experience all of those things sometimes, but that doesn't mean I believe that I turn into a werewolf during the night and sleepwalk my way into hunting for prey without realising what I'm doing.'

'No,' I replied, '*you* don't. But some people do.' Learning of two in one week was unusual, though.

'People are dumb.'

I shrugged. 'Put it another way. Have you ever looked up symptoms on an internet-based medical site and come away convinced you have cancer?'

'No.' Then he looked away. 'But I did once think I might have dengue fever.'

Liza leaned back in her chair. 'Isn't that a mosquito-borne disease found in tropical countries?'

'It's very serious,' Fred said.

'Had you visited any tropical countries at the time?'

'Does Wales count?'

I smiled slightly. 'People can be persuaded into believing a lot of things,' I said softly

'That's all very well,' Liza said, 'But it doesn't help us with Lance Emerson. What are we going to do about him?'

I considered the options. 'There's something not right about him, but we've no evidence that he's done anything illegal.'

'Yet,' Fred muttered.

'We only have a few dark whispers about him. We don't have any *evidence* that he's done anything illegal.' Lisa repeated my words.

'Not here in London.' I quickly outlined what I'd learned from Kennedy. 'If he's persuading people that they're supe when they're not...'

'That's not illegal.'

'Or if he's recruiting supes to his weird cult...'

'That's not illegal either.'

'It is if they move out of the supe zone in London and up to the Borders,' I said.

Fred intervened. 'But it's the supes who would be breaking the law, not Emerson.'

I thought about what Nathan Fairfax had said, that Emerson had a black heart and a silver tongue. 'Regardless of what the law says, we have enough reasons to boot him out of the summit. In fact, we don't need a reason to boot him out.'

Fred looked at me. 'I'm sensing a but.'

I nodded. 'As long as Emerson is here, we can keep an eye on him. If we throw him out of the summit and get the DeVane Hotel to eject him, he'll be out there getting up to all sorts and we won't know what. I don't have a good feeling about him, and I have no doubt that his reasons for being here are less than savoury, but I'd rather know where he is and what he's doing.'

Liza shrugged. 'It's your funeral.'

I'd died seven times so far, and I hadn't yet enjoyed any sort of funeral. 'I'll speak to DS Grace and get him to sign off on this. We can always change our minds and kick Emerson out later, if we have to. Unless the druids or Lukas come up with something concrete against him, I think this is our best option.'

I checked my watch. 'The champagne reception starts in a couple of hours and we have a lot of other guests to consider. The supe summit is too important – we can't let concerns about one man derail it.' I hoped I wouldn't live to regret my words.

CHAPTER EIGHT

I WASN'T USED TO WEARING A DRESS; I TEND TOWARDS LOOSE-fitting trousers that allowed for greater ease of movement. I certainly wasn't used to wearing to a slinky long black cocktail dress with a plunging neckline and a face full of make-up. Unfortunately, I didn't feel sexy – I felt kind of stupid.

'I'm sorry I couldn't find out anything useful about Lance Emerson,' Lukas called from the other room. 'But if he's at the reception there will be a lot of eyes on him. All my vampires have been pre-warned.' He walked into the bathroom adjusting his pristine white cuffs.

I turned towards him and he gaped. 'Too much?' His jaw worked. Damn it. Yeah, too much. I looked ridiculous.

Lukas found his voice. 'We don't have to be there tonight,' he said in a low, husky tone. 'We could stay in our room. The others will manage perfectly well without us.' His black eyes glittered. 'You look too good for a bunch of shady supes.' He strode towards me, reached for my waist and pulled me towards him. 'In fact, D'Artagnan, you look good enough to eat.' He dipped his head towards the base of my neck and his lips brushed a line of feather-light kisses across my bare collarbone.

I gave a delicate shiver. 'You look pretty damned delicious yourself, my Lord Horvath.'

'I look like a waiter. I hate tuxedos,' he grunted.

'It suits you.' It was true. The fabric moulded to his frame and the perfect tailoring revealed a hint of the sculpted body underneath. 'You look less like a waiter and more like a model from an over-sexed aftershave advert.'

He raised a single eyebrow. 'Over-sexed?'

'Not now.' I flashed a grin. 'But maybe later.'

'I'll hold you to that.' He stepped back, put a hand in his pocket and pulled out a narrow box. 'Here. I thought you might want to wear this.'

Slightly wary, I took the box from him and opened the lid. Nestled against black velvet was a ruby necklace. The multitude of shimmering gems were shaped into teardrops in a silver setting. The colours were extraordinary. 'Bloody hell.'

'Funny you should say that,' he said. 'It's called the Tears of Blood.'

'That's … creepy.'

Lukas shrugged. 'It's an old piece. I didn't name it.' The light in his eyes grew more intense. 'But I should tell you that it has a meaning. If you wear it, the vampires will understand that meaning, as will most of the werewolves and a lot of other supes. Not all of them will like it.'

'It's silver,' I said drily. 'It goes without saying that the wolves won't be keen.' Lukas didn't say anything. I met his eyes. 'What?' I asked. 'What's the meaning?'

'That our relationship is more than casual. It's usually worn by the Lady of the vampires.'

'I'm not a vampire.'

'No.' He watched me intently. 'But our relationship is more than boyfriend and girlfriend. You could say that it's our equivalent of an engagement ring.'

My mouth was suddenly dry. 'In that case,' I whispered, 'I'd be honoured to wear it.'

His expression transformed in an instant from watchful and quiet to blazing with triumph, laced with a measure of relief. I hadn't realised until then that he was nervous. He picked up the necklace and fastened it round my neck. It was cold and heavy, but it felt oddly comfortable. 'It suits you.'

I swallowed. 'Thank you.'

Lukas lowered his lips to my ear. 'I know you still doubt me sometimes, D'Artagnan, but I will never lie to you. I promise you that.'

I smiled at him and slipped my hand into his. I could trust him. I let myself relax. I *would* trust him.

* * *

I DEPOSITED my crossbow with the DeVane Hotel receptionist. I wasn't naïve enough to walk into a supe-filled room without it near at hand, but I wasn't stupid enough to carry it. It would only be seen as a provocation – or as a suggestion that the police didn't trust all the supes in the room to play nice.

The receptionist handled it gingerly, clearly afraid that it might go off. I watched as she placed it in the safe behind the desk. She breathed out heavily, relieved to have it out of her line of sight. I smiled my thanks and crossed my fingers that I wouldn't have to retrieve it in a hurry because I needed to use it.

Lukas and I walked hand in hand into the bar. Several heads turned in our direction and several eyes widened at the sight of the glittering necklace around my neck. I kept a fixed smile on my face despite the tightening in my shoulders when I saw how many supes were in attendance, including werewolves from all four clans.

While Lukas headed off to the bar to get us a couple of drinks, I made a beeline for Ladies Sullivan and Fairfax. Before I was ten metres from them, two werewolves stepped into my path and barred my way.

I looked from Buffy to her companion and back again. 'Are you playing the role of bodyguard tonight?' I enquired. 'You do know this is a party, right? There won't be any trouble.'

'You don't know that,' Buffy returned.

'I do,' I told her, 'because I won't allow it.'

She gave a peal of laughter. 'Immortality is going to your head, DC Bellamy. You're starting to think you're some kind of god.'

My smile didn't flicker. I understood the werewolves well enough to know that they appreciated gargantuan claims and loud boasts of power. 'Make that goddess,' I returned.

Buffy's eyes dropped to the necklace. It was obvious from her expression that she recognised it and understood its significance. 'I don't know of any goddesses who belong to the bloodsuckers.' She widened her eyes. 'But I'm not as clever or as educated as you are.'

I snorted. Yeah, yeah.

DS Grace appeared at my shoulder. 'Good evening,' he said to Buffy, the perfect picture of a polite police officer. I could have kicked him. 'I trust you're enjoying yourself so far.'

Buffy simpered and I stared at her. 'Oh, it's so fabulous!' she said. She raised her glass to him. 'Though I think these bubbles are going straight to my head.' She staggered slightly and collided with Grace's body. He was forced to put a hand out to steady her. 'You're so strong, detective,' she purred. 'And you have such quick reflexes.'

I rolled my eyes. DS Grace looked pleased. 'Call me Owen.'

'Owen? What a beautiful name.' She curtsied, dipping so low and yet so gracefully that it was impossible not to be impressed. 'Just like its owner.'

'You're too kind,' he murmured. He looked over her shoulder. 'Is it possible to gain an audience with your alpha?'

'Of course, Owen!' Buffy immediately stepped to the side. 'You're always welcome.'

Translation: I wasn't. I pretended I was anyway and stuck so closely to Grace that Buffy had no choice but to let me past.

'She's very dangerous, isn't she?' he murmured to me.

'Oh yes.'

'I thought so.' He sighed. 'Oh well.'

Lady Sullivan raised a hand. 'Detective Sergeant Grace. It's wonderful to see you,' she drawled. She looked at me and sniffed, her tone altering enough to be on the edge of disdainful. 'And you, DC Bellamy.'

'Have you found my missing werewolf yet?' Lady Fairfax asked.

Grace glanced at me. 'We were going to ask you the same question.'

I relaxed slightly. DS Grace wasn't quite the fool that everyone thought he was.

Lady Fairfax folded her arms. 'We have not.' She looked pissed off about it. I felt relieved for Nathan, albeit baffled as to where on earth he'd disappeared to.

'I'm surprised, detective, that you don't take care about what your staff do.' Lady Sullivan's tone was cutting. 'I hoped that Supernatural Squad would remain impartial towards all supes, but I can see that's not the case.'

My eyes narrowed as I recognised that my cold-shoulder treatment had nothing to do with Nathan Fairfax and everything to do with Lukas's necklace. The werewolves obviously believed that I was firmly on the side of the vampires. They didn't understand me at all.

'I can assure you that all our officers are both fair and unbiased, Lady Sullivan,' Grace said. 'We follow the laws of this land and we don't take sides. Justice is impartial.'

It wasn't the best answer he could have given; I doubted there was a single person in the room who believed that justice meted out by the laws of this land was ever impartial.

Both alphas' lips curled simultaneously.

'We're done with you now,' Lady Sullivan said. 'Go away.' She took Lady Fairfax's arm and they strolled away with a large entourage of werewolves trailing in their wake.

DS Grace stared after them. 'At least I was polite.'

'The wolves don't like polite, sir,' I said. 'They like power.'

He straightened his back. 'We are the arm of the law,' he declared, a tad too loudly.

He ought to stop bringing that up. I patted him on the arm. 'Yes,' I agreed. 'But the law isn't particularly kind where supes are concerned.'

'You don't seem to agree with either supe law or human law, Emma.'

I chose my words carefully. 'There are aspects of both which are ... troubling.'

'So why do this? Why be a detective?' His gaze was curious rather than censorious.

I leaned towards him. 'I like to catch bad guys.'

Grace smiled slightly. 'Speaking of potential bad guys, I don't see this Lance Emerson anywhere.'

He was right. I'd been keeping an eye out and hadn't caught sight of either him or his freckled assistant. 'He'll be here,' I said. 'He won't miss an opportunity to schmooze with supes.'

'You say that like you know him.'

'I know his type,' I replied darkly.

Grace's sighed. 'Unfortunately, so do I. Very well, I'm prepared to trust your instincts. Allowing him to stay at the summit is probably a good idea, especially as he appears to be human. We have enough problems as it is without people believing we're anti-human.' He pulled back his shoulders. 'I keep getting interview requests from this terrible Chambers-May woman. She seems to believe that Supe Squad despises humans.' He smacked his chest. '*I'm* bloody human!'

'She's been causing problems for me, too,' I admitted.

Grace stiffened. 'Speaking of problems,' he muttered.

I followed his gaze. He was staring at Liza. 'What?' I asked, confused.

'Look at what Liza is wearing! It's completely inappropriate!'

I frowned. She had on a pretty emerald-green dress that was offset her red hair perfectly. There was nothing inappropriate about it.

'I'm going outside to check on the protestors. There are more there now than there were before, and we have to keep tabs on them.' He marched away before I could speak.

Lukas reappeared holding two champagne glasses. 'Is DS Grace alright?' he asked.

I pursed my lips. 'Beats me.'

'Sorry I took so long. Kennedy was up there and demanded my attention. I think he's been sitting at that bar all day.'

It was highly likely. I glanced over to see if I could spot the golden-eared satyr but there were too many people blocking my view. 'Look how many are here, Lukas. Lots of supes came, and plenty of humans too.' A brief thrill of delight rippled through me. 'I'm finally beginning to think that the summit might be a success.'

'It was your idea. You deserve the credit.'

I smiled at him. 'I don't really. Others did most of the planning.' Then my smile vanished. 'You know who I can't see, though?'

Lukas's mouth flattened. 'Lance Emerson.'

'Indeed. The Chief is still not here.' I took a sip from my glass. 'I'll give him five minutes. If he doesn't show, I'll get Kennard to send housekeeping to his room so we can make sure he's not up to anything.'

Lukas didn't respond. His eyes were focused on something across the room. 'Something's wrong,' he said.

I stiffened. 'What is it?'

He pointed. Wilma Kennard was standing in the doorway to the bar; her right hand was covering her mouth and she looked as pale as a damned ghost. My stomach dropped.

I pushed through the crowd with Lukas on my heels. 'What's wrong, Wilma?' I asked softly. 'What's happened?'

The relief that flashed across her face when she saw me didn't ease my fear in the slightest. 'You need to come with me,' she said. 'It's urgent.'

'What?' I asked. 'What is it?'

She swallowed. I'd never seen her look nervous or frightened before, but there was no denying she was now. 'It's better if you see it for yourself.'

'Wilma—'

She lowered her voice. 'One of the guests has been found in the spa. He's dead.' Her ashen face probably meant murder rather than death by natural causes. Nausea rolled in my stomach. 'Which guest?' I demanded. 'What's his name?'

She drew in a shuddering breath and I had a horrible sinking feeling. I knew what she was going to say.

'I think,' she murmured, 'it's a man called Lance Emerson.'

Shit. Bloody damned fucking shit.

CHAPTER NINE

THE SPA WAS ON THE OTHER SIDE OF THE HOTEL. AT LEAST THE distance meant we didn't have to worry about any supes with sensitive noses noticing the scent of blood.

'I haven't called 999 to bring in the other police yet,' Wilma said, as we marched quickly towards the suite of spa rooms. 'It seemed wise to speak to you first.'

I shot her a quick glance. She was a clever woman, and she understood the implications of a dead body at the first supe conference. The longer we kept this under wraps, the better. We couldn't keep a death quiet for long, but we had to manage the flow of information and ensure that the details were only revealed when we understood what had happened. As long as we could justify keeping a murder quiet, and public safety wouldn't be compromised as a result, the law was on our side.

'I appreciate that,' I murmured. 'If you could send someone across the street to find DS Grace, that would be helpful.'

She nodded and pulled a member of staff aside. I reminded myself to breathe and stay calm. This was my job; I was trained for it and I'd dealt with far worse situations. It was imperative that I kept an open mind. We couldn't just be fair and impartial, we had to be *seen* to be fair and impartial.

I stopped in my tracks and turned to Lukas. 'You have to go back to the reception.'

He frowned. 'Somebody has died. I can't go and sip champagne.'

'You have to. You can't be at the crime scene, Lukas. This is for Supe Squad to deal with. The vampires can't be seen to be getting involved – not yet.'

His face shuttered. 'You mean because a vampire might be the murderer.'

'I didn't say that.' I touched his arm and lowered my voice. 'Caesar's wife must be above suspicion in every way. This is about protecting you, your vampires and all the other supes in the hotel. You have to go back and act like nothing's happened.' I gazed into his eyes. 'And you have to pay attention. I need to know who's there and who's absent. Who is drinking more than they would normally? Who is acting strangely?'

'It sounds like you already believe a supe is the murderer when you don't even know for sure that a murder has been committed.' Barely suppressed anger rippled through his voice. He didn't like being told what to do. I understood that – I didn't like it, either. But this was what had to happen and deep down Lukas knew it.

'Lukas,' I said. 'Please.'

He clenched his fists then released them. 'Okay,' he said. 'Okay.'

'Thank you.'

He remained where he was for a moment, his black eyes searching my face. 'You know, D'Artagnan,' he said softly, 'it's not going to matter. The fact that there's been a murder here will be more than enough to condemn every supe for the rest of time. In the blink of an eye, we've gone from an event that could have changed everything for the better to one that could destroy any progress we make with the humans. The summit that you planned to improve our circumstances will end up being the death of us instead.'

I set my jaw stubbornly. 'It won't.'

'You can't promise that.'

'No,' I conceded, 'but I can do my best. And my best is pretty damned good.'

To Lukas's credit he didn't argue, but I could see black shadows of doubt in his face. Frankly, I couldn't blame him for those.

* * *

WILMA KENNARD HAD POSSESSED the foresight to place a guard in front of the spa suite. He nodded as we approached. 'Has anyone else come this way?' I asked.

'No, ma'am. You're the first two people since I was asked to stand here. The spa closed two hours ago. There's nothing else beyond these rooms, so there's no reason for anyone to come here.'

Okay. I took a deep breath and gazed at the immaculate glass-fronted doors of the spa. 'Who found him?' I asked Wilma.

'One of the hotel cleaners. She's pretty shaken up. She's in the staff room with a cup of very sweet tea.'

'I'll need to speak to her.'

'She'll stay as long as you need.'

'Thank you.'

'The only other person who's been inside is me,' Wilma said, 'and that was only to confirm that Mr Emerson is dead. I didn't touch anything.'

I nodded my appreciation and swallowed. My mouth was dry and my stomach rolled unpleasantly. No matter how many times I did this, or how often I died, murder messed with my head, but the day I became blasé about investigating suspicious death was the day I should find a new career.

'Nobody else is to enter these rooms unless I or DS Grace say so.' I glanced down at my bare hands. I was wearing a damned cocktail dress; I didn't have any forensic kit or protective equipment.

'Here.' Wilma held out a box of disposable gloves. 'I thought you might need these.'

Bless her. I extracted two and put them on.

'The body is in the massage room,' she told me. 'It's the first door on the left after the welcome desk.'

I pulled back my shoulders and pushed open the spa door. There were several elaborate arrangements of fresh orchids around the reception area. I sniffed; strangely, although my nostrils tickled slightly, I couldn't detect any heady floral scent.

I glanced at the slightly ajar door to the massage room but didn't rush towards it. Instead I took my time and looked slowly round the spa's reception area for anything out of place. There was a small seating area with neatly fanned magazines on top of a low table. A darkened computer screen sat on the reception desk, and there were floating shelves along the far wall. Most were occupied by small plants in pretty pot holders, but one shelf held three candles. I walked over and peered at them. None of the candles were lit but their wicks were black and stubby and the wax in the centre of the largest one looked soft, as if it had only recently been extinguished.

I glanced round once more to make sure I'd not missed anything, then went towards the four doors beyond the desk. I ignored the open massage-room door; I wanted to know what lay beyond the closed doors.

The first led into a large room with leather-covered chairs, footstools, sinks and an array of expensive-looking beauty products. Nothing seemed disturbed or out of place. It was so clean that I suspected any dust that dared to sneak in would immediately be scared away.

I tried the second room. It was a dressing area with clean white robes hanging on hooks, three empty cubicles and a bank of lockers, none of which were closed. The wallpaper had a pink tinge and there was a large photograph of a serene mountain view on the wall.

There was another door at the far end. The door knob clicked, indicating that it was locked. I pursed my lips and went to the third room. It was identical to the previous one, even in the artwork, but the wallpaper was blue. I snorted. A room for women and a room for men, then. The far door in this dressing room was also locked.

As I turned to head for the last room where I knew I'd find Emerson's body, the hooks and hanging gowns caught my eye. Four hooks but only three white gowns. I paused and looked round once more, checking the narrow cubicles. There were no clothes or shoes waiting for their owner to return. The lockers, where items might have been placed for safekeeping, were open and empty. I tapped my mouth thoughtfully, then I pivoted and headed for room number four.

The door was open but I had to nudge it with my foot to slip inside. I stood at the threshold and gazed at the scene.

'Hey there.' I spoke softly. Needless to say, Lance Emerson didn't respond.

There was no point in checking his pulse; he was most definitely dead. His naked body was sprawled across the massage table facing upwards. One heavy leg dangled over the side and his head lolled off the end. His staring eyes were fixed on me. Feeling foolish and uncomfortable, I stepped to my right to avoid his dead-eyed gaze. I had to take care not to disturb the blood pooling beneath his corpse.

His throat had been slit from ear to ear. The weight of his head, combined with the depth of the slice, had made the wound gape open and the flesh rip. I wasn't certain, but it looked as if the blade had cut through his windpipe. A single arc of blood was splattered across the wall to his left. He'd died quickly, albeit gruesomely.

Emerson was a large man and he must have tried to fight back in the few seconds when he'd realised what was happening. Whoever had done this must have used considerable strength and put a speedy stop to any defence. And strength meant supe.

There was no sign of his clothes or the missing robe, and I couldn't see the murder weapon. Lying on the centre of his chest was a white card. I edged round the table to get a better look. It was a business card. An embossed logo with the letters SP in black was etched onto it, then Emerson's name and a mobile phone number underneath.

'Jesus H Christ.'

The sound of DS Grace's voice made such an impact in the silent, death-filled room that I jerked, jumping backwards as my heart nearly leapt out of my chest. I gasped loudly and narrowly avoided colliding with a table of glass bottles filled with coloured liquid. I was irritated with myself for such an extreme reaction, but DS Owen Grace wasn't looking at me. His focus was wholly on Emerson.

After a few long seconds, he dragged his eyes away from the body and onto me. 'We have a problem.'

That was the understatement of the year.

* * *

'We should release a statement immediately.' Grace's arms were folded and a muscle ticked angrily in his cheek. There was certainly no sign of the dimple that so irked Liza. 'We have to get everyone in here and as many police as possible. We have to talk to the press, and we have to start interviewing every guest in this hotel straight away. We have to be seen to be carrying out a full-on, guns-blazing investigation. Neither Supe Squad nor the Metropolitan Police can hide from this shocking crime. The most likely scenario is that somebody staying in this hotel is responsible. Security is tight and strangers aren't wandering in off the street. We've made sure of that.'

DSI Barnes, who'd arrived here straight from her home and was the only one of us not in formal evening wear, looked at me. 'Emma?'

I lifted my chin. 'I'm not suggesting that we don't investigate Lance Emerson's murder with all the energy we can muster. And I'm not suggesting that we try to brush anything under the carpet.'

'But?'

I exhaled. 'A loud, noisy investigation won't help us find the murderer, it will just make the supes here close ranks. Besides, Lance Emerson was here for the supe summit so it's possible he was a supe himself. That means his death falls under Supe Squad's remit.'

'What kind of supe do you think he was?' Barnes asked.

'I don't know. There are plenty of undocumented supernatural species out there. It's one of the reasons we're holding the summit. We need to know who the supes are – and *what* they are.'

'There's nothing to suggest he was supe,' Grace argued.

'He was attending the summit,' I repeated. 'Isn't that enough? Plus we've all seen the protestors outside and we all know that anti-supe sentiment is on the rise. Everyone in the hotel is immediately under suspicion. Until we can point to a culprit, it won't be one supe who's blamed but *all* supes. Okay,' I conceded, 'Emerson was probably human. To a lot of people out there that means his life was worth more than a supe's. In the short term, fingers will be pointed and the summit will collapse. In the long term, attacks on supes will increase and more of them will go into hiding, which will cause bigger problems in the future. Any efforts to improve human–supe relations will be set back by decades. We can't rule out the possibility that the motive for this murder was to upset the summit and do just that.'

'Neither can we pretend the murder didn't happen!' Grace snapped.

'I'm not saying that we should,' I returned in a far calmer tone than I felt. 'But if we deal with this badly, we'll have half of the delegates running away to avoid being accused. If we stay calm, we can keep them all here and investigate everyone in the hotel without raising too much suspicion. All the guests have been advised to stay in the hotel grounds. It won't be difficult to spot anyone who tries to slip away.'

'The press will find out sooner or later,' Barnes pointed out. 'While I agree that there are good reasons not to release an immediate statement – and to limit the investigation to Supe Squad for now – we can't conceal Mr Emerson's murder for long. The fact that you were already looking into him and considering removing him from the summit is not a good look either.'

I licked my lips. Lance Emerson's unfortunate death hadn't changed my feeling that he was not a good man. As far as I could discern, he was a dodgy cult leader who used sacrifice and the suggestion of the supernatural to his own advantage. More than one person had spoken ill of him. However, this was hardly the time to share my opinion of a dead man.

'Keeping the investigation with Supe Squad will help us catch the killer and prevent widespread panic amongst the delegates and the people who are watching. There are 478 people attending this summit. Most of them are supes and all of them are suspects. They'll talk to us because they know us and they want the summit to succeed. That's more than enough motivation to help us.'

'I understand what you're saying, Emma – in fact, I believe you're right.' DS Grace glanced at Barnes. 'Despite our lack of resources, I think that Supe Squad has a better chance of finding the perpetrator than a homicide team from the Met. But if there's any suggestion of a cover up, we'll be crucified. Forget the supe summit – Supe Squad won't survive.'

Barnes raised her hands and both Grace and I fell silent. 'This is a delicate situation,' she said. Her expression was sombre. She wasn't a great fan of supes, but she'd backed the summit from the start. As she'd already told me, she was aware that any violence directed towards the supes could erupt into retaliation against humans. Unfortunately, there were very few scenarios where this wasn't going to turn into a shitshow for everyone.

Barnes continued. 'Here's what will happen. The summit officially starts tomorrow and is due to last four days. I'll give you half that time to find the person responsible for Lance Emerson's murder. Once that time is up, the pathologist should be able to confirm whether Emerson was human or not. If he turns out to be a supe, you can continue. If it's revealed that he's human, I will call in an investigative team from outside. Either way, we will release a statement after forty-eight hours. It's highly unlikely you'll manage to fend off any leaks for much longer than that.'

Both Grace and I opened our mouths to argue but Barnes stared us down. 'In the meantime, you will need to keep the journalists at bay. It's up to Supe Squad to solve this murder in the next two days.'

'We can't do it with just the two of us,' Grace protested.

'You've got PC Hackert, and I'm sure Liza May will also provide back-up. I imagine you can also get some of the more senior supes to help you without interfering too much, though I'll leave that to your discretion. Supe Squad always has been a law unto itself so you have more leeway than other Met Police departments. I'll provide a small forensics team and a pathologist, but don't be under any illusions. Unless you find the murderer quickly, there is little chance that Supe Squad will come out of this well.'

'I'm a supe,' I said. 'That's no longer a secret in London. If all this goes to hell and we don't find the perp, I'll take full responsibility for any failures in the investigation.' I hoped my voice didn't sound shaky. 'I have total confidence in my own abilities to find this fucker.'

I pointed at DS Grace. 'You should stay out of the murder investigation, that way you'll have full deniability. You can say that you were focused on security for the summit.'

Grace drew himself up. 'I most certainly will not. You'll be vilified, Emma. We're a team. Regardless of any professional disagreements, I won't throw you to the wolves. Not human ones and not supernatural ones.'

I met his eyes. 'Somebody needs to be around to pick up the pieces if Lance Emerson is confirmed as human and we don't find his killer. You're the best person for that.'

'She's right,' Barnes said. 'We can't afford for Supe Squad to be dismantled or destroyed because of one case.' She turned to me. 'But don't lose sight of the fact that a man is dead. Lance Emerson is a victim and he deserves the best we can offer him. At the end of the day this isn't about helping supes or maintaining Supe Squad's integrity, it's about finding a murderer.'

My tone was grim. 'Noted.'

'Forty-eight hours, Emma. You'd better get to work.'

CHAPTER TEN

THERE WERE A THOUSAND THINGS TO DO AND NOT MUCH TIME TO do them in. I weighed up where to start. There was no doubt that I needed the supes on my side if I was going to have any chance of success, so I made a decision to avoid seeking out Emerson's assistant or speaking to the hotel cleaner who'd found his body. Instead I strolled into the champagne reception as if nothing untoward had happened. I had to be both subtle and swift, and hope that none of my anxiety showed on my face.

The room was full. Under any other circumstances, I'd have been thrilled to see so many supes and a smattering of humans in one place indulging in polite conversation. There were vampires talking to werewolves, and pixies talking to ghouls. There were two druids explaining to an interested human why they avoided advertising their skills. I recalled that the human had requested an invitation to the summit because he was curious about some long-dead ancestors who may have been supes. I spotted one of the ghouls in amiable conversation with a very drunk Kennedy. This was good; this was what it was supposed to be like.

A small orchestra of gremlins was playing in the corner, their music mingling with the gaps in the buzz of chatter. The atmosphere was optimistic and positive. Even Lady Sullivan seemed to be smiling. It was a shame I was about to ruin the evening for several people.

I was barely five feet into the room when Lukas appeared at my shoulder. There was an easy smile on his face and he lowered his head to drop a kiss on my lips. His voice when he spoke told a different story, however. 'So?' he asked. 'What's going on?'

I smiled at him for the benefit of anyone watching and murmured in his ear, 'He's definitely been murdered. I need to get several people out of the room so I can talk to them without the others noticing.'

'Tell me who and I'll make it happen.'

I breathed out. At least there was someone here I could trust. I grabbed a champagne glass from a passing waiter and gave Lukas several names. 'The Supe Squad suite,' I said. 'In five minutes. Make sure Liza comes along, too.'

I raised my head and caught Fred's eye. Looking confused, he frowned at me but I gestured towards the lobby area and he nodded. Pretending to take a sip from my glass, I stepped away from Lukas and completed a fast circuit of the room, engaging in brief pleasantries with several guests. Everything is fine, I projected. Things couldn't be going any better.

Then I wheeled around and ambled out to where Fred was waiting. 'What's going on?' he asked. 'And where the hell have you been? You missed the opening speeches. Honestly, until you've heard Lord McGuigan wax lyrical for twenty minutes about the merits of fellowship, you haven't learnt the meaning of boredom.'

I wished I were bored; I fervently wished I could be bored. 'Come with me,' I told him. 'I'll fill you in along the way.'

* * *

By the time Fred and I got to the suite, he was pale and twitching with worry. 'This is bad, boss. This is proper bad.'

'I know. We need all our wits about us. Stay frosty.'

'Easier said than done,' he muttered.

He could say that again. I poured myself a glass of water. I'd barely taken a few sips when there was a knock on the door and the first group of people arrived. Lukas had done me proud; I was standing in front of ten of the most powerful supes in the country. I didn't know what strings he'd pulled to get them here so quickly and without complaint or dramatics. It certainly wasn't typical of them to be so obedient. These were people who didn't enjoy being directed around or told what to do.

I mouthed thank you to Lukas who inclined his head and sat down next to Lady Fairfax. Sometimes it was definitely a positive to be dating the vampire Lord himself.

'I'll make this fast because you all need to get back to the reception,' I said.

Phileas Carmichael Esquire, the gremlin solicitor whose legal knowledge might come in handy at some point during the next forty-eight hours, sniffed loudly. 'I don't see why. The canapés are appalling and the champagne is definitely second rate.'

Albert Finnegan spoke. 'At least you can eat something. As this is a supe summit, you'd think that the DeVane Hotel would be able to accommodate *all* supes.' Thankfully, there was a twinkle in his eye. Surely nobody would really expect dead human flesh to be served up outside of a ghoul household.

Ochre, a rather outspoken pixie who was known for pushing for greater pixie representation, and the mild-mannered druid representative, Andrew Ashead, suddenly looked green around the gills.

Mosburn Pralk, the manager of the Talismanic Bank, crossed his legs. 'Let's hear what DC Bellamy has to say, shall we?'

Lady Sullivan sighed audibly. 'If we must.' She glanced at her watch. 'This is all very tiresome.'

I drew in a breath. 'In the last few hours,' I said, my voice expressionless, 'a man was murdered in the spa rooms of this hotel. It's not yet been confirmed, but it's more than likely he was human.'

If I'd been expecting the small assembly of supes to not take the news seriously, I was mistaken. Each one of them snapped to attention, minute tells in every face indicating that they fully understood the implications of my words.

'He was here to attend the summit and was already under investigation for some ... anomalies. It seems likely, given the security we have in place around the hotel, that the murder was committed either by a member of staff or a guest. As we all know, most of the current DeVane Hotel guests are supes.'

Lady Carr stared at me. 'So you're telling us that a supe murdered a human in this hotel under our noses this very evening?'

My answer was swift. 'No. I'm saying that a *probable* human was murdered this evening and everyone in this hotel is a suspect.'

'But supes will be blamed,' Ochre said. 'By tomorrow morning every tabloid in the city will be declaring our guilt.'

'No werewolf did this,' McGuigan spat. 'We're not bloodthirsty like some around here.'

'And no vampire did this either,' Lukas said, his eyes flashing. 'None of my people would be so foolish as to jeopardise the summit or kill a human.'

'It certainly wasn't a damned pixie!' Ochre rose to her feet.

I'd barely started and things were already descending into chaos. 'I need you all to calm down,' I said.

Lady Sullivan glanced at Finnegan. 'Who was it?' she asked with an air of faux innocence. 'Who was talking about eating human corpses?'

Albert Finnegan had always struck me as a mild-mannered gentleman who placed great emphasis on old-fashioned politeness. The sudden blazing rage in his face at Lady Sullivan's implication was striking.

I opened my mouth to bring order to the room but I was beaten to the punch. 'Will the damned supernatural lot of you shut the hell up?' Liza's voice carried from the back of the room. Her tone was piercing enough to make everyone turn and look at her folded arms and straight-backed figure. She glared with enough venom to quell any further dissent. 'DC Bellamy has brought you here for a reason – and it's not to allow you to accuse each other of murder. Let's listen to what she has to say and deal with this bloody situation like adults!'

She was worth her weight in gold. There were a few grumbles of dissent but the supes returned their attention to me. Even Lukas looked shamefaced.

I gave a small, satisfied smile. 'Thank you, Liza. At this point, I'm not accusing anyone of anything. We're pursuing several lines of enquiry. Believe me, we will do everything in our power to find the person responsible for this man's murder – but we need your cooperation. If it turns out that one of the supe guests killed him, we need to identify and deal with him or her as quickly and efficiently as possible. We can't give the outside world any more ammunition against supes. The murderer, no matter who they are, must be found and brought to justice, otherwise we might as well pack up now and let future supernatural generations deal with whatever bullshit is thrown at them.'

I gazed at each of them in turn. 'The last thing we need is this sort of finger-pointing panic to spread to the other delegates. Consequently, you can't tell anyone else what has happened for the next two days.'

'What happens after two days?' Lukas asked.

'Then it's out of Supe Squad's hands and all hell will probably break loose. The Met will take over and an outside team will be brought in.'

There were several hisses. 'My people will not be dictated to by a bunch of coppers who don't know us or our ways,' Lady Sullivan declared. 'If the Met takes over, my wolves and I will leave the hotel immediately. We will not be subjected to a witch hunt by the humans.'

There were several nods of agreement. I drew in a breath. 'That's why we need your help and cooperation. If we can locate the killer quickly, everybody wins.' My voice hardened. '*Everybody*.' There was silence.

I continued. 'Do whatever you can to keep everyone inside the hotel. There's more than enough going on with the summit to keep them occupied, so there's no reason for anyone to leave. Watch the delegates and let Liza, PC Hackert or me know if anyone is acting strangely. Without alerting suspicion, find out if anyone was missing this evening. However, you need to stay away from the main investigation until we know more about what's going on and who is responsible. Any suggestion of your involvement could be disastrous if one of your own turns out to be the killer. And it goes without saying that if one of your people *is* the culprit, you can't stand in the way of what happens next.'

'There is no chance a werewolf did this,' Lady Sullivan said. This time, everyone in the room glowered at her. She sighed and tutted. 'But,' she continued, as if she were doing us a massive favour, 'in the unlikely event that a Sullivan werewolf is responsible, I will do nothing to impede the investigation or its consequences.'

'Nor will I, if a Carr wolf did this,' Lady Carr interjected

'Nor will I,' agreed Lady Fairfax.

'If one of mine is the murderer, I will hand him or her over myself,' Lord McGuigan declared.

'I think I speak for all of us when I say that we all want this bastard to be found and made to pay for their actions,' Mosburn Pralk said. 'None of us will stand in your way.'

That had gone better than I'd hoped. 'Thank you. And if there is anyone whose whereabouts between the hours of five and nine this evening are not accounted for, let us know. Now you should all return to the reception before your absence is remarked upon.'

The supes started to file out until only Lukas remained. Liza coughed pointedly then she and Fred left the room. As soon as the door closed, Lukas took three long strides and wrapped his arms round me. 'Are you alright?' he asked roughly.

'No. But yes.' I buried my face in his shoulder. 'I didn't want this.'

'Nobody did.' He squeezed me tighter. 'Two days isn't long.'

'It'll be enough. I'll find the bastard who did this. Nobody will ruin this summit.' I gritted my teeth. 'Nobody.'

'They'll be sorry when you catch up with them,' Lukas said.

I certainly hoped so.

CHAPTER ELEVEN

FRED AND I SAT DOWN IN FRONT OF ROSA CARNE, THE unfortunate cleaner who'd discovered Emerson's body. 'Thank you for waiting so long,' I said gently. 'I'm sorry you had to find Mr Emerson that way. If you need a break at any point, or you feel you can't speak, say the word. We'll go at your pace.'

Rosa was shaky but resolute. 'I'll be fine. I used to work in a hospital so I've seen plenty of death. It was a shock and it wasn't pleasant, but I'm alright. Ask me whatever you need and I'll do my best to answer.' She was made of strong stuff.

'Can you talk us through what happened leading up your discovery? We'll record what you say, but you're not under any suspicion. We only want to make sure we don't miss anything.' I placed my phone between us and pressed the record button.

Rosa swallowed. 'My job is to clean the spa after it closes at the end of the day. After I'm done there, I'm supposed to help with turn-down service in the hotel rooms. We're busier than usual because of the summit, and some members of staff are worried about our guests. They don't want to knock on the door of a werewolf or a vampire while they're alone and then end up – uh, you know...'

This certainly wasn't the time and place to persuade Rosa that the hotel workers had no reason to be worried about the supes. I gave her a sympathetic nod and she looked relieved.

'Anyway,' she continued, 'I was going to pair up with one of the older room attendants, so I started work earlier than normal. Usually I wouldn't start on the spa till later but I wanted to get it out of the way. The spa staff had already gone, but I knew as soon as I walked in that something wasn't right.' She wrung her hands in her lap. 'I should have thought more of it at the time.' Her voice dropped. 'I was so stupid.'

'You weren't stupid at all,' Fred told her. 'You could hardly have anticipated what was in there.'

She gave him a weak smile but we knew she wasn't convinced.

'What gave you the idea that something wasn't right?' I asked.

'The candles, for one thing,' Rosa said. 'They're a fire hazard and they're against hotel regulations, even in the spa. The lights were off and three candles had been lit. I thought maybe it was a supe thing and an exception had been made, so I just blew them out and put them on a shelf.' She pulled a face. 'There was music playing, too. During the day, there's soft music in reception – you know, chimes and bells and calming vibes. The staff normally turn it off before they leave but this time they hadn't and it was louder than usual.'

No doubt because loud music might drown out the sound of any screams, I thought grimly

'I can't stand that stuff,' Rosa said, 'so I turned it off and started cleaning the reception area. I wiped down all the surfaces and vacuumed. Then I did the changing rooms.'

'Was there anything out of place? Any clothes left behind?'

She shook her head. 'No. In fact, the male changing room was cleaner than usual.' She bit her lip. 'There was a bath robe missing and I thought someone had maybe nicked it. That happens quite a lot. Some people will steal anything that's not nailed down. We once caught a guest trying to walk out of the front door with a coffee table.' She paused. 'It wasn't even a nice coffee table.'

I smiled, recognising that Rosa was clinging onto absurd, everyday details so as not to think too much about the gruesome death. 'I went into the changing rooms,' I said. 'There's a locked door at the far end of each of them. Where do they lead?'

'The sauna, steam room and swimming pool. Those doors are always locked unless a spa guest wants to use them. It stops other guests wandering through to the spa by accident,' Rosa explained. 'But because of the summit, all those areas have been closed since midday today. Ms Kennard didn't want werewolves changing shape and then clogging up the pool filters with their fur.'

I remembered that had been a concern during the planning stages of the summit. It hadn't bothered me; we weren't here for a holiday. 'Who holds a key to those doors?'

Rosa frowned. 'Cleaners like me. Management. The pool attendant. Security staff.' Her shoulders dropped. 'Lots of people.'

Fred leaned forward. 'And when you arrived, was the main door to the spa locked as well?'

'Normally it is.' She looked away. 'Today it wasn't.' Guilt coloured her words, as if the simple fact that a door had been left unlocked should have alerted her.

I glanced at Fred. 'Can you check the swimming pool area, just in case?'

'I'll go now.'

I watched him leave and then pushed on. 'So you cleaned the changing rooms. What next?'

Rosa's voice was barely audible. 'I went to the massage room.'

'Was the door open or closed?'

'Closed.' She drew in a shuddering breath. 'I opened it and saw the ... the ... body. At first I couldn't work it out. I thought maybe it was a joke. A sick joke, but a joke nonetheless. But deep down, I knew it wasn't. All I could do was stare at him. It felt like my feet were stuck to the floor. I don't know how long it was before I ran out of there to find help. It felt like forever.' A solitary tear trickled down her cheek and she made no attempt to brush it away. 'I'm fine, though. I'm absolutely fine.'

I didn't think she was fine at all. 'Nobody ever talks about the people like you, Rosa.'

Her eyes flew to mine.

'How many times have you heard about a body that was found in the middle of nowhere by a jogger or a dog walker?' I said. 'Nobody ever thinks about what it's like for them to come across something so horrific, but they're affected by what they've seen for the rest of their lives. It's not fair that this happened to you. You've dealt with it well so far, but it's only been a couple of hours. Sometimes it can be weeks or months before the full impact hits you. I'll speak to Wilma and we'll arrange transport to get you home safely. I'll also arrange for a victim support counsellor to contact you tonight. You're a victim in this, too.'

Rosa looked as if she wanted to disagree, but there was a flicker of relief in her face as well. Sudden death never affected just one person; the impact could invade dozens of lives even when murder wasn't a factor and the victim was unknown. Sometimes the aftershocks were more powerful than the earthquake itself.

* * *

'HERE's a list of all the members of staff who have keys and access to the spa rooms and beyond.' Wilma passed over a sheet of paper. 'I've also had all the relevant CCTV footage from five o'clock onwards put onto a memory stick and given it to your colleague, Liza. But I should warn you in advance that we don't have any cameras around the spa or in the corridors leading towards it. It's one of the areas in the hotel where our guests appreciate some privacy.'

I grimaced, although that wasn't unexpected. I glanced

beyond her to where the champagne reception was continuing in full swing in the bar on the opposite side of the DeVane lobby. 'Any sign of Lance Emerson's partner?' I asked.

'She's still in their room.' Wilma looked at me meaningfully. 'She called down to reception ten minutes ago and asked if she could be connected to the spa phone to speak to Mr Emerson.'

Oh. 'She thinks he's still there. She thinks the spa is open.'

The hotel manager nodded. 'It would appear so.'

'That begs the question why Emerson went to the spa,' Fred said.

'Or,' I added, 'who lured him there.'

We all exchanged looks. 'Do you know his partner's name?' I asked Wilma.

'We have her listed as Moira Castleman. She made the initial room booking. I believe the summit records have her attending as Lance Emerson's assistant. She only booked the one room.'

'So either they're trying to save money or they're intimately involved.' I thought about the conversation I'd overheard in the hallway. There hadn't appeared to be much in the way of romance between them, but I'd only caught a snippet. I glanced at Fred. 'Ms Castleman has to be our next stop. This isn't going to be pretty.'

Fred nodded at something over my shoulder. 'We have a temporary reprieve,' he said.

I turned and followed his gaze, feeling some of my tension dissipate when I saw who was walking towards us.

'Well,' Laura said, 'that's quite some circus you've got out there.' She smiled easily. Obviously the protestors weren't going home any time soon.

'There's quite a circus going on in here, as well,' I told her. I knew from my own experience that Laura wasn't the sort of pathologist who let much shake her. I'd come back from the dead for the first time in her morgue and she'd taken my fiery reawakening in her long-legged stride.

'Then it's just as well I came with reinforcements.' She jerked her thumb at the two moustachioed figures carrying heavy bags coming up behind her.

'Barry and Larry!' I grinned at the familiar faces of the two forensic technicians. This was getting better and better.

'Good to see you, Detective Constable Bellamy. Set anything on fire recently?' Barry asked.

There was still a scorch mark on Lukas's spare bed where I'd resurrected a few days earlier, but the least said about that the better. I laughed weakly. 'I didn't think you two worked in the city.'

'We were close by so we were called in. Something about a murder that needs to be kept on the QT?'

Ah. That had to be Barnes's doing. She was keeping any potential taint away from the Met and outsourcing forensics to another police force in order to detach blame from anyone who might end up in the hellfire of condemnation after all this was over. It was a smart move.

'You don't have to involve yourselves if you don't want to,' I told all three of them. 'This case could blow up in our faces, so I won't blame you if you'd rather withdraw. There's no pressure to stay.'

A female vampire chose that moment to sashay past us towards the restrooms. She was wearing a skin-tight pleather catsuit that left nothing to the imagination. Barry and Larry stared after her.

'You're drooling,' Larry told his partner, wiping his own mouth with the back of his hand.

The vamp, well aware of her effect, pushed open the restroom door and glanced over her shoulder at our little group. She winked saucily at Barry and Larry before disappearing.

'We're happy to stay,' Barry said. 'Since the events in Barchapel, I've learned to … appreciate the benefits of working with supes.'

'It's no great hardship,' Larry agreed. 'We can learn a lot from this sort of environment.'

'I'm sure,' Laura said drily. 'Don't worry, Emma. We've got you covered.'

'You guys are the best,' Fred said.

'You can say that again,' Barry grinned.

'You guys are the best,' I told them. I meant it, too.

CHAPTER TWELVE

FRED AND I STOOD OUTSIDE THE HOTEL ROOM DOOR. 'I HATE THIS part,' he muttered. 'What do we do if she flips?'

'We don't know how she's going to react. Bear in mind that she's as much a suspect as anyone else. She might have killed her boss.'

'I doubt it,' Fred said.

'Why?'

He gave me a long look. 'Because that would make our lives too easy.'

Yeah. I sighed; he was probably right. I gazed at the door for another moment then I raised my fist and knocked sharply.

It opened so quickly that I wondered if Moira Castleman had been standing on the other side watching us through the spyhole. She was dressed for the champagne reception in a short, tight, black dress that skimmed her thighs and was scooped low at the front. Her dark hair was tied neatly in a chignon with jewelled clips holding it in place. Her expression wasn't that of someone who was ready to party, though; her brow was creased with worry and her freckles stood out in sharp relief against her pale skin.

'Ms Castleman?' I asked. 'Moira Castleman?'

'He's not here,' she said quickly. 'I'm sorry but you'll have to come back another time.' She started to close the door but I wedged my foot into the frame.

'I'm Detective Constable Bellamy,' I said. 'This is my colleague PC Hackert. We're here to talk to you, not Mr Emerson. May we come inside?'

Moira Castleman's eyes widened. She was clearly unused to anyone wanting to speak to her rather than her boss. 'Uh...' She blinked rapidly. 'Uh...'

'It's important, Ms Castleman.'

She swallowed and glanced down the empty corridor. 'Okay,' she said nervously. 'But Mr Emerson will be here soon and he'll be really pissed off if he finds you in our room.'

We'd not given any indication about why we wanted to speak to her, but she was already exuding the same vibes as a terrified gazelle. People often react like that when approached by the police, but I wondered if there were more to it than that. Was she scared because of Emerson's motives for attending the supe summit? Or was he a bully who kept her in her place through fear?

I reminded myself that she worked for Emerson and might well be part of his mysterious cult. Until I knew more about her, I couldn't jump to conclusions.

She stepped away from the door and Fred and I went in. Although the room was nice, I knew that it was one of the smaller, cheaper ones. I noted the tuxedo hanging up, waiting for Emerson to return from the spa, and I also noted the double bed.

I pointed to the small table and chairs by the window. 'Why don't we sit down?'

Moira bit her lip and nodded but remained standing while Fred and I made ourselves comfortable. Rather than take the spare chair, she perched on the side of the bed and stared at us. 'What is this about?'

'Are you sharing this room with Lance Emerson?'

Her eyes darted from side to side. 'What if I am?' she asked defensively, folding her arms across her chest.

I took a deep breath. 'I'm afraid that I have some bad news, Ms Castleman.'

She started to blink rapidly and a flush rose up her neck until it reached her cheeks. 'What – what do you mean?'

I had to be very careful to leave no ambiguity while breaking the news to her as gently as possible. 'A body has been found in the spa,' I said. 'We believe it's Lance Emerson. It appears that his throat has been slit.'

Moira Castleman didn't move a muscle. All she did was stare.

'Lance Emerson,' I told her, 'is dead.'

She stood up then she sat down. A moment later she stood up again. 'No,' she whispered, 'that doesn't make any sense.' She shook her head. 'It's not him. It can't be.'

'We're fairly certain it is, but his body will need to be formally identified once the scene has been secured and he's been taken to the morgue.'

Moira Castleman was already walking to the door. 'I have to go there. I have to see him.'

Fred reached her before I did. 'It's not a good idea right now,' he said gently. 'He's being attended to by our technicians. It's a crime scene and we have to investigate it – that means we can't let anyone into the room where he was found. We'll take you to him as soon as we can, but right now we need to ask you some questions.'

I nodded. 'I know it's difficult, Ms Castleman, but Mr Emerson's murderer is out there and we need to find them as quickly as possible. We have to keep everyone else safe. We need to speak to you about Lance and find out all we can about him so we can bring whoever did this to justice.'

'Not Lance.' She raised her head and stared at me. 'You can't call him Lance. Nobody called him that.'

I watched her. 'What should I call him?'

'The Chief,' she said. 'He liked to be called the Chief.'

Of course he did.

'Then the Chief it is.' I smiled, trying to convey that I would do whatever I could to respect him so she would feel that I was on her side.

'I'll answer whatever questions you have,' she said shakily. She pointed to the bathroom. 'Can I have a minute to myself first?'

'Of course. Can we fetch you something? Make you a cup of tea, or get you some water?'

'No.' She set her mouth into a taut line. 'Please.' Her voice was strained. 'I need a moment alone.' She disappeared into the bathroom, closed the door and locked it.

Fred and I exchanged glances as we heard a choked sob. I grimaced and started to look around. There might be something in the room that could help us better understand Emerson – and who might have wanted to kill him.

My gaze fell on a card on one of the bedside cabinets. I bent down to examine it, taking care not to touch it. The hotel's logo was embossed on the top. Underneath, in typed script, it read: *Mr L. Emerson. Thank you for your kind patronage at the DeVane Hotel. We wish to offer a free sports massage to show our gratitude for your custom. We've taken the liberty of booking you into our spa at 6pm on Wednesday evening.*

I frowned as I took out my phone and snapped a couple of photos of it. Then Fred cleared his throat and pointed to something on the desk by the opposite wall.

There was a pile of expensive-looking leaflets. Each one was identical and proudly displayed the words *The Perfect Path To Power and Redemption* next to a glossy photo of a serene mountain scene. Fred raised his eyebrows questioningly and I nodded. He gingerly picked up the top leaflet and opened it.

We heard the toilet flush and a few seconds later Moira Castleman reappeared. She noted the leaflet in Fred's hands but her expression didn't alter. Her skin was still red and flushed, and there was a dull horror in her eyes, but it didn't appear to affect her resolve. 'I'll answer any questions you have,' she told us. 'Anything to get the person who did this.'

'Thank you,' I told her. I meant it. While I'd still keep an open mind, I sincerely doubted that anyone would possess the acting chops to appear as upset as Moira Castleman did. She was devastated by the news of Emerson's death. Any chance that she was involved in his murder seemed remote. 'Shall we sit down again?'

She nodded and this time she sat on one of the narrow chairs. Fred grabbed a glass, filled it with water and handed it to her. Her hands shook as she took a tiny sip. She nodded again, indicating that we could begin.

I started with the formalities. 'You and the Chief are here for the supe summit. Was the Chief supernatural? Is that why you're here?'

Moira recoiled slightly. 'He's human,' she declared, more loudly than was necessary. 'He was definitely human.'

I wasn't surprised, although I did feel a brief stab of disappointment. The news that a human had been murdered at the first-ever supernatural summit would cause untold damage. I kept my expression neutral. 'And do you know who is the Chief's next of kin? Is he married?'

'Marriage is an outdated institution that the government uses to promote the yoke of ownership and obedience,' Moira said, with the tone of someone repeating a mantra that they didn't believe. 'No, he isn't married.' She swallowed and a spasm of pain crossed her face. 'He *wasn't* married,' she amended. 'His parents are dead and he doesn't have any brothers or sisters. We're his family.'

'When you say "we", who do you mean?'

She nodded at the leaflet in Fred's hand. 'The Perfect Path,' she said. 'That's who.'

'Tell us about the Perfect Path.'

A tiny furrow creased her forehead. 'I don't see how that's relevant.'

I didn't miss a beat. 'We don't know who murdered the Chief or why. We need to find out as much as possible to help us build a picture of him.' I didn't tell her that his body had been found with one of his cards carefully placed on top of it, something that suggested that whoever had killed him had done so because of his business practices.

Moira was obviously reluctant, but she put down her glass of water and drew in a breath. 'We help people who need our help. The Chief helped me, and now I help him help others.' Every time she repeated the word 'help', her voice rose. She seemed to realise she sounded odd and explained. 'Vampires and were-wolves and pixies and all of those creatures shouldn't exist. They're not natural, they're aberrations that disturb the natural order.'

I bit my tongue hard but Moira Castleman didn't appear to notice.

'But it's not their fault – they can't help what they are. Other people blame them but at the Perfect Path of Power and Redemption we *save* them.' Despite her grief, her eyes shone with fervour. 'The Chief takes away their monsters. He saves them. It hurts him so much to do it, and I've seen him screaming in agony, but he's prepared to sacrifice his own well-being to save others. He can save supernatural monsters from themselves, make them whole again.' Her face fell. 'Now he's gone, nobody can save them. They're doomed. Without the Chief, they're all *doomed.*'

Okaaaaaaay.

Fred's mouth was hanging open. I nudged him sharply and he snapped it shut. 'Just so I understand what you're saying,' I said, 'the Chief takes the, uh, monster out of supes and makes them human?'

Moira nodded vigorously. 'Yes.'

'How does he do that?'

'It's a secret process and it takes a long time. It's not easy, you know.'

'No,' I murmured, 'I don't imagine it is.'

'It's different for every type of supe.'

'Uh-huh.' I thought about the woman who'd walked into that little Cumbrian police station and claimed she was a werewolf when she most definitely was not. Then I thought about Night Stalker Jim who'd been convinced he was a vampire when the truth couldn't have more different. 'So,' I said aloud, 'supernatural conversion therapy.'

'Yes. You don't believe it,' Moira said. 'A lot of people don't, but I've seen it with my own eyes. I've seen vampires turned into humans, and werewolves change in a matter of weeks.' She closed her eyes briefly and said, 'And me. I changed too.'

'You used to be a supe?' Fred asked.

'I was part demon.'

Demon? That was a new one on me.

'It was inside me, an evil that threaded through my veins and made me do bad things,' Moira said. '*Terrible* things. I shoplifted, I took drugs, I hurt everyone I came into contact with and I didn't care.' She shuddered. 'And then the Chief found me. He saved me.'

'How old are you?' I asked.

'Twenty.'

She sounded like a troubled teenager who'd been easily manipulated by an older man with a dark agenda.

'I've been free of the demon for almost a year now, though I have to be vigilant. It could come back and invade me again. The Chief makes sure I keep myself safe.' Her body sagged. 'But I won't be safe now. Without the Chief, the demon will return.' For a moment, terror lit her face. 'I can't protect myself without him.'

I took her hands and squeezed them, then spoke as diplomatically as I could. 'I think you're much stronger than you give yourself credit for.'

She smiled weakly in return.

'Is this why you and the Chief came to the summit?' I asked. 'To help other supes and – remove their, uh, monsters?'

'Yes. They don't want us here. They stopped the Chief from giving a presentation explaining what he could do, but we came anyway. That's the kind of good person he was.' Her voice dropped to a whisper. 'He was our saviour, and now he's gone we're all damned. Even you, detective. You can become infected and nobody will be able to stop it. The Chief was our only hope.'

Infected? Good grief. It was becoming harder and harder to maintain a neutral expression. Moira Castleman was also clearly unaware that I was unashamedly a supe. This wasn't the time to reveal that particular truth. Forget that Lance Emerson was supposedly doing the impossible; his behaviour was unethical, unwarranted and wholly unwanted.

'You've already been here for a few nights,' I said. 'Have you spoken to many supes?'

She gave a sudden, brilliant smile. 'Lots. The Chief has approached many different monsters.'

My stomach tightened. If that were true, there were plenty of supernatural beings who could be responsible for his murder. If the Chief had walked up to a vamp, a wolf or even a pixie and claimed that he could drive the supposed *monster* from their body, he'd handed over a motive for his murder.

'Do you have a list of the supes he spoke to?'

'He had a notebook. He kept meticulous notes,' Moira said proudly. 'All the names are in there.'

I brightened. That would be helpful. 'Can I have a look at it?' I asked.

'He took it with him to the spa when he went for the massage. He always kept it beside him.'

Shit. There was nothing left at the spa, not even Emerson's clothes. 'We didn't find anything there,' I told her. 'Do you know the names of the people he approached? Could you remember them and write them down for us?'

Moira sucked her bottom lip. 'You think one of them did this. You think it was one of the monsters he was trying to save.'

I was prepared to grant her leeway, given the situation she was in and the sudden onset of grief she must be experiencing, but I was getting mightily tired of the word 'monsters'. 'We're exploring every avenue. But we won't jump to any conclusions.'

'I'll try and remember,' Moira said. 'I'll try and write them all down.'

'Thank you.'

'But I already know who killed him.' She spoke without emotion.

Fred and I stared at her. 'Who?' I asked. 'Who was it?'

'Nathan,' she whispered. 'It had to be Nathan.'

The werewolf's face flashed into my mind. 'Who's Nathan?'

'A wolf,' she said. 'He was the Chief's most trusted friend. He used to be a werewolf but the Chief saved him and drove the beast from his body. Then Nathan let his monster back inside his heart and it overtook him. It was Nathan Fairfax who did this. He lured the Chief out with the fake promise of a free massage, and then he murdered him. He did it, I know he did.'

Her eyes held mine. 'It's not Nathan's fault. He wasn't strong enough to beat the wolf so you can't blame him for what he did. He's a good person really – but he's also very dangerous.'

'Do you know where Nathan is now, Moira?'

Her eyes widened with fear. 'He'll be out there on the streets. Now he's killed once, he'll have the taste of blood in his system and he'll want to kill more. He won't be able to help himself. You have to find him, detective. And you have to stop him.'

CHAPTER THIRTEEN

IT WAS AFTER ELEVEN O'CLOCK WHEN WE REGROUPED IN THE SUITE with Liza. Moira had refused our attempts to call someone on her behalf, and the formal identification of Lance Emerson's body would wait until the morning. There was a great deal more I wanted to ask her but it was late and she was struggling to cope with the shock. We left her in the solemn, unsettled peace of her own grief with the promise to call on her first thing next day. In the meantime there was plenty to discuss.

'Do you think,' Fred asked hesitantly, with a nervous side glance in my direction, 'that there's any chance at all that the Chief could do what she said?'

I snorted. 'Beat the supe out of supes? I'll believe that the day I see Satan himself ice skating to work. It's a scam, a nasty scam that preys on people's fears. All he had to do was find someone vulnerable, persuade them they're a supe and promise to banish the supernatural from them in return for wads of hard cash.'

'Then why did he come to the summit?' Fred asked. 'Why would he want to mingle with real supes?'

This time it was Liza who answered. 'Legitimacy. It's like those adverts in magazines that say, "As seen on TV". A few well-posed photographs of Chief Lance Emerson hanging with a bunch of famous supes would go a long way to encouraging his targets to believe his claims. Maybe he was hoping to be thrown out. There's plenty of press lurking around who could capture the moment – and any publicity is good publicity. He was clearly a wanker who took advantage of vulnerable idiots. Frankly,' she gave a loud sniff, 'it's a good thing that man is dead.'

I gave her a long look. 'You can say what you want in here,' I told her. 'But make sure you don't repeat anything like that outside these four walls. Any publicity might be good publicity for the likes of Lance Emerson, but the same is definitely not true for Supe Squad.'

Liza's nose wrinkled. 'Give me some credit. I'm not a fool like Moira Castleman. I know how important this investigation is and how vital it is that we handle it delicately.' She made a show of looking around. 'Speaking of handling things, where's our esteemed boss?'

'DS Grace is keeping out of this investigation.'

Liza's eyes narrowed. 'What?'

'In the event that things go tits up over the next few days,' I explained, 'he can claim ignorance and maintain his position at Supe Squad without any problems. You two are merely following my orders so you'll be fine, too. Any come back will land on me.'

'What?' She put her hands on her hips. '*What?* You've got to be kidding me? That slimy, little—'

'It was my suggestion, Liza. As long as we find Lance Emerson's killer before his murder turns into a circus, there won't be a problem.'

'Fucking Grace,' she muttered. 'Fucking—'

I held up a hand. 'Enough already. It's a done deal and it's the price that has to be paid to keep the summit running as smoothly as possible. I take it the champagne reception is still going on?'

She glared at me as if this were all my fault. 'It's barely getting started. They'll be going for hours yet.'

I nodded. 'Good. Has anything come out of the CCTV footage?'

'Very little. I still have to trawl through the previous days' footage and see if we can spot Emerson hanging around the hotel and talking to anyone. As for this evening's footage, there aren't many cameras near the spa area but I've pulled off a few images of supes who were nearby at the time.'

'Okay. You and Fred need to work together to identify who those people are. Fred, can you speak to the hotel staff who are working this evening and see if they've noticed anything out of ordinary?'

He nodded.

'Focus on the ones who hold keys to the spa and swimming pool. See if they still have those keys or if they've misplaced them.' I raised an eyebrow. 'And don't forget that our murderer might be a hotel worker. Let me know immediately if anyone seems to be acting suspiciously.'

'Will do, boss.'

I rubbed the back of my neck. There was more. 'We'll also need an update from Laura, Barry and Larry in the spa, and to touch base with the supe leaders about anyone who's missing. There's the question of Lance Emerson's belongings, too.' I held up the spa invitation card I'd taken from Moira Castleman. 'And we need to know whether this is genuine or not. It will be a long night and there's a lot to cover. Do you think the two of you can handle it alone?'

Liza still looked pissed off. 'Well, if Owen bloody Grace won't grace us with his majestic presence, I guess we'll have to.'

'Where will you be, boss?' Fred asked.

'I'm going to try to track down our two top suspects,' I said grimly. 'Nathan Fairfax and Night Stalker Jim.'

'You couldn't find them before,' he said. 'How will you find them now?'

I gave him a humourless smile. 'This time,' I told him, 'I'll have a secret weapon.'

* * *

THE ORCHESTRAL GREMLINS had been replaced by two pixies bellowing out the best of Gloria Gaynor. Although they were singing with considerable gusto, I winced. Karaoke had never been my thing. Kennedy was swaying on the makeshift dance floor in front of them. I'd never taken him as much of a dancer but he was proving me wrong.

At least some people were enjoying themselves. The point of the champagne reception was to encourage different relation-ships to form to loosen tensions. It seemed to be working – at least for most of the attendees.

Lukas instinctively sensed the moment I walked into the busy reception. His head turned and his eyes met mine across the room. He'd unfastened his bow tie and undone the top button of his crisp white shirt. His black hair was more mussed than it was the last time I'd seen him. The faintly unkempt look gave him a raffish air and I caught my breath.

'Alright?' he mouthed.

I half-nodded, half-shrugged. Seeing him helped to reassure me, even though he wasn't the person I was looking for. I gave him an apologetic look, knowing he'd understand that I had to focus on other things right now, then glanced around. Lukas wasn't the only person watching me. I acknowledged the glances from ghouls and goblins and Lord McGuigan, then made a beeline towards my occasional nemesis.

Lady Sullivan was sitting on a raised chair by one of the large windows. Her beta wolf, Robert, was murmuring in her ear but he withdrew when I approached. I sat down in his chair. He shooed the other werewolves away and sent me a dark look of warning that could have meant just about anything. Whatever. His opinion was the least of my concerns.

'I hope you're not here to tell me you're about to arrest one of my wolves for murder, Emma,' Lady Sullivan said.

'No,' I replied. And then, because I couldn't resist, 'Not yet, anyway.'

Her eyes flashed. 'I have been making inquiries. No Sullivan werewolf was anywhere near the spa at any point today. I know the other clan alphas can tell you the same.'

'Thank you for looking into the matter,' I said politely. 'I don't suppose you've ascertained whether any wolf was approached by the victim?'

'None of them have spoken to him,' she said, a tad too quickly. She obviously didn't know for sure. 'Is that why you're here? You wish to interrogate my innocent people further?'

'No,' I said, 'I'm here to ask for a favour. I need to search for Nathan Fairfax and another man. Both are somewhere in London and I have to find them. They're involved in some way with Lance Emerson, the man who was killed. It's vital that I speak to them.'

She raised her eyebrows. 'You mean the Nathan Fairfax who was in your custody and whom you let escape.'

I didn't bother to respond.

'London is a big place. It won't be easy to find them,' she said. 'I take it the favour you're looking for involves the nose of one of my wolves.'

I was glad that I didn't have to voice the request. 'Only temporarily. And only because time is of the essence.'

Lady Sullivan didn't hesitate. 'Take Buffy.'

I gave the werewolf alpha a sidelong look.

'She's the best,' Lady Sullivan said.

I couldn't disagree. 'Okay. Thank you.' Curiosity got the better of me. 'I know Buffy is good, so why is she ranked so low?

She could challenge plenty of other wolves for their position and probably win.'

For once, Lady Sullivan didn't take offence at one of my questions; in fact, she seemed to appreciate it. 'I've dissuaded her from making any challenges for now because at the moment she can learn more as a foot soldier. Buffy will be alpha of this clan one day and I want her to have a full and proper grounding before then. A fast path to success only leads to a sharp fall to failure.' She met my eyes. 'Don't tell her I said about her becoming alpha. Her ego is already big enough to match mine. It doesn't need to be inflated any further.'

I glanced at the glass in Lady Sullivan's hand before returning my gaze to her eyes. She smiled at me, a slight lack of focus in her pupils. I almost laughed. She was drunk, not drunk enough to fall over or make a fool of herself but definitely to the point where her tongue had loosened and her mood was merry. This would be the perfect opportunity to delve deeper into Lady Sullivan's psyche and get her to open up – except I had a damned murder to solve. Bugger it. I'd probably never get a chance like this again.

She might have been tipsy but she'd certainly not lost her wits. She wagged her finger at me in warning as if she knew exactly what I'd been thinking. 'Robert is a breath away,' she murmured.

I looked over. He was still glaring at me as if he were certain I was taking advantage of his alpha. 'No need to worry.' I smoothed down my dress and prepared to stand up but Lady Sullivan's hand shot out to stop me.

'You underestimate him, Emma.'

I was puzzled. 'Who?'

'I know you think that you're being fair and even-handed, and that you treat all of us the same, but your relationship with him means that you act differently towards the bloodsuckers. You're always prepared to go toe to toe with me or one of the other alphas when a young wolf acts up, but you turn a blind eye when a vamp does the same.'

I instantly felt defensive. That wasn't true. I didn't have the same trouble with the vampires. They didn't cross the line in the way that the werewolves often did.

'And now,' Lady Sullivan continued softly, 'you're wearing his token.' She gestured towards the heavy necklace hanging round my neck. 'Did he tell you what it means? That he's informing the entire world that you belong to him?'

'Actually, he did say something to that effect,' I retorted. 'But I don't belong to him, I belong *with* him. There's a world of difference.'

'Is there?'

Yes, there was. 'We keep our professional and personal lives separate.'

Lady Sullivan took a long sip from her glass. 'And that's very commendable. It's also probably true, but you won't always be able to do that. You need to be prepared for the day that your priorities clash with his. He's been around for a long time – and yes, I do believe he cares for you. He may even genuinely love you. But he will also always be Lord Horvath and he'll always be a vampire. Just … be careful. I know I'm a vicious bitch sometimes, but that doesn't mean I wish ill on you. Guard your heart.'

My skin prickled with irritation. I was a whisker away from snapping at her to stop interfering and trying to manipulate me for her own ends, but when I looked at her expression I didn't get the usual sense of calculation and guile. Misguided and unwelcome or not, Lady Sullivan meant well.

'It's taken a long while for me to trust him fully,' I said finally, reining in my temper. 'And he more than deserves my trust.'

For a moment, she didn't speak. When she did, her face had changed and I saw she had resumed her usual attitude. 'Whatever,' she said dismissively. 'I'm sure you're right.' She raised a finger towards Robert. 'I'll have Buffy meet you out the front.' She turned away to indicate that our conversation was over.

I glanced round, my eyes searching out Lukas. His head was bowed as he spoke to a small group of vampires but he felt my gaze and looked up and his eyes softened. I smiled at him and he smiled back. No, I'd come too far and travelled too hard a road to get to this point. I didn't only trust Lukas with my life, I trusted him with my heart and that wouldn't change.

It *was* possible, I conceded, that I didn't examine the vampires' actions to the same extent that I did other supes'. I wasn't stubborn enough or stupid enough not to question myself or to reflect on my behaviour, so I'd take on board what Lady Sullivan had said and think about it. But nothing material between Lukas and I would change. I was his – and he was mine.

CHAPTER FOURTEEN

ONLY A HANDFUL OF PROTESTORS REMAINED ACROSS THE STREET from the DeVane Hotel as Tallulah and I chugged round to the main entrance from the underground car park. I memorised each face. Anyone who was hardcore enough to stay out this late and in this weather definitely felt like they had a point to prove. Although they were now DS Grace's problem, making a mental note of who possessed strong anti-supe ideology couldn't be a bad thing.

I was fixed on one protestor in particular, squinting to try and read the words on his cardboard sign, when the flash of a camera briefly illuminated my face and Tallulah's interior. I heard a shout and saw Buffy dart out from the front door of the hotel and lunge towards someone. Shit. That was all we needed.

I sent a quick, wistful glance towards my crossbow, which I'd retrieved from the hotel reception and placed on the narrow seat behind me, then I left it where it was before fumbling with Tallulah's door and jumping out. Buffy was engaged in a tussle with that bloody columnist, Juliet Chambers-May. My stomach tightened in dismay.

'Give me that fucking camera!' Buffy screeched, her fingers curved into claws as she tried to grab it.

'You have no right to it, you ugly animal,' Chambers-May hissed, taking a swipe at Buffy's head.

I pushed my way between them and forced them apart. 'Stop it! Stand back the pair of you!'

Juliet Chambers-May raised a manicured finger and pointed at Buffy. 'That she-wolf assaulted me. I demand you take action.' She glared at me. 'You're the police. Do something!'

'You're not supposed to be here,' Buffy spat back at her. 'You're hanging around spying on people and taking photos of them without their knowledge.'

'That's not against the law,' the columnist scoffed. 'But attacking someone is.'

'I wasn't attacking you,' Buffy snapped. 'I was trying to take your camera.'

Juliet's eyes widened. 'So now you're admitting to theft? In front of a police officer?'

I was aware of a few ragged protestors watching us avidly from across the road and of the simmering tempers of the women in front of me. I passed a hand in front of my face and sighed. 'Okay,' I said. 'Let's all take a breath. Ms Chambers-May —' I began.

'Call me Juliet,' she interrupted, as if we were supposed to be friends.

Fine. 'Juliet,' I said. 'The press are not allowed in this area at the moment, as I'm sure you're aware. There are rooms in the hotel for your use, but we have made it clear that journalists must use the east entrance and keep away from the lobby. It's a condition for all press who are attending the summit.'

'Because you don't want us to see the protestors over there?'

'You can see – and talk – to the protestors whenever you like,' I said. 'But our delegates deserve some level of privacy. The Press Association agreed to that.'

Buffy folded her arms smugly across her chest. Then, horror of horrors, she stuck her tongue out. I should have been grateful that she didn't start chanting na-na-na-na-na.

I turned to her. 'Buffy, it is not your job to police the press. You cannot take away a journalist's camera. You cannot attack a journalist. You cannot attack *anyone*.'

Her smirk disappeared. 'I wasn't attacking her.'

'You know what you did.' I took a breath. 'Any further breaches like this and you'll be removed from the summit and formally cautioned.'

'You're the person she was photographing. I was trying to help *you*.'

I wasn't convinced that was true. Buffy was probably looking for any opportunity for a brawl, though it was curious that Juliet Chambers-May was more interested in photographing me than the other supes attending the summit. A picture of me wouldn't sell as many papers as one of Lukas. Suddenly I was worried. Did she already know that Lance Emerson had been murdered?

Juliet snorted derisively, then tilted up her nose. 'Leaving your own summit so soon, detective? A rat deserting a sinking ship?'

I tried not to rise to her bait and chose my words carefully. 'I have other matters to attend to.' I paused and gazed at her. There was a red welt down her arm from where Buffy had scratched her. I swallowed and took a big gamble. 'Tell you what, once the summit is over, I'll grant you a full, no-holds-barred interview.'

Juliet's clever eyes gleamed. 'You mean in return for not causing a stink about the assault I was just subjected to?'

I didn't reply.

She ran her tongue over her lips and I caught a flash of brilliant white teeth that suggested either dentures or excellent dentistry. Juliet Chambers-May had certainly enjoyed a full array of cosmetic procedures. 'Very well,' she said. 'I will expect to sit down with you first thing on Tuesday morning.'

'I can't wait,' I told her, lying through my own less-than-perfect teeth.

She inclined her head and stepped away. 'Good night, detective.' Then she paused and looked at Tallulah. 'So go on, then. What other matters do you have to attend to? Where are you heading to at this hour?'

'Goodbye, Juliet,' I said firmly. I stalked to my purple Mini and climbed into the driver's seat.

Buffy tugged at the door handle on the passenger side and slid in beside me. 'That woman is an aberration,' she muttered

I wasn't going to disagree with that. 'Do me a favour, Buffy,' I said. 'Stay away from her and, no matter what happens, do not attack anyone else.'

'I didn't atta—'

I raised a hand to silence her. It wasn't yet midnight and this was already proving to be a horrendously long night.

* * *

OF THE TWO suspects who'd mentioned the Chief before his death, Nathan Fairfax was top of my list so we went to the Supe Squad building first. It was a relief that Stubman was absent from his usual position outside the hotel next door.

I glanced up and down the dark, silent street then unlocked the front door and led Buffy inside. She whistled when she saw the bashed-in interview room door. 'You do have a winning way with people, don't you, DC Bellamy?'

I sent her an irritated look. 'It's been some time since Nathan Fairfax was in here. Although the room hasn't been used since then, I'll understand if you can't pick up his scent. And it's been raining, so the trail might have vanished. If there's nothing to follow, let me know.'

Buffy rolled her eyes. 'Puh-lease. This will be like taking a bone from a wolf cub.' She walked round the small room sniffing repeatedly, while patches of fur appeared and then disappeared across her skin. Unspent energy rolled off her body. Despite the circumstances, watching her was fascinating.

She paused in the middle of the room with her eyes half closed, then nodded. 'Okay,' she said. 'I've got it. I'll follow the scent and you can follow me.' She grinned suddenly. 'If you can keep up.'

Finally, a challenge that I might be able to meet. 'Lead the way.'

Buffy burst out of her clothes, her body twisting as her human form merged into that of her wolf. Although the interview room was small and the table and chairs took up at least half of it, she avoided knocking into anything as she transformed. Her shaggy head turned to me and she offered a wolfish grin. A split second later, she took off.

Bounding down the hallway, she paused at the front door only long enough for me to open it for her. There were some things a werewolf couldn't do, and twisting doorknobs was one of them. It didn't stop her for long and within moments she was hurtling down the street. I closed the door behind me and sprinted after her. I'd keep up with Buffy if it damn near killed me.

I followed her down to the first crossroads. She stopped there briefly, not to allow me to catch up but to ascertain where Nathan Fairfax's lingering scent was leading. Then she turned left, away from Lisson Grove where all the clans resided. She wove down the empty street while I ran after her, crossing my fingers that she'd at least locate the area where Nathan Fairfax vanished if not the man himself. Of course, if he'd grabbed a taxi or hopped onto a bus, it would be much more complicated. I hoped that wasn't the case.

Buffy stopped at a lamppost and I came to a juddering halt next to her, trying not to breathe too hard. 'He peed against this?' I enquired with raised eyebrows.

Though she rolled her eyes and shook out her fur in disgust at my pathetic attempt at a joke, Buffy made it clear that Nathan had paused briefly here. I glanced round. He must have run out of Supe Squad at high speed; with the long road stretching behind him, this would have been a good place to stop and check to see if anyone was following.

Buffy trotted across the road, her head dropping as she sniffed the ground. She returned a moment later and tried moving ahead. I grimaced. Had she lost his scent? I was disappointed, even though this had been a long shot from the start. She pawed at the pavement and whined, then her head jerked up, her nostrils flared and she took off again.

We crossed another intersection, and another. Much more of this and we'd end up back at the DeVane Hotel where we'd started. Then another thought struck me and I faltered mid-step. The DeVane Hotel wasn't the only landmark up ahead.

Buffy hadn't noticed that I'd stopped. She continued to plough on ahead, but it didn't matter that she was pulling away from me. I already knew where she was heading.

She rounded another corner and vanished so I picked up my feet and darted after her. When I caught up with her, she'd stopped again. This time she was on the edge of St James's Park. 'He went in there, didn't he?' I asked.

Buffy's ears twitched and she nodded. I gritted my teeth. Almost every wolf in the country used this park during the full moon. I didn't ask her to continue to follow Nathan's scent because it was lost for good now amongst the many other werewolf smells. But he'd come here – and so had Nightstalker Jim. Although we'd found neither of them, I'd learned something. It wasn't good, but it was something.

* * *

BEFORE WE HEADED BACK to Tallulah and she returned to her human form, Buffy and I checked out the interior of the park. It was a pointless mission. She located a few traces of old blood – including, somewhat gallingly, my own – but there was nothing relating to Nathan Fairfax or Night Stalker Jim. Both of them had mysteriously appeared, created a disturbance, mentioned the Chief and disappeared. And now that Chief – Lance Emerson – was dead.

Jim had been in possession of a dangerous knife with a sharp blade. Could that have been used to slit Emerson's throat? Did Nathan Fairfax sneak into the hotel, lure Emerson to the spa and set Jim the grisly task of murder? And if he did, then why?

Buffy gave me a long look. 'You're thinking so hard that I can literally hear the cogs turning in your brain,' she told me.

I tutted. 'You can't *literally* hear me thinking.'

'It's a figure of speech.'

'Literally is a figure of speech? You know that makes no sense, right?'

Buffy smirked. I was glad someone was enjoying themselves. 'You know,' she said, 'it would have been faster for us to walk to the hotel than go to Supe Squad to retrieve your stupid car.'

'There are still protestors hanging around. You walking past them, either as a wolf or stark naked, would only add fuel to their fire.'

She bared her teeth. 'It would be fun.'

'No, it wouldn't. Besides,' I said as I directed Tallulah into the hotel's car park, 'I might need the car later. It's better to have her close by.'

'Her? This hunk of junk is not a girl, it's definitely a boy. No girl would permit herself to get into this state.'

In my opinion, Tallulah was looking rather good right now. She'd been to the carwash last week, so she was far cleaner than usual. I sniffed. 'Don't diss my baby.' As I hopped out, I gave her purple bonnet a brief caress.

Confusingly, Buffy stayed where she was. I ducked my head back into the car. 'Do you want me to fetch you some clothes so you can walk through the hotel lobby without baring your arse?'

'Don't be ridiculous.' Her face was red and she was biting her lip. 'I have a lovely arse and I'm proud to show it off.'

'Then why—'

She tugged at the seatbelt. 'It's stuck,' she muttered. 'I can't release it.' She clicked the button several times and tugged again, her frustration growing.

I watched her for a moment or two, until my amusement gave way to concern. The harder Buffy tried to free herself, the more the seatbelt tightened across her body. 'Maybe you should apologise to Tallulah,' I suggested slowly.

Buffy's stared at me. 'Are you trying to tell me this car is sentient?'

I didn't think so. It didn't seem credible; Tallulah was a car, nothing more, nothing less. But all the same... 'Give it a shot.'

Buffy muttered something under her breath then stopped scrabbling at the seatbelt. 'I'm sorry, alright? I didn't mean to call you a hunk of junk. You're beautiful, Tallulah.'

Nothing happened. She tried to release herself again but the seatbelt resolutely refused to give way. 'I can't believe I just apologised to a car.'

I walked round to the passenger side. 'It's probably jammed. I'll help you.' I opened Buffy's door and reached down for the seatbelt catch. My fingertips had barely grazed it when there was a click and it slid free.

Buffy leapt out of the seat and bolted out of Tallulah at high speed. She glared at the car and then at me as I grabbed my crossbow from the rear seat. I strapped it to my back. I'd have to keep it with me from now on, regardless of how threatening it looked. There was a killer on the loose.

'I'm sure it was a coincidence,' I said. 'She's an old car.'

Buffy wrapped her arms around her body. 'I'm off to find

some clothes and go back to the party,' she said. 'I need a damned drink.' She raised her foot as if to kick Tallulah's front wheel then thought better of it and moved away.

'There's one last favour I need before you start downing more champagne,' I said. 'But don't worry, it doesn't involve driving anywhere.'

Her eyes narrowed to slits. 'Just as fucking well.'

CHAPTER FIFTEEN

Wrapped in a white spa robe in the middle of a bloody crime scene, Buffy looked incredibly out of place even though she didn't act it. She walked pensively round the small room, barely registering Emerson's corpse.

'Transport is already arranged,' Laura told me. 'As soon as it arrives, I'll take Mr Emerson's body to the morgue and begin a thorough post-mortem. Not that there's much doubt about how he died.'

I nodded and flicked a glance at Barry and Larry. 'How about you two? Have you found anything I can use?'

'It's a clean scene so far,' Barry said.

Larry grimaced. 'Yep. We've found various clear fingerprints that we'll have to cross-check against staff members and other visitors to the spa, but given their positions I don't think any of them belong to the killer. The only clear matches we can find around the massage table and the door belong to Lance Emerson.'

That wasn't surprising. The massage table would have been sanitised between spa sessions and, with the amount of essential oil being used here, the door handles were probably cleaned regularly.

Larry continued. 'We've also come across several smudged partial prints, including some near the victim's body, but none of them are distinct enough to be used for identification. The killer was probably wearing latex gloves.' He smiled cheerfully at me. 'Don't be completely disheartened, DC Bellamy. Contrary to popular belief, fingerprints can still be found on surfaces even if gloves are worn, especially when they're made of something thin, like latex. It's early days and we'll keep looking. We might still find something we can use.'

I'd keep my fingers crossed but I wouldn't bank on results. Emerson's murder had been obviously premeditated. While it was possible the killer might have made mistakes such as putting too much trust in a thin pair of gloves, they'd also been prepared.

Barry seemed to agree with me. 'Whoever murdered your man here knew what they were doing. It looks as if the victim came in of his own accord, undressed, lay on the massage table and was killed there.'

I considered his words. 'You don't think Lance Emerson suspected anything was wrong until the blade entered his neck?'

'It doesn't appear that way,' Laura said. 'He has no defensive wounds. It looks as if he died quickly. The murderer was strong and swift. Everything indicates that this was business and not personal.'

'Like an assassination?' The thought that there was a professional assassin who'd been hired to kill Emerson chilled me. That would mean we were looking for two perpetrators, rather than one.

'Possibly.'

I swallowed. A professional hit would make my life much, much harder.

Buffy, who had been silent up to that point, lifted her head. 'A supe did this.'

I stared at her. She wouldn't point a finger at our own kind unless she was sure. 'Why do you say that?' I asked.

'You know my nose is far more sensitive than yours.' She wasn't boasting, merely stating a fact.

I nodded. That was why I'd dragged her into this.

'Verbena and wolfsbane have been used in the public areas of the hotel because of the summit. The smell is particularly strong in the lobby but it fades away as you move into other areas. It's very faint on the higher floors where the rooms are, but you can still smell it in most places here on the ground floor. Your nose has grown accustomed to it, so you won't notice the different intensity in the same way that a werewolf does.'

Buffy was right; I'd definitely registered the heady scent the first time I'd entered the hotel but I hadn't paid much attention to it since then.

Larry frowned. 'Verbena and wolfsbane?'

'They're herbs that only supes can pick up on,' I explained. 'We use them to determine who's a true supe and who's not.' It was a shame that Night Stalker Jim or the Cumbrian woman who'd thought she was a werewolf hadn't known about them. The herbs could have saved them a lot of trouble.

'That's not their only use, detective,' Buffy said. 'One of them is called wolfsbane for a reason.'

Uh-oh. 'Go on.'

'When verbena and wolfsbane are distilled to their purest form and used in concentrated quantities, they act as covering agents for other scents. The combination you use in the Supe Squad building and in Tallulah isn't particularly strong, and neither is the stuff that's been used in the rest of the hotel.' She smiled faintly. 'That's a good thing. As werewolves, we don't appreciate being scent-blinded. In here, though, it's a different story. I reckon that the verbena and wolfsbane in here was concentrated enough to force out any other smells around the time that man was murdered.'

She met my eyes. 'I'm not talking about the odours of death or blood, I'm talking about the scent trail of the murderer. Only a supe would have thought of that and taken action to guard against it. Nathan Fairfax could have rubbed his body odour all around this room but I can't smell him because of the herbs that were used in here when the murder occurred. For that matter, I can't smell any other supes.'

I stared at her. 'Wait here,' I said suddenly. I whirled round and ran out of the massage room, returning a moment later with one of the candles that Rosa Carne had extinguished and which I'd noticed when I'd first entered. I sniffed it. Damn it, Buffy was right. It definitely smelled like wolfsbane and verbena. I'd been an idiot for not noticing it before.

I held it out to Buffy but she recoiled. 'That reeks. Get it away from me or it's all I'll smell for days.'

I handed the candle to Barry, who placed it in a ziplock bag. 'We'll put a rush on it at the lab,' he said, pre-empting me. 'Don't worry.'

But I was worried, very worried. Emerson had been targeted. He'd been lured out of his hotel room to this place, which had been set up as a kill zone. The murderer had made an effort to conceal their presence, and they'd murdered him without a sniff of a conscience.

Despite my earlier concerns, I no longer believed that this death had anything to do with the summit. This was about Lance Emerson himself; all roads led to the Chief and the man that he used to be. Focus on him, I decided, and you'll find the killer.

'I can hear those cogs turning again,' Buffy said.

This time I didn't rise to the bait. 'Thank you for your help. I'd appreciate it if you kept this quiet. I know you'll speak to Lady Sullivan but—'

Buffy held up her hands. 'Chill. I won't say a word to anyone.' She mimed zipping up her lips. 'Am I free to go now?'

I nodded. She didn't smile but she did give the four of us a warm look. For all her bluff and posture, she was on our side. 'Find this fucker,' she said simply, then she turned on her heel and walked out.

I looked at the others. I might have told DSI Barnes that I'd take the lead and find the killer, but I had little idea what I was doing when it came to crime-scene management. The best I could do was to follow Laura, Barry and Larry's lead.

Apparently my thoughts were more obvious than I'd realised. 'We'll finish bagging and tagging,' Larry said. 'We'll take care of matters here so you're free to investigate other avenues.'

'Okay,' I said. Then more quietly, 'Thank you.'

There was a muffled call from outside the door of the spa. I stiffened and turned to see what the problem was. When I saw Fred's drawn face, relief washed over me. At least it wasn't a member of the press who'd sneaked through, or a wandering supe who'd sidled in to cause problems.

My relief was short lived – Fred had come for a reason. Judging from his face, he and Liza had found something. I nodded at Wilma Kennard's guard and went out. 'What is it?' I asked.

'We've found something on the CCTV.'

'Something good?'

Fred's mouth flattened into a thin, grim line. 'Something.'

* * *

'I'VE MANAGED to isolate several useful clips from the footage,' Liza said. She'd hoisted her green dress up so she could tuck one leg underneath her and tied up her red hair out of the way. A half-empty mug of coffee sat next to her laptop screen. The party, at least as far as Supe Squad was concerned, was well and truly over.

'Emerson spent some time wandering around the hotel lobby and bar after he checked in on Monday. The more supes who started to appear, the more time he spent hanging around.' She gave me a meaningful look and gestured at the screen. 'He approached a lot of people. Here.'

I pulled over a chair and sat beside her. The DeVane Hotel might not have had CCTV in the areas where we wanted it, but the cameras they did have were high tech. The images were sharp and clear and there was no mistaking Emerson's tall figure as he lumbered around. I leaned in more closely, as if I could reach into the screen and pluck him out to quiz him and get a better grasp of what he was up to.

'This is from Tuesday. He approached this man.'

I watched as Emerson engaged a lanky, depressed looking fellow with dark hair tied in a pony tail. They spoke for several moments then Emerson motioned to Moira Castleman, who was standing quietly beside him. She passed Emerson a leaflet and he passed it to the man. I recognised it immediately as one of the Perfect Path's glossy brochures. A black scowl crossed the man's face. Obviously annoyed, he thrust the leaflet back at Emerson and stalked off.

'And then,' Liza said, clicking on the mouse, 'there's this from later that day.'

The next clip was of Emerson and Castleman in the bar. She nodded towards an older woman sitting alone nursing a cocktail. Emerson looked at the woman and shook his head, then he jerked his thumb towards another woman near the window. A moment later he stood up and walked towards her.

'He's recruiting for his daft cult,' I said.

Liza agreed. 'We've identified each of Tuesday's targets as humans. He spoke to this woman for about an hour – I can show you the rest of the footage, if you like. She took a leaflet but we don't know whether she tried to contact him later, or vice-versa. Kennard has looked up these people on the hotel system and they all checked out on Wednesday, so I don't think they're high on our list of suspects.'

I scratched my head. 'He only approaches people who are on their own. He's looking for those who are vulnerable individuals who don't have back-up. He seeks out humans who appear to be soft targets, tries to convince them that they're supes and says that only he can do something about it. And, for all Moira Castleman believed in what her boss was doing, she appears to be in on the act.'

'They don't seem to be doing very well,' Fred pointed out. 'Everyone they spoke to appeared … unenthusiastic. Even that last lady.'

I shrugged. 'Maybe it's a kind of "throw spaghetti at the ceiling" logic. Sooner or later something will stick. If he's after wealthy clients, the DeVane Hotel is the right choice. People who stay here have money.'

We stared at Emerson's flickering image.

'He's a wanker,' Fred said baldly. '*Was* a wanker.' He sniffed. 'I tracked down those druids like you told me. They're as skittish as kittens and only one of them seemed keen to talk, but he confirmed that this is what Lance Emerson was doing. He pretended to be all magical and wise, but really he was a grubby conman. He tried to insert himself into the druid community for a while, but they saw through him quickly enough. Unfortunately for everyone else, the druids keep to themselves and it didn't occur to them to flag up Emerson as a problem.'

I sighed. Hence the need for something like the supe summit.

'That's all very well,' Liza interjected, 'but it doesn't explain why he started approaching supes and trying to recruit them as well as humans.'

'Kennedy,' I said. 'He tried to get Kennedy to join him.'

'That sloshed satyr's not the only one.' She clicked her mouse again. 'Here is Lance Emerson trying to chat to a vampire.'

I watched as Emerson smiled charmingly at the vamp, who smiled back. Within two minutes, however, the vamp was trying to stuff a Perfect Path leaflet down Emerson's throat. Literally.

'The vamp's a French bloodsucker,' Fred said. 'I've already checked. He's giving a presentation on how Paris has made itself more welcoming to supes. It sounds like the supes are being forced into acting like performing seals, gremlins dressing up as gargoyles at Notre Dame and that kind of thing. I don't think his speech will be a big hit. Anyway, he's been at the champagne reception since it started and before that he was seen talking to some American werewolves in the lobby. I don't think he's our guy.'

'That was Wednesday. We also had this on Wednesday.' Liza moved onto another clip, this time of Emerson talking to a werewolf. The wolf listened politely for several minutes, but when Emerson gave her a leaflet she took one look at it, stood up and walked away.

'He's not having much success,' I commented.

'It doesn't seem to stop him from trying,' Fred said. 'We've found lots of other examples.'

I thought about it. 'It might be worth looking into his financials,' I said finally. 'There's something desperate about him. He might have convinced a human that he could beat the supe out of them with witchery and magic, but he couldn't actually beat the supe out of a real supe. So why was he so focused on recruiting supes?'

'Maybe he was lying for so long that he's started to believe what he was saying.'

Maybe. I thought about Nathan. How had the ex-Fairfax werewolf come to know Emerson? They'd lived in the same area, so maybe they'd been neighbours. Or maybe there was more to it.

'Is this what you wanted me to see?' I asked. 'Is this the "something"?'

Fred shook his head. 'No.' He glanced at Liza and she nodded.

'I found footage from the hotel lobby that includes Emerson. It's from this morning and...' She paused. 'Well, watch it for yourself.' She cued the next clip. 'Here we go.'

The camera was trained on the seating area to the left of reception. In the corner I spotted Emerson's now-familiar figure talking to a woman. Her head turned and I immediately recognised Juliet Chambers-May. The journalist smiled and seemed eager to take one of the Perfect Path leaflets, which she folded carefully and placed in her bag. Fodder for her next column, no doubt. I rolled my eyes.

Liza clicked her tongue. 'Not this bit,' she muttered. She fast-forwarded the footage. 'There,' she said. 'This is part you need to watch.'

Chambers-May had disappeared from view and Lance Emerson was sitting on one of the chairs. His legs were splayed wide, taking up a great deal of space, and he was scratching absentmindedly at his groin. He clearly hadn't noticed the camera.

'I don't—' I began.

'Wait,' Liza said.

A minute or two passed. Emerson took out more of his leaflets and spread them artistically across the coffee table, then reached for a copy of that day's *Daily Filter* that someone had left behind. He unfolded it, scanned the front page and flipped the newspaper to the back page for the sports news. That was when a small figure came up behind him with a knife and pressed it to his throat.

I jerked. 'Jesus.' I stared at the small female as she muttered something in Emerson's ear. He was rigid with what looked like genuine fear.

'We've not identified her yet,' Liza said, 'but she's obviously a pixie. We'll have her name shortly.'

'There's no need,' I told her. 'I know who she is.' I gazed at the spasm of vicious hatred on Belly's face as she made a sawing motion with her knife in exactly the same spot where, hours later, Emerson's throat had been slit. Shit.

CHAPTER SIXTEEN

Dawn was only a few hours away. It wasn't long until the keynote speakers were due to cough into their microphones and launch the first-ever Supernatural Summit with suitable aplomb and gravitas. Neither of those facts affected the party atmosphere at the reception.

The free champagne had been drunk, so it was now more of a 'tequila shots and over-priced liqueurs' reception. A lot of the remaining supes were creatures of the night, so it wasn't surprising that they were still going strong. Karaoke had been abandoned in favour of huddled chats and boogying around the dancefloor. Simply breathing in the alcoholic fumes and glancing at the slack, drunken faces was almost enough to give me a phantom hangover.

The majority of the werewolves had gone but most of the vampires remained. I felt Lukas's eyes on me as I walked slowly through the room. There was no immediate sign of Belly or her friends and none of them were answering their doors, but they'd all been three sheets to the wind when I'd met them earlier – and that was hours ago.

I scanned around for any pixies until my gaze alighted on a

group of five of them who were dancing enthusiastically. I exhaled. The tallest one, who had bubble-gum-pink hair in a soft cloud around her head, had been one of those drinking cocktails with Belly earlier in the day. She even looked vaguely sober. I made a beeline for her but I didn't get very far.

'Lord Horvath would like to speak to you,' said the pale-faced vampire who moved in front of me.

My stomach tightened. Lukas was still watching me with hooded eyes and I mouthed an apology. He didn't react but I knew what he was thinking.

'Please tell him that I'll find him at the earliest opportunity, but I have to deal with other urgent matters first.'

'He was very insistent.'

'I'm sure he was,' I said calmly. 'I will speak to him as soon as I can. I can't speak to him right now.'

'But—'

'It's alright, Heron,' Lukas rumbled as he abandoned his shadowy corner and walked over. 'You may go.'

Clearly relieved, the vampire slid away.

'Lukas,' I said, 'you know this is not how I wanted to spend my night but I don't have a choice. I've got limited time.'

'You look stressed.'

'I *am* stressed.'

'I can help, D'Artagnan. What's happened tonight affects all of us, not just Supe Squad. You don't have to shut me out. I want to find the murderer as much as you do – probably more.'

I reached out, my fingers grazing his. I wanted to keep him away from the investigation so he could honestly deny any involvement and he wouldn't be tainted if I didn't find Emerson's killer, but I'd already involved the werewolves by asking for Buffy's help. Maybe Lady Sullivan was right and I did treat both groups differently because of my relationship with Lukas. Anyway, Lukas was more than capable of looking after himself.

He certainly didn't need my protection – though maybe I needed his help.

'There are two suspects we can't find.' I'd locate Belly under my own steam, but she wasn't the only person I needed to talk to. I held Lukas's black-eyed gaze. 'You've met one of them already.'

'You mean Nathan Fairfax.'

'I do. The other suspect is the human who was causing problems at Trafalgar Square.'

'The one who doused himself in blood?' Lukas scowled. 'The one who stabbed you?'

'That wasn't his fault,' I reminded him.

'You shot yourself in the head.'

'That wasn't his fault either.' I squeezed his fingers to tell him to avoid pursuing the subject further. 'Both of those men knew the Chief, both of them mentioned him, and both of them disappeared somewhere in the vicinity of St James's Park.'

'That can't be a coincidence,' Lukas said. 'And that damned park is a stone's throw from here.'

'At this point we only want to talk to them,' I cautioned. 'There's no evidence that they were involved in Emerson's murder. They might well be completely innocent.'

'But until you speak to them, you won't know for sure,' Lukas said grimly

'Indeed. And we have to find them to speak to them.'

'I can help with that. The vamps here are more sober than you'd think. Once it became clear how serious the situation was, I forbade them from drinking.'

I raised an eyebrow. 'I don't imagine that was popular.'

'Like I said, D'Artagnan, the death of this man affects us all.'

I nodded, conceding the point. 'Buffy lost Nathan Fairfax's scent in the park, and she couldn't pick up Jim's.'

'I've got more tools at my disposal than my nose, plus I have a few ideas where they might have gone to hide. Leave it with me. I'll find them.'

The unshakeable confidence in his voice was reassuring, even if I wasn't convinced he could live up to his promise. 'Thank you.'

'You have your phone with you?' he asked.

'Yep.'

He cupped my face with one hand. 'Good. Take care out there.'

'You too,' I said softly.

Lukas's lips brushed mine, making a tingle ripple across my skin, and the tiniest smile lit up his eyes. He knew exactly how he made me feel. He tipped an imaginary hat in my direction and I curtsied. A moment later, we walked off in opposite directions.

It wasn't easy to get hold of the pink-haired pixie. She glanced in my direction when I approached, but her eyes flicked away as I drew close. She was obviously far more interested in dancing than she was in speaking to a member of Supe Squad. I waved at her and she ignored me; I tried speaking but she pretended not to hear. In the end, I stepped between her friends until I was standing directly in front of her. She rolled her eyes but nodded briefly when I pointed to a quiet corner.

'Are you going to arrest me for dancing, detective?' She jigged around, her body still moving in time to the music.

'I'm looking for someone,' I said. 'As soon as you tell me where she is, I'll get out of your hair and you can go back to your big-fish little-fish routine.'

The pixie sighed. 'Go on, then. Who are you after?'

'Belly.'

Her body language altered instantly from relaxed to something far more wary. She folded her arms across her chest and her eyes narrowed. 'What do you want with her?'

'I have to speak to her. It's important.'

'It's four o'clock in the morning.'

'Like I said, it's important.'

The pixie gave me an assessing look. I had no doubt that she was fully aware of Belly's assault, and it was good that the pixie community rallied around one of its own – but it wasn't good that none of them had sought to report what had happened.

'Belly's had a difficult time,' the pink-haired pixie said.

I nodded. 'I know.'

'If you make life more difficult for her...'

I couldn't make any promises. 'I have to speak to her,' I said. 'The sooner the better.'

She sighed. 'Fine. She's in room 211.'

'I've checked her room. Nobody's answering.'

'It's four in the morning,' she repeated. 'I guess she's sleeping.'

Perhaps. I'd knocked pretty hard on her door and called through to announce myself so as not to scare her, but she wouldn't have heard me if she was drunk and out for the count. Normally I wouldn't wake someone up at this hour but I didn't have a lot of time to spare. And I was investigating a bloody murder. A very bloody murder.

'Alright.' I stepped back to let the pixie return to her friends.

Something flitted across her expression and she called me back. 'She was pretty drunk earlier. I didn't see her here at the reception – I don't think she came. But if Belly's not in her room, she might be having a late-night swim.' She shrugged. 'Or early-morning swim. Depends on how you look at it. She said she was planning to take a dip.'

I stiffened. Did Belly swim a lot? The pool led directly to the spa. 'The pool is closed,' I said. It had been temporarily shut to prevent the werewolves from messing with it. In any case, Fred had checked the pool and reported it was empty.

A flash of amusement lit the pixie's face. 'Sure,' she said. 'I guess she didn't go for a swim then and she really is asleep.'

Damnit. 'Thank you,' I said aloud.

'Don't fuck up Belly,' the pixie said.

I swallowed. 'I'm not planning to.'

* * *

I CALLED Fred and told him where to meet me then moved quickly towards the DeVane swimming pool. Even under normal circumstances, none of the guests should have had access to the pool at this hour and there was no reason to believe that someone petite like Belly had killed Lance Emerson. She was a pixie and they weren't exactly renowned for their strength. Besides, she'd hardly still be hanging around the area if she'd committed murder.

The person who'd slit the Chief's throat had planned it – and that would include creating an alibi for themselves. It wouldn't include loitering near the scene of the crime hours after it had occurred, would it? I felt a shiver of doubt. Other criminals had been caught for more stupid reasons.

I passed through the hotel lobby. Wilma Kennard was no longer anywhere to be seen and I hoped she was getting a few hours' rest. It had been a long night for all of us and it wasn't going to end any time soon. I nodded acknowledgment to a giggly gremlin swaying her way towards the lifts. I veered past the corridor on the right, which led to the spa, and took the left-hand passageway instead.

As soon as I pushed open the double doors, I could smell the chlorine. The chemical scent was mixed with the wolfsbane and verbena that were still in evidence. Chlorine probably didn't have the same numbing effect on werewolves as the herbs did, but then I doubted any werewolves had wandered down here for a swim during the party.

I strode down the carpeted corridor until I reached the final door marked with a sign for the swimming pool. I reached for the door handle and it rattled as I shook it. It was indeed locked. I knelt down and examined the lock. It didn't look as if it had been tampered with.

'I've got a master keycard,' Fred called to me from behind.

I glanced round. 'There was definitely no sign of anyone anywhere in the pool area when you checked?'

'There wasn't a soul. I walked round with one of the hotel staff and they said nothing seemed out of place.'

Okay, that was good. This was probably a dead end. The chances were that Belly was fast asleep in her room, or simply refusing to answer her door at four o'clock in the morning. Who *would* answer their door at that time? Her mention of a moonlit swim had probably been nothing more than bravado.

'Can you open it up?' I asked. 'I want a quick look around. It's unlikely, but Belly might have come in here.'

'No problem, boss.' Fred unlocked the door and held it open for me.

The swimming pool reception area was larger than the spa's and much darker. I fumbled around for a light switch and finally located one behind the main desk. There was a faint buzz of electricity and then the room was illuminated. I blinked a few times and looked round.

Everything was quiet; everything seemed normal. There was a vending machine filled with energy bars and 'health' drinks. There were a few chairs and a large laundry trolley piled high with used towels that were waiting to be picked up later today. The walls displayed artful photographs of professional looking swimmers, and there were a few healthy plants dotted around. I couldn't see any candles. I sniffed the air but the smell of chlorine pervaded everything – at least as far as my senses were concerned.

There were two changing room doors. Fred headed for the one marked male while I walked into the female one. I was pleasantly surprised to see that it was a relaxed green colour rather than the traditional pink of the spa.

I wandered round three times. There was no sign of anyone. I checked every cubicle. Nothing. Nada. This was beginning to feel like a wild goose chase.

Rather than go back into the reception area, I headed for the opposite door which led to the swimming pool. Despite being empty and closed, it was illuminated with lights that, coupled with the tiny blue tiles inside the pool, gave the water an inviting aquamarine hue. Hell, even I was beginning to be tempted by the idea of a swim.

I walked round the edge of the pool towards another door. It was also locked but Fred quickly appeared and opened it. We checked the sauna and the steam room and examined the two locked doors leading to the spa changing rooms. It was all in order. Nobody was here, certainly not Belly. I shrugged and turned to leave.

My phone rang as I reached the far side of the swimming pool. I glanced at the caller ID and paused to answer, waving to Fred to carry on.

'Hey, Laura.'

'Hi, there!' She sounded far too chirpy. 'The transport is here so I'll head to the morgue with Mr Emerson. I'll start the post-mortem straightaway and let you know what I discover as soon as I'm done.'

'Thanks, Laura. I'll understand if you need to catch some sleep first, though.' I looked round the pool again. A swim wouldn't be appropriate but maybe I could grab a quick shower to freshen myself up.

'Pah. Sleep is for sissies and cats. I am neither. You need this done, and I'll do it for you.'

'You deserve a medal for all the stuff I keep putting you through.' I frowned towards the far end of the swimming pool where there was a raised area that seemed to lead to a jacuzzi. Next to it was another large laundry trolley. Why were there two laundry trolleys? Why was there one here and one in reception?

Laura laughed. 'That's what I keep telling everyone. I'll settle for a drink next time you're free.'

'That much I can do.' I started to walk to the trolley. 'How long do you think the post-mortem will take?'

'About three hours, give or take. Most of your supes will still be asleep by the time I get the results to you. Don't expect anything too surprising, though we might get lucky with skin scrapings. Emerson might have scratched his attacker and there might be some underneath his nails that we can use.'

'That's a lot of mights.'

'Yeah. I wouldn't hold my breath, I'm afraid. But I should be able to tell you more about the weapon and there could be something useful. You never know what stories the dead can tell you.'

I came to a halt by the trolley and glanced inside, then I looked at the jacuzzi.

'Emma?'

My answer came out as a croak. 'Don't leave yet, Laura.'

Her voice changed immediately. 'What is it?'

'There's something else you need to look at before you go.' There was a tight pain in my chest. 'No, not a something. A someone.'

I dropped the phone and reached in to grab Belly's body, pulled her out and started CPR.

CHAPTER SEVENTEEN

'SHE'S BEEN DEAD FOR HOURS,' LAURA SAID. 'YOU COULDN'T HAVE saved her.' Her expression was grim and tight. 'I won't know for sure until I do a full examination, but early indications suggest that she drowned.'

'Is there any bruising?' I asked quietly. 'Is there any sign that someone held her under the water?'

'There are no visible signs that's what occurred, though it's always possible.'

'I know it's early days, but can you tell how long she's been dead for?'

Laura shook her head. 'I can't, I'm afraid. This isn't like the movies and it's not that simple to put a time of death on a body. I'd say it's been several hours, but anything more specific would only be a guess.'

Fred was pale and shaking. 'I didn't see her. When I walked through here before, I didn't see her.'

This wasn't the time for recriminations. We were working with a skeleton crew – and that was because of me. 'Unless you came right up to the edge of the jacuzzi and peered in, you wouldn't have,' I told him. 'This isn't your fault. I almost missed her too, Fred.'

He didn't appear comforted. All three of us gazed down at Belly. For the briefest moment, overwhelming sadness choked me and my eyeballs stung with the threat of tears. I swallowed them down and turned to Barry and Larry who were focused on the contents of the laundry trolley. 'What do we have?' I asked.

The two moustachioed technicians turned to me, their expressions as identical as their grooming. 'We have one bloodied white robe that matches the other ones from the spa, and several bloodied towels. There's also one complete set of male clothes – chinos, a white shirt, a pair of socks and two size-thirteen matching shoes. Obviously we can't confirm it, but they appear to belong to Lance Emerson.'

Jesus.

'And we also have this,' Larry said. 'It was at the bottom of the jacuzzi.' He held up a clear bag containing a long-bladed knife. The jacuzzi water had wiped it clean of blood, and it would need to be matched to the wound on Emerson's throat, but we all knew that it had to be the weapon used to kill him.

Fred remained pale but raised his eyebrows. 'We're all thinking the same thing, right? We have Belly attacking Emerson on CCTV, clear as day. Then she's found less than fifty metres from Emerson's corpse with his clothes and blood next to her, not to mention the murder weapon. She murdered him.'

'And what? Drowned herself out of guilt?' Larry looked dubious.

Laura frowned. 'Emma said she was drunk at lunchtime yesterday. Alcohol and water are not a good combination, even if the water is shallow. Her death might be misadventure.'

'She killed a man and then decided to take a jacuzzi?'

'Maybe she needed to wash off the blood,' Fred suggested. 'The jacuzzi was here. She stopped to clean herself and the knife, started to enjoy the water and fell asleep. She drowned by accident.' He pulled a face. 'It's a stretch but it could fit.'

Barry glanced down at Belly's body. 'She's pretty small. Do pixies have supernatural powers that I'm not aware of? Could she have overpowered a large man like Emerson?'

'She came at him from behind while he was lying face down. He was vulnerable. She might not have needed a great deal of strength,' Fred said.

'It's not as simple as you think to slice someone's throat,' Laura argued. 'It wouldn't just require a strong stomach and a good blade, it would require a very strong hand.'

Reluctantly, I played devil's advocate. 'She was recently attacked herself, so she might have been working on her self-defence skills.' Not that Emerson's murder could ever be construed as self-defence. And I still didn't believe that a pixie could possess the sort of strength required to saw through someone's neck. Especially a drunk pixie.

'Could Lance Emerson have attacked her?' Fred asked.

'It's possible,' I conceded. 'It would explain why she went for him in the lobby. But it's unlikely. He lived up in Cumbria – it would be easy enough to check if he was in London at the same time as Belly. Anyway, I was told that she was attacked by three human lads, not one human man. However, there's something else that we haven't considered.'

'That she came here for a secret swim and surprised the killer, who drowned her to keep their identity secret?'

'There's that,' I said, 'and Lance Emerson's little black notebook. Moira Castleman told us he always kept it with him and that he took it to the spa with him.' I pointed at the clothes and towels. 'There's no notebook here. Somebody else is definitely involved because somebody else has Emerson's diary.'

'Maybe Emerson lost it. Maybe Moira Castleman was mistaken and it's back in their hotel room hidden under a pillow.'

It was possible but, apart from the missing notebook, everything pointed at Belly as the culprit.

'What did she do?' Laura asked. 'On the CCTV footage? How did she attack Lance Emerson?'

I looked at her grimly. 'She got hold of a knife and held it to his throat.'

'Oh.' She bit her lip. 'Which hand did she use? Left or right?'

'Left hand,' Fred said.

I nodded, visualising it. 'Yeah,' I agreed. 'She used her left hand.'

Laura smiled. 'That's what I thought.' She looked at Belly's body. 'She's not wearing any clothes but she still has her watch on her right hand. That's typical for lefties. You know that only about ten percent of the population are left-handed, right? It's an odd statistical fact that is the same for supes as it is for humans.'

I gazed at her. 'Is that odd statistical fact significant?'

'Oh yes.' Her smile grew. 'I don't need to complete a post-mortem to tell you that the mortal wound on Lance Emerson's neck was made by someone who was right-handed. Poor Belly did not kill him.'

* * *

BY THE TIME Belly's and Emerson's bodies had been taken away, together with the evidence that had been found, my head was pounding. Barry and Larry were going to spend the best part of the day examining the area and searching for anything that could help us pin down who was responsible.

I jumped in and out of the shower, changed my clothes and knocked back a triple espresso. I was ready to face the world, as much as I'd ever be. The first keynote speech was due to start in two hours. That gave me time to speak to the pixies – but it certainly wasn't a conversation I was looking forward to.

DS Grace paced up and down the room. 'Maybe I should do it.'

I shook my head. 'No. It still makes sense for you to keep out of the investigation. According to DSI Barnes' orders, I've still got almost thirty-six hours to look into the deaths.'

'Another dead body changes everything.'

'I didn't know Belly,' I said, 'and I only spoke to her once a few hours before she died, but her death is still devastating. It will send shockwaves through the pixie community. She's a victim, too.' I winced, remembering the rancour in Belly's voice as she'd told me she *wouldn't* be a victim.

I pointed towards the windows. 'The number of protestors out there has quadrupled since yesterday. Almost all of them are anti-supe. The vast majority of people in this country aren't going to give a shit about a pixie because they don't see her as one of them. Laura won't confirm it until after the post-mortem and the initial lab results, but we're fairly sure that Lance Emerson was human. As far as those people out there are concerned, his death is the only important one. Belly matters to us but not to them.' I met Grace's eyes. 'So in that sense, sir, nothing has changed at all.'

'How many corpses will it take, Emma? How many more deaths will there be before this is over?'

I didn't answer his question because I couldn't, but there was one concession that I could make. 'I'll see what the pixies say. If they want us to cancel the summit out of respect, that's what we'll do.' Maybe it would be for the best; maybe this had been a losing battle from the moment that Emerson's corpse had been found. Maybe it would take a miracle to change public opinion of supes. A sense of defeat washed through me and I felt my shoulders sag.

Grace raised his eyebrows in surprise. 'You'd be prepared to cancel for a supe death but not for a human death?'

'It's the supe summit, not the human summit,' I said. Then I sighed. 'But you're right. A second death changes things.'

Several emotions flitted across Grace's face. 'There won't be another chance to do this. If the summit falls apart now, you'll never get supes – let alone humans – to agree to another one. An event like this won't happen again, at least not for a long time. Hopefully the pixies will see that.'

I blinked.

'I'm not against the summit, Emma, any more than I'm against supes or against you,' DC Grace said

I glanced down at my feet. Although it sometimes felt like I was battling the whole world, it wasn't true. It would never be true. A little of my depression eased. 'Thank you, sir.'

At that moment Liza came in, walked over to her laptop and sat down. Her pretty green dress had been replaced by smart trousers and a blouse, but Grace's cheeks flared red all the same. His eyes tracked her movements before he looked away again, then Liza glanced in his direction and her eyes travelled up and down his body. Oh. *Oh.*

Grace shook himself. 'There's something I *can* do,' he said. 'Belly's parents live a stone's throw from here. If I inform them of what's happened before you speak to the rest of the pixies, it will save you some time. Maybe they can shed more light on the attack she suffered.'

Not only would that be genuinely helpful, but it also meant I wouldn't have to knock on the door of a deceased person's loved ones. It was one of the worst parts of the job and I was happy to pass it over to Grace.

Liza drew in a sharp breath and we both turned to look at her. 'What is it?' I asked.

'Here,' she said. She swivelled the laptop screen. 'Take a look at this.'

It was a news article that, for a moment, filled me with dismay. Despite my best efforts, the press had got hold of the details of Lance Emerson's murder. Then I realised the article wasn't about him – it was about me.

The headline was in large, bold letters: *Why Does Supe Squad Hate Humans?* Underneath it was an unflattering photo of me. I realised it must be the picture Juliet Chambers-May had taken the previous night before Buffy tackled her.

'The gist appears to be that you're putting humans in danger by hosting the summit,' Liza said.

Wait until they found out one of those humans had been murdered by a supe at the very same summit, I thought ruefully.

'It says that you only care about supes and you have no business policing them because you're a supe yourself.'

I'd have argued the opposite but it wasn't worth worrying about just then. Juliet Chambers-May could write whatever she wanted. In fact, if I didn't find the killer by the time my deadline was up, it might stand everyone else in good stead because it put me in an excellent position to be the fall guy.

'Does it say anything about Emerson? Or about any kind of death?'

Liza shook her head. 'Nothing's mentioned.'

I breathed out. I wasn't going to look a gift horse in the mouth; the longer we could keep the salient facts quiet, the better.

'She interviewed Stubman and he had some choice words to say,' Liza continued.

I snorted. 'I bet he did.'

'And she said that you're the vampires' stooge because you're going out with Lord Horvath and you're wearing his necklace. The Tears of Blood.' Liza glanced up. 'Is that really what it's called?'

I shrugged. I wasn't wearing the damned thing now, and it wasn't anyone else's business what jewellery I put on. There were far more important things to worry about.

'That bloody woman,' Grace muttered.

'She's entitled to write whatever she wants. It's her job and her prerogative. It doesn't help me but it doesn't harm us, not as much as it could,' I said firmly. 'Forget about her and focus on what we have to deal with. Got it?'

'Sometimes I regret the day I agreed to come to Supe Squad,' Grace said to himself,

I couldn't blame him.

He sighed and looked at Liza again before returning his attention to me. 'I'll go and speak to Belly's family. Keep me in the loop, will you, whether I'm involved in the investigation or not?'

'Liza can do that, can't you, Liza?' I said.

'If I've got time.' She turned back to the laptop. 'I've got plenty of other things to do.'

There was a moment of awkward silence then I clapped my hands to break the tension. 'Let's get to it, people.'

CHAPTER EIGHTEEN

ACCORDING TO WILMA KENNARD AND THE HOTEL'S KEY-CARD system, Moira Castleman hadn't left her room all night. I returned to her room while I waited for DS Grace to message me that he'd spoken to Belly's family. There was no answer when I knocked, so I slipped a note underneath the door asking Moira to call me as soon as she could. Then I headed downstairs to the Rose Room and called the pixies to order.

Not many of them were there. The champagne reception had continued until after six in the morning; no doubt many of the delegates were in bed nursing hangovers. Belly's friends were present, however, and so was the young pixie with the bubble-gum-pink hair.

From the mutters, whispers and narrow-eyed sidelong glances, most of them had worked out who I wanted to speak to them about, even if they didn't know why. I'd considered speaking only to Belly's best friends, but word would spread quickly. It would be better to speak to most of them immediately and avoid inaccurate rumours.

I drew in a breath and wished my hands would stop trembling. 'Thank you all for coming.' My voice was shaky and too quiet. I coughed and tried again. 'Thank you for being here.'

There were a few grunts and nods. The pink-haired pixie stood up and glared at me. 'Where is she?' she demanded. 'Where is Belly? Have you arrested her? Is that why you're here? Are you blaming her for the murder of that stupid human? Emerfuckson?'

I jerked. 'You know about what happened to him?' I thought we'd kept Emerson's murder quiet apart from telling a few important supes. I looked at Ochre, the older pixie who'd been in attendance when I'd spoken to the supe leaders, but she merely shrugged. She'd probably told all the pixies about Emerson straight after I'd asked them to meet me here.

Several pixies rolled their eyes then the pink-haired one spoke again. 'Of course we know about him. And no, we've not spoken about his murder to anyone outside of the summit and we won't. We know you don't want the humans to find out about it yet.'

Another of the older pixies laughed coldly. 'Yeah. We're all aware what will happen if people out there think we killed a human while we were drinking champagne. The tabloids and the Twitterati will say that we danced on top of his bloody corpse.' He put his hands on his hips. 'But that doesn't change the fact that there is no way Belly would have done this. No. Way.'

Everyone in the room seemed to agree. I didn't know whether they genuinely believed that or they were closing ranks around their friend, but I suspected the former. I hoped it was true. 'She's not been arrested.' I paused. 'But I do have some very bad news.'

They stilled immediately; the shuffling stopped and the scowls ceased. I could have heard a pin drop. I coughed once more. 'I'm sorry to say that we found Belly's body this morning near the hotel swimming pool. She was in the jacuzzi. She appears to have drowned.'

There were several gasps of horror and at least three pixies collapsed to the floor. One of them, a woman whom I recognised as one of Belly's friends, let out a heart-wrenching wail of anguish.

I looked down at my feet then looked up again. The very least the pixies deserved was someone who would look them in the eye.

Ochre was pale but her voice was steady. 'Was it murder, detective? Or an accident?'

'I don't know.'

'For fuck's sake!' someone else yelled. 'You could be honest with us!'

I winced. 'I am being honest. There's nothing to suggest she was murdered, but we can't rule it out. Not yet, not until we know more.'

A male pixie shook his head. 'It must have been the same person who killed the human bloke. There's no other way there would be two suspicious deaths within hours of each other.'

I'd already discussed this with Liza and Fred. We'd debated how much information to tell the pixies and decided to share everything. The pixies had known Belly and might be able to help us with the investigation, and they deserved to know because she was one of their own.

'Next to where Belly was found, we found a pile of bloody towels and clothes that we believe belonged to the human who was killed,' I explained.

'See?' The male pixie waved his hands. 'I told you! The same fucking person killed both of them!'

Ochre stared at me. 'That's not what you're saying, is it, detective? You're saying that Belly might have been the one who killed the human after all.'

I met her eyes. 'We are ruling nothing out at this stage. *Nothing*. There is some evidence to suggest that Belly didn't kill him but somebody seems to want us to think that she did.' I drew in a deep breath. 'We have Belly on camera earlier in the day holding a knife to the human's throat.'

The pink-haired pixie moaned. 'Yeah, but he deserved that.'

Ochre looked at her. 'Why do you say that, Flax?'

Flax's eyes shifted from left to right. Tears were running freely down her cheeks and she was shaking.

'Please,' I urged her. 'Don't hold anything back. Any details you can tell me will be useful.'

Flax shuddered and sighed. She got to her feet with some difficulty and waved off a helping hand from the pixie closest to her. She choked slightly, but when she looked at me her eyes were clear.

'Belly was late and checked in after we did. That human guy, Emerson, followed her into the lift and then to her room. She told us that he kept talking at her, saying he could help her, take all her worries away. It wasn't what he said that bothered her, though. He grabbed her arm at one point and it completely freaked her out.'

There was enough rage in her words to cut through her grief. 'It reminded her of those human blokes who attacked her because that's what they did too. They followed her down the street and then one of them grabbed her arm.' Her voice dropped. 'After that, they all piled in.'

Lance Emerson had been looking for real supes to join his fake cult and Belly would have been the perfect target. She looked vulnerable and she was on her own. Emerson would have thought her ripe for the picking. My lip curled. I'd investigate Emerson's death it to the best of my ability but I wouldn't mourn his death.

'That's why we went to the bar and started drinking so early,' Flax continued. 'We were trying to cheer her up, to get her to relax. But then she saw Emerson in the lobby and...' She shrugged. 'She might have been over-enthusiastic in her retaliation.'

That was an understatement. 'None of you tried to stop her

from attacking him?' I said. None of Belly's friends had been close enough to be picked up by the CCTV camera.

Flax folded her arms across her chest defiantly. 'I handed her the damned knife,' she said. 'We were close to her and we wouldn't have let things get out of hand. But Belly needed to do it. She needed to know she could stand up for herself if she needed to.'

I wasn't convinced by that logic, but I understood it.

'She didn't hurt him,' Flax said. 'Not even slightly. She only wanted to scare him and make sure he stayed away from her for the rest of the summit. No matter what it looks like on film, Belly wasn't violent. She wouldn't have hurt a fly.'

Hmm. 'Was she at the champagne reception? Did anyone see her?'

Almost all of the assembled pixies shook their heads but it was Flax who answered. 'No,' she said. 'We left the bar around four, long before the reception started. That was when Belly atta —' she swallowed and amended her words '—*spoke* to Emerson. Then she said she was going to have a lie down and maybe go for a swim when she woke up. She didn't ever make it to the reception.'

I nodded my thanks. 'Is there anything else?'

'She didn't kill him,' Ochre said. 'She wouldn't have.'

I nodded again and took a deep breath. 'We can call a halt to the summit. The keynote speeches aren't due to begin for another twenty minutes. I'm more than prepared to cancel everything in Belly's memory. A lot has happened and—'

'Don't you dare.' Flax looked furious. 'Don't you bloody dare cancel this summit. It's not what Belly would have wanted, and it's certainly not what we want. If you cancel the summit in her name that makes her the victim she never wanted to be. The purpose of this event is to find ways to get on better with the humans. We want them to recognise us as real people, not as

monsters. That's what the summit has been designed for, right?'
When I didn't immediately answer, her voice rose. 'Right?'

'Yes. That's right.'

'If Belly hadn't been attacked last month by those fucking freaks, we wouldn't be here right now. It was the snowball that became an avalanche.' Her tiny hands clenched into fists. 'Don't let that avalanche bring down the mountain.'

I stared at her then at all the others. Ochre allowed herself a tiny smile in my direction; it didn't quite reach her eyes but it was enough.

'Thank you,' I said quietly. 'Thank you all.'

* * *

I TOOK up my position at the back of the main hall. I certainly didn't have time to listen to all the speeches but it was important for the delegates to see that Supe Squad was here, even if only for a short while. Besides, I thought, as I watched the stony-faced pixies file in, if *they* could sit and listen politely, the least I could do was be here for the start.

I looked round. There was no sign of Lukas's dark head. It was hours since I'd last heard from him, and several other vampires whom I knew were also missing. I slid out my phone and sent him a quick text. Maybe, I thought hopefully, he'd found Nathan Fairfax.

Despite the missing vampires, almost every chair in the auditorium was occupied. There were hundreds of supes inside this one room – probably the first time such a thing had ever happened. Whatever else was going on, relationships would be forged here and alliances would be made. The more that supes could stop thinking of themselves as distinct groups, from vampires to werewolves to pixies to gremlins to whatever, the more of a united front we could present to the human world. I almost felt a return to my earlier feelings of hope and optimism.

This was where we could start to create a better society for everyone. Or at least we could if the summit attendees would stop dying.

Reverend Knight, looking dapper in his crisp white dog collar, strode up to the stage. It had been a calculated move to get a human to give the first keynote speech; the significance of a man of God opening the first-ever supe summit wouldn't be lost on anyone. The good vicar understood what a big deal this was and he'd been delighted to be asked. He tapped the microphone once, cleared his throat and smiled beatifically.

'This is an historic moment,' he intoned. 'Never before has something of this magnitude happened in this country. The supernatural world has had many trials and tribulations, but this event proves how far we have all come. I am honoured to be invited to be here today, and I am fortunate to count many of you in the audience as my friends.

'When I first arrived in my new parish, I was terrified of you. I didn't understand supes – I *couldn't* understand supes. I lived in a world where to be supernatural meant that you were strange, unnatural.' He touched his chest. 'Now, having been forced to confront my own prejudices, I know that I couldn't have been more wrong. If I can overcome my preconceived ideas about the supe community then so can the rest of this wonderful country.'

It was a bit heavy-handed but it got the point across. Reverend Knight continued speaking while Liza leaned in to my ear. 'We've checked the CCTV footage again,' she murmured. 'Belly was seen exiting the lift and heading in the direction of the swimming pool at about five-thirty yesterday.'

So she didn't go to lie down. She'd gone up to her room and then headed to the pool soon after that, just before Emerson had been killed. The fake spa invitation he'd received was for six o'clock.

'The doors to the pool were locked at midday,' I whispered.

'She could have picked the lock,' Liza suggested. 'Or nabbed a key from somewhere.'

Or Emerson's killer had got there before her. Perhaps they had their own key and had used the route via the swimming pool to get into the spa. Perhaps they'd not locked the door behind them and Belly had thought the pool was still open. Unless she really was the killer, which seemed unlikely even without her friends' avowals. She'd been getting drunk in the bar, not forging fake spa invitations or sourcing anti-werewolf candles. I pursed my lips.

Liza nudged me sharply in the ribs with her elbow. I let out a surprised yelp and turned to glare at her. At least a third of the audience turned round to glare at me. 'Heads up,' she muttered and jerked her head to the right.

I followed her gaze, my heart leaping in my chest when I saw Lukas stride into the auditorium. He was here, thank goodness. His gaze swept round the room and settled when he found me. He was still wearing his tuxedo from the night before but it looked considerably more rumpled and dirty than it had done the last time I'd seen him.

I breathed out and nodded eagerly when he pointed towards the exit. Reverend Knight would have to finish the rest of his speech without me.

CHAPTER NINETEEN

'I WAS GETTING WORRIED ABOUT YOU. YOU'VE BEEN GONE FOR hours.'

Lukas wrapped his arms round me. 'Now you know how I feel most of the time.'

I managed a smile. 'We've had trouble here.'

'So I've been hearing.' He held me tight for a moment before releasing me. 'Was she murdered? The pixie?'

'I don't know. Hopefully Laura can tell us in the next hour or so, but she's got two bodies to deal with now rather than one. It might take longer.'

I looked behind him. He seemed to be alone. 'Where are your other vamps?'

'I found trouble, too,' he told me. 'They're doing what they can to manage it while I came here to find you.'

I held my breath. 'Nathan Fairfax?'

Lukas shook head. 'The other one. The human.'

My eyes widened. Night Stalker Jim. 'Where is he?'

He grimaced. 'It's easier to show you than to tell you. We're having some … problems with him. He says he'll only to talk to you. He's not far from here but it will be faster if we drive, and we'll avoid the protestors outside. You can't hear them in here but they're deafening out there.' He tilted his head, a question in his eyes. 'Did I hear right? Did Juliet Chambers-May write a nasty article about you and publish it this morning?'

I shrugged. 'Yeah. It's not an immediate concern.'

Lukas scowled blackly. 'Hmm.'

'Leave it, Lukas. It's not an issue.' I looked him up and down. 'Why don't you go and get changed whilst I bring Tallulah out front?'

'Sounds like a plan.'

He kissed me and headed for the lift. I watched him go and noted one of the hotel staff grinning at him as he passed by. My brow creased. Once upon a time, Lukas had informed me that he'd bribed several of the DeVane Hotel staff members for information on some of their guests. I hadn't approved of it then, and I didn't approve of it now. And someone who could be bribed by a vampire Lord into passing on gossip might also be bribed to hand over a copy of a hotel master key. It was certainly another lead worth pursuing.

* * *

LUKAS HAD BEEN RIGHT about the protestors. Looking across from the front of the hotel, they were less of a sea of angry faces and jiggling placards than an ocean. As Tallulah's engine ticked over, I gazed at them. They weren't confined to any particular age group; I could see kids and teenagers next to white-haired pensioners.

There were no longer any marriage proposals or pro-supe declarations. The supe fans had most likely been intimidated into leaving by the others whose red-faced rage at the supes' audacity for daring to exist, let alone come together for a conference, was shockingly intimidating. Plenty of uniformed Met police officers had been drafted in to keep them away from the hotel, and nobody was broaching the temporary steel barriers, but they still made me nervous. I couldn't begin to fathom where all that hatred came from.

There was a tap against the window on the passenger side of the car and I jumped, before cursing myself for doing so. It was only Lukas. I noted that he'd decided against changing into anything inconspicuous; quite the opposite, in fact. He'd plumped for full vampire-Lord fancy dress, with a frilly white shirt, a flamboyant blood-red cloak and matching top hat. I knew he was making a point. He wasn't ashamed of what he was and he wanted everyone across the street to know it. All the same, jeans and a T-shirt wouldn't have been a bad idea. Not that I was going to say anything. He could wear whatever he wanted to, even a damned top hat.

He flashed a grin and reached for Tallulah's door handle. The crowd of protestors roared at him and he doffed his hat. Then he rattled the door. I frowned. It wasn't locked. Lukas tried again, and again the door wouldn't open.

Reaching across, I tried it myself. I tugged and then I yanked, but it seemed the car door was well and truly stuck. I grimaced and mouthed to Lukas to wait a second.

At that moment there was a loud bang from the protestors and I ducked instinctively. What the fuck was that? It sounded like a bomb. I raised my head and looked: a firecracker. It had only been a firecracker, nothing more than a daft scare tactic. I exhaled. Nobody was trying to kill us.

Somewhat shakily, I put my hands on the steering wheel. 'Tallulah,' I said aloud, 'can you please let Lukas in?'

There was no response. I felt even more stupid than Buffy had done when she'd apologised to the car the previous night. Nevertheless, I tried again. 'Please, Tallulah. This isn't the time for fun and games. Just let him in.'

After a second, there was a loud click. Lukas tried the door handle again and this time it swung open without a single rusty creak. He took off his ridiculous top hat and slid inside. 'What's up with the car?'

'I don't know.' I gave Tallulah's interior a suspicious look. 'I really don't know.'

He opened his mouth. Suspecting that he was going to say something less than complimentary about her, I motioned him to stay quiet. His eyes narrowed slightly but he got the message and focused on me instead of Tallulah. 'You looked scared when that firecracker went off,' he said softly.

'It was unexpected, that's all.' I paused. 'I know you've had to deal with this sort of thing for a lifetime, but it's not easy to be confronted with so much hate and anger.'

Lukas paused for a moment before speaking again. 'It looks like a lot of people and, yes, they are scary. But when you think about how many humans live in London, it's only a tiny percentage who've come out to protest today. Most of them are here because they're afraid of us. Fear is a more powerful motivator than hate.'

I nodded. He was right. I knew all that and I'd been expecting large numbers of protestors today, but it was one thing to be aware of what was happening and quite another to experience it in person. 'Where are we going?' I asked.

'Just the other side of St James's Park. It's not far.' He reached across and squeezed my hand. 'Are you alright?'

'Yes.' I nodded firmly. 'Yes.' I told my stomach to stop churning and put Tallulah in gear. I had to focus on the road, not the furious faces watching me. 'Let's see what Night Stalker Jim has to say for himself.'

* * *

I PARKED Tallulah in the first spot I could find. Both the driver door and passenger door opened easily. I carefully stroked Tallulah's bonnet. 'It's okay, old girl. It's okay.'

Lukas raised his eyebrows and I shrugged, then gave him a pointed look. He'd put the top hat back on and the red cloak was swirling round his ankles in the light breeze.

'You like my outfit?' he enquired.

'I have no words.'

Lukas smirked. 'You know you've made an impact when the love of your life is rendered temporarily speechless. You did the same to me when you put that black dress on last night.'

'Honestly,' I said, 'I'm not quite sure whether to laugh or cry.'

His smirk grew to a grin. 'Maybe when all this is over, I'll give you a personal fashion show.'

I met his gaze 'Less is more, sweetheart.'

'I'll bear that in mind.' His eyes glittered, then he shook himself and pointed behind me. 'There,' he said. 'That's where we're going.'

I swivelled round. I couldn't work out where he meant.

'Cockpit Steps,' Lukas said.

I finally spotted the narrow alleyway and the curving steps leading down and away from us. 'Really?' I asked doubtfully. I'd walked those steps plenty of times. They were named after the Royal Cockpit Inn that used to be a popular place for the barbaric sport its name memorialised. Thankfully, the pub had long since been demolished, and Cockpits Steps was a handy shortcut that tourists rarely noticed. Only thirty metres long, it was hardly a good place to hide out for a long period of time.

'Trust me,' Lukas murmured.

'I'll do my best.'

We walked towards the start of the alleyway. As we drew close, a vampire stepped out from the shadows and inclined his head. 'Lord Horvath. Detective Constable Bellamy.'

'Has he made any attempt to leave?' Lukas asked.

'No. We've kept the entrance sealed as you requested. It's quiet now, but there were a few people passing by and walking the steps not long after you left.'

Entrance? There was no entrance anywhere along Cockpit Steps. I shot Lukas a confused look.

He smiled slightly. 'Sometimes it's easy to forget that there's a lot more to London than the surface suggests. I'd forgotten about this place myself until I walked past the entrance. Even then, I only checked it on a whim. I should have thought of it earlier, but it's been disused for so long. Buffy is young – she wouldn't have known it exists any more than you do.'

Now I was more puzzled than ever, but I reserved judgement and followed Lukas's lead to the start of the steps. I peered down them. There were another two vampires stationed halfway along and probably more round the corner, but there was still no entrance. There was no magic door.

'Did you come here?' I asked. 'When there was still cockfighting, I mean?'

Lukas shook his head. 'No, that was well before my time. But I've been to the pit on more than one occasion.'

'The pit no longer exists.'

He held up his index finger and leaned in towards me. 'That's what they want you to think. Officially cockfighting ended in the early seventeenth century, although reports suggest it continued for some time after that. The cockpit was turned into a theatre for Charles I. Nowadays the building is used by the Cabinet for government business.'

Lukas gestured beyond the high wall. 'That's not the part we're interested in.' He pointed at the stones beneath our feet. 'There's another pit underneath here that still exists. It was used for fighting until the 1970s. Not cocks, though. Well,' he amended, 'not cocks of the feathered variety. People were prepared to pay a pretty penny to watch supes duke it out in an arena.' He rubbed his cheek. 'They probably still would.'

'You're saying there's an old fighting pit right below where we're standing?' He nodded. 'And that supes used to fight each other in that pit?' Lukas nodded again. 'And you're saying that there's access to it? And Night Stalker Jim is down there now?'

'Yep. In theory, anyone can get in if they know how.' He gave me a meaningful look. 'But nowadays no human would know, not without supernatural help.'

I folded my arms. 'So somebody supernatural showed Jim the secret entrance.' My mind flitted through the possibilities. 'Do we know who?'

Lukas's gaze was steady. 'He called out a name when we first tried enter.'

'Go on.'

'Nathan.'

I already knew that Jim and Nathan were connected via their knowledge of Lance Emerson, so I shouldn't have been surprised. 'Very well,' I said quietly. 'How do I get in?'

Lukas tapped one of the stones with his shoe. 'Here,' he told me. 'And here.' He bent down and placed his right hand on a weathered, scratched stone and his left hand on an identical one half a metre away. 'I think this is how that game Twister was invented.' He jerked his head towards a third stone. 'You see that slab with the moss round the edges? There's a hole to the side of it. You need to...'

I knelt down and stuck my little finger into the hole.

Lukas smiled. 'That's it.'

I waited. 'Nothing's happening.'

'Be patient.'

I was beginning to think this was some kind of prank. If so, I wasn't even faintly amused. 'Lukas—'

All of a sudden there was a muted rumbling and the ground started to shudder. I jumped with shock.

'You have to be quick,' one of the vampires called. 'People are heading this way.'

'We'll be twenty seconds,' Lukas replied.

And then, beneath my eyes, the ground opened up.

I stared at the dark hole. 'I ... uh ... I...' What the hell? How was that possible?

'They're almost here,' the vamp hissed.

Lukas grabbed my arm. 'In we go.'

The hole was pitch black; there was no way of telling how deep it was. 'But...'

'Now, Emma.' And with that, he jumped in.

I sucked in a breath. There was no choice. I closed my eyes and followed him.

CHAPTER TWENTY

EXPECTING MORE OF A DROP THAN THERE WAS, I LANDED gracelessly in a heap. Before I'd untangled my legs, the opening above our heads slid closed. A moment later, I heard several pairs of feet clip-clop along the alleyway and pass directly over us.

'That's unbelievable,' I whispered. 'How can people not know this exists?' I scrambled to my feet. It was still pitch black and I couldn't make out a single thing. Despite Lukas's presence, I felt a surge of cloying, desperate claustrophobia. Sometimes pure darkness reminded me too much of my own deaths. I gulped and felt my heart rate speed up.

'Relax,' Lukas said. He slid out his phone and switched on the torch light function. I gasped with relief. 'Once upon a time,' he murmured, 'flaming torches would have been provided.'

'I'll put in a complaint on TripAdvisor.' My voice sounded weak and shaky even to my own ears.

I brushed off the clinging dirt and looked around. Although there was soft, sandy earth on the floor, the walls were smooth, much like you'd find in any old basement. It wasn't so spooky down here. I shuddered. Nope. Not spooky at all.

'There are lots of hidden places like this,' Lukas said. 'If there are stories about somewhere being haunted, there's usually a concealed room or building nearby.'

'So ghosts don't exist, but secret passageways do?'

'Welcome to Supe City, D'Artagnan.' He winked.

Yeah, yeah. I peered down the corridor. Lukas's light only stretched so far. 'I take it Jim is down that way?'

'Indeed. It's not far.'

I swallowed. Just as well.

'Are you okay?' Lukas asked.

'Peachy.' I gritted my teeth. 'Let's get this over and done with as quickly as possible.'

We set off and I counted the steps in my head. Seven. Eight. Nine. There was a faint scraping sound. Was that a rat? I swallowed. Probably. Rats were okay; I could deal with rats. Ten. Eleven. Twelve.

I glanced at the walls on either side. There were suspicious dark blotches on various different spots. 'Is that blood on the walls?'

'Sometimes the fights continued beyond the actual fighting pit itself,' Lukas said,

Great. 'Remind me never to go for a city walk with you again.'

Lukas chuckled, the sound bouncing off the walls and creating an eerie effect. Not that we needed eerie sound effects, given the creepy atmosphere and shadowy dark corners.

'Who's there?' a male voice called. 'Who's out there?'

I stiffened. That was Jim. It had to be.

'I'm warning you! I'm a scary vampire! If you get too close, I'll suck your blood. There'll be nothing left of your body except a dried-out husk.'

Yep, that was definitely Night Stalker Jim.

Lukas raised his voice 'It's Lord Horvath. I brought DC Bellamy with me, like you asked.'

There were a few seconds of silence. Lukas and I kept moving quietly towards a heavy oak door that flickered into view as the light reached it.

'Is she mad at me?' Jim asked finally.

I cleared my throat. 'I'm not mad, Jim. Not at all.'

'You sound mad.' He sounded accusing. 'Your voice is shaking.'

'That's because I'm afraid of the dark.'

There was a rattle. The oak door opened and Jim's pale face, free now of blood, peered out. He didn't appear to be wearing any clothes beyond a grubby pair of Y-fronts, although there was a woollen blanket draped round his shoulders. It was an improvement on the last time we'd met. 'You're scared of the dark? Really?' he asked.

I nodded. 'Really.'

'I've got candles in here,' he said. 'You can come in, if you like.' He glared at Lukas. 'But not him. He's a vampire, like me. He'll try to attack me and kill me because I didn't stay in London like I was supposed to.'

'Is that what the Chief told you?'

Jim's eyes went wide. 'You know the Chief?' He looked beyond my shoulder. 'Is he here?'

'I'm afraid the Chief is gone, Jim.' I was deliberately vague. 'And the things he told you about supes aren't true. I promise you, they're not true at all. Lukas won't hurt you.'

'I don't believe you.'

'It's true.' I took a step towards him. 'Things have been hard for you recently, haven't they? It makes sense that you wouldn't know who to trust or who to believe.'

Jim's gaze shifted nervously from me to Lukas and back again. 'Yeah. That's right.' He started to scratch himself, starting on his upper arm and moving down across his chest and stomach. The wounds I'd spotted when he was on the plinth at Trafalgar Square were healing, but there were red marks up and down his body.

'You're having withdrawal symptoms, aren't you? You were

taking some kind of drug before, but now you don't have any left.'

'Nathan said he'd get me some more. He promised.' Again he looked beyond me. 'He'll be back soon.'

'That's good.' Brilliant, in fact. Despite what we'd found next to Belly, Nathan Fairfax remained high on my list of suspects. There was no real evidence against him, but there was more than enough reason to doubt his innocence. 'Before he returns, why don't we take you out of here and get a doctor to see to you? You look like you could do with some medical attention, Jim.'

He shied away. 'No! No doctors! They're all quacks! The Chief told me I couldn't trust doctors and I know he was right.'

It was a shame that Lance Emerson was dead. I'd have loved to get him in a room and find out why he'd persuaded a vulnerable man who obviously required medical care that doctors weren't to be trusted. 'Okay,' I soothed. 'Okay. Let's go into your room where there's more light. We can have a chat there. And don't worry about Lukas. He's been a vampire for a long time and I know he can help you.'

Jim started scratching himself again. 'I don't know. I don't know. I don't think it's a good idea.' He shivered. The thin blanket wasn't doing nearly enough to keep him warm.

Lukas untied his cloak and shrugged it off. 'I won't come in if you don't want me to, Jim,' he said quietly. 'But you're cold. Why don't you take this? It might help warm you up.'

Jim glared at him, then he shivered again and grunted assent. Lukas reached across and draped the cloak round him. As he did so, his fingers brushed against Jim's skin. 'You're safe,' he murmured. 'We won't hurt you. You can relax.'

The skin-to-skin contact and vampire trickery did what needed to be done. Jim exhaled and his shoulders sagged. 'Alright,' he said. Some of the tension left his face. 'Alright. You can both come in.'

I smiled softly, then Lukas and I followed him into the depths of the old fighting pit.

* * *

JIM HAD BEEN RIGHT: there was certainly more light. Everywhere I looked candle flames were dancing, illuminating the corners of the circular room which was far larger than I'd expected. I had to remind myself that Londoners were going about their business over our heads, completely oblivious to this bizarre underground cavern.

Where we were standing must have been the fighting floor. Surrounding it were rows of wooden benches that would have seated several hundred spectators. I toed the dirty floor. A lot of pain had been experienced here. Candlelight didn't make the place any less creepy.

I noted a canvas bag on the floor with more candles inside, empty burger wrappers and several bottles of water. I glanced at the two bed rolls; Nathan and Jim must have been sleeping here. No wonder they'd found it so easy to stay out of sight and avoid being caught. It wouldn't have been my choice of venue, but it certainly served a purpose.

'How long have you been here, Jim?' I asked gently.

He raised his shoulders in an awkward shrug. 'I don't know. What day is it today?'

'Friday.'

He counted off his fingers. 'Maybe a week?'

'Did Nathan bring you here?'

Jim nodded. 'He said it was safe. He told me not to leave.'

My mind flitted to Jim dancing on the plinth. 'But you did leave, didn't you? That's when I saw you at Trafalgar Square.'

His head dropped. 'Nathan was very angry with me.' He jerked up and stared at me. 'I hurt you. Are you alright? I didn't mean to hurt you.'

175

'I'm fine,' I soothed. 'I told you.' I stretched my arms out wide as if to prove the point. 'See? I'm perfectly fine.'

Lukas snorted quietly but I ignored him. 'Did you come to London with Nathan?'

'He's my friend. He brought me here. He said we could do sightseeing together.'

'Uh-huh. Where did you meet him?'

'In Cumbria.' Jim's eyes travelled up and down my body. 'You're really not hurt, are you?'

'No,' I said cheerfully, before steering the conversation back to where I needed it to be. 'Where in Cumbria?'

'At the Perfect Path, of course. Nathan's the lieutenant.'

I stiffened. 'Nathan is part of the Perfect Path?'

Jim nodded vigorously. 'Oh, yes. He helps people, just like the Chief does.'

'Are you part of the Perfect Path, too?'

Desolation crossed his face. 'I used to be,' he whispered. 'But then Nathan said I had to leave. I didn't want to leave! I'm not cured yet! I'm still a vampire!' He stared at my throat. 'I could drink your blood. I could drink it all now.' He licked his lips, an edge of madness flashing in his eyes. He lunged forward, his hands outstretched as he tried to grab me.

Lukas stepped swiftly between us. 'You don't want to drink her blood,' he said. 'It doesn't taste very nice.'

Jim dropped to his knees and covered his face with his hands. 'But I'm a vampire,' he said mournfully. 'I have to drink blood. I don't want to, but I have to.'

Lukas and I exchanged glances. 'Why did Nathan tell you to leave Perfect Path, Jim?' I asked.

His face took on a melancholy, confused cast. 'I don't know. He said he'd help me but that I couldn't stay. He said the Chief was dangerous.'

'Uh-huh. And when was the last time you saw the Chief?'

He mumbled something.

I knelt down. 'Jim?'

'Two weeks ago, in Cumbria. He held a meeting with us all. He said he had special plans and that things were going to be different. He promised he'd help more of us and prevent future infections.' His eyes suddenly shone. 'He said he'd save us all.'

Jim was obviously another true believer. 'What about Nathan? When did Nathan last see him?'

'I dunno.'

'Did he see him here in London?'

Jim's head jerked up. 'The Chief is here? Where?' He scrambled up and whipped round, as if expecting to see Lance Emerson suddenly emerge from the shadows. 'Can I see him? Where is he? I have to go and speak to him. I need his help. He's the only one who can save me. You have to understand. He's the only one!' Jim's voice was rising, hysteria punctuating every word.

I reached for his shoulder and squeezed it. 'It's okay, Jim,' I said. 'Don't worry.'

He sucked in several sharp breaths. I waited until he'd calmed somewhat and then met his eyes. 'I only have one more question, Jim. I need you to answer me truthfully.'

'I never lie.'

'I'm glad to hear that.' I smiled at him. 'Was Nathan here with you yesterday?'

He nodded vigorously. 'Yes.'

'Did he go out at all? Did he leave you on your own at any point?'

'No. We stayed here together. He only left this morning. Yesterday,' he said, 'we played I Spy.' He leaned in towards me and dropped his voice. 'I won.'

'Good for you.'

He beamed proudly. 'Can I have some of your blood now?'

I shook my head sadly. 'No, Jim. You can't.'

He started to shake. 'Please. Pleeeease!'

I squeezed his shoulder again. In all good conscience, I couldn't continue this any longer. Jim was in dire need of professional help, and my questions were only making him more agitated.

One thing was clear: he hadn't known that Emerson was in the city so he couldn't have been the one to kill him. But Nathan Fairfax certainly could have done it. Jim had provided Nathan with an alibi, but he was very confused and I couldn't take what he'd said at face value.

I still didn't understand what was going on here and what the werewolf's role had been with the Perfect Path Of Power and Redemption – but it certainly wasn't looking good.

CHAPTER TWENTY-ONE

WE WAITED UNTIL THE AMBULANCE HAD BUNDLED JIM INSIDE AND taken him away. He didn't refuse to go with the paramedics, but he did keep repeating over and over again that Nathan would be angry with him for not staying underground.

I had no idea how Jim had become involved with Nathan Fairfax, Lance Emerson or the Perfect Path, but there was no doubt in my mind that he was a victim. I sent a silent prayer after the flashing blue lights, hoping that he'd receive the care and attention he so desperately needed. Then I turned to Lukas.

'It's likely that Nathan Fairfax will come back here sometime soon,' I said grimly. 'We mustn't scare him off before that happens. If we can catch him by surprise, we can haul him in for questioning, find out what's going on and if he killed Lance Emerson. Jim said they stayed together yesterday in the pit, but it's not easy to keep track of time when you're underground. He might have fallen asleep or been confused. We need to get hold of Nathan and speak to him.' This time, I promised myself, I wouldn't let him break down any doors and run away.

'My vampires will wait for him in the pit. They'll deal with him when he shows up.'

'He's a werewolf. He's strong.'

'That's not a concern.'

'He can't be hurt,' I warned. 'We still don't know what his role is. Harming him isn't the answer.'

'He'll be fine, D'Artagnan. My vamps know what to do.'

I breathed out. Okay.

'What do you think?' Lukas asked. 'Do you believe that Nathan Fairfax killed Lance Emerson and the pixie?'

I shook my head. 'I've got no bloody clue,' I said. I was telling the truth. Nothing about this was neat and tidy; maybe it never would be.

I glanced at my watch. The speeches would be over by now. There was a break scheduled and then the first workshops would begin. In half an hour's time I was supposed to be in the Rose Room at the DeVane Hotel debating the best way to approach the government to change some of its more draconian supe laws. I sighed. So much for all that.

My phone rang and I drew it out. Laura. No doubt she was calling with information from the post-mortems. I held my breath and answered. 'Hey.'

'Hi, Emma. I thought you might pick up quickly.' Laura's tone was dry.

'Have you got something for me?' I asked.

'I've completed the post-mortem on Belly. Given the question marks over the manner of her death, it seemed wise to begin with her rather than Emerson.'

I nodded. That was good. 'And?' I asked.

'Cause of death was drowning. I've sent blood off to the lab, but it'll take them a while to confirm the level of alcohol in her system or whether any drugs are present. There's no indication of bruising or defensive wounds on her body. It's still early days, but so far it doesn't look like she was attacked and held under the water. Barry and Larry have confirmed that evidence at the scene matches those findings. If she was pushed under the water, she'd have thrashed about and tried to free herself but there was no spilled water around the jacuzzi. To be honest, Emma, there's nothing to suggest that she was murdered. It looks like a tragic accident – she had too much to drink, went for a dip and fell asleep.'

I passed a hand over my eyes. That poor young woman. But a tragic accident didn't explain how she'd ended up with the murder weapon and Lance Emerson's bloody clothes next to her. I picked at a hangnail and wondered if placing them with her had been opportunism on the part of Emerson's killer.

'Thank you,' I told Laura. 'I appreciate the fast turnaround.'

'You're welcome.' She sighed. 'What a mess. I'm going to take a break. I'll get to Emerson's post-mortem shortly.'

'Thanks, Laura.'

'You stay safe out there. Happy hunting.'

'Bye.' I hung up and looked at Lukas. 'You heard that?'

He took my hand. 'Yes. I'm sorry about the pixie. She deserved better.'

She definitely did. I smiled sadly. 'Come on, we need to return to the hotel,' I said. 'There are still plenty of people to talk to before Nathan Fairfax shows up.'

* * *

LUKAS WENT to the Rose Room to check on the start of the main summit discussions, while I went to the Supe Squad suite to check in with Liza and Fred. When I opened the door and saw that Moira Castleman was sitting by the window talking to Fred, I strode over and sat down beside them. Good: I had plenty more questions for her.

'Hi, Moira,' I said. 'Thanks for coming to talk to us again.'

She nodded stiffly. 'I heard you knocking on my door,' she said quietly. 'I'm sorry I didn't answer. I needed a bit more time.'

'I understand.' I looked her over. She was pale and wan, but she was composed and there was a determined tilt to her chin. She was refusing to let her grief overcome her. I respected that.

'Have you found him yet? Have you found the Chief's killer?' she asked.

'You're talking about Nathan Fairfax. We want to speak to him but we don't know for certain that he's responsible.'

Her face twisted into a snarl. 'He did it. I know he did.'

'We're following several leads and looking into a number of people. It's important not to jump to conclusions.'

She glared at me. 'You're protecting him because he's a werewolf, right? You're protecting the wolves instead of protecting humans. You don't see that there's a monster inside of you and inside of him. One day that monster will overcome you – it will overcome all of you.' She spoke with the fervour of a true convert. Her sentiments probably matched those of the protestors across the street.

'Supernatural doesn't mean monster, Moira.'

'Well, you would say that, wouldn't you? I looked you up and I know you're one of *them*. You're infected, like everyone else here. You should have told me that last night.'

It was none of her business what I was. 'You told us last night that you used to be a demon,' I countered. 'That you were one of *them*, too.'

She folded her arms across her chest. Damn it. I should have softened my tone because I needed Moira on my side. A combative interviewee wouldn't help me.

'I'm not a demon any more,' she said defiantly. 'The monster inside me has gone.' She touched her chest. 'It might come back one day, but it's not there now. I'm safe.' She met my eyes. 'You're not.'

Fred leaned forward. 'I'm human, one hundred percent. You can trust me.'

She stared at him then turned, closing herself off from me. 'In that case,' she said tightly, 'I'll talk to you.'

He smiled gently at her. I knew he'd get more out of her than I would so I pulled back slightly, indicating that Fred had the lead.

'We've been looking at the CCTV footage from around the hotel,' he told her. 'We wanted to track the Chief's movements to see who he spoke to.'

Moira lifted up her chin. 'Nathan killed him. There's no point in looking at anyone else.'

'We have to be sure. We have to look at everything.'

She sniffed. 'Okay.'

'You said you were going to give us a list of all the people the Chief approached.'

'If you have the CCTV, you don't need the list.'

I was beginning to wonder if she was being deliberately obstructive.

'It would still help us, Moira,' Fred said.

She stared at him for a moment then reached into her pocket and took out a folded piece of paper. 'They're all here. I don't know all their names but I wrote down as much detail as I could. Supe *and* human.' She gave me a narrow-eyed look. 'I'm trying to be helpful.'

'You're being very helpful,' Fred reassured her. 'You have no idea how much we appreciate this. Can you tell me how you decided who to speak to?'

'I don't understand.'

'On the footage we watched, it seemed like you and the Chief were deliberately selecting people to approach.'

'Yeah.' She hesitated. 'So?'

'What kind of people were you looking for?'

'They're not people, they're monsters.' This time she didn't look at me. '*She's* a monster.'

This was a different Moira Castleman to last time. The shock and grief she'd felt earlier had coalesced into bitter rage that was directed wholly at supes. She was hurting and looking for someone to blame, and we were a convenient target. Supes were always a convenient target. I resisted the urge to speak because I knew it wouldn't help. Not right now.

'How did you decide who to approach, Moira?' Fred repeated.

Her tone was flat when she responded. 'Some refuse to see the truth but some are more willing to listen. It's just the way it is. We were looking for the monsters who were prepared to listen.'

'How could you tell who'd listen?'

'The Chief could tell.'

'If they listened, Moira, and if they accepted the Chief's help in getting rid of their … monsters, what would have happened next?'

Her eyes flicked away from Fred. 'They'd have come up to Picklecombe in Cumbria. That's where we live – that's where the Perfect Path is. They'd have come with us and the Chief would have helped them. Their monsters would have been forced to leave and they'd have been saved.'

Hallelujah, I thought sarcastically.

'We've never heard of demons,' Fred said gently. 'And from other reports we've received, some of the people the Chief was trying to help were never supes in the first place.'

'That's ridiculous!' Moira said firmly. 'Just because *you've* never heard of a demon doesn't mean they don't exist. I know what was inside me, and so did everyone else that the Chief helped.'

Fred nodded. 'Did the Chief ask the people he helped for money?'

Moira sat straighter and looked at him as if he were stupid. 'Of course he did!' she snapped. 'He couldn't live off air. None of us can! He only asked for what was reasonable, though.'

'Did you give him money, Moira?'

'I don't have any money. I paid what I owed in other ways.'

'Such as?'

She waved her hands around in frustration. 'I don't under-stand why you're asking all these questions. He's dead, he's the victim, and you're treating him like he was some kind of criminal!'

'The more we know about the Chief, the better chance we have of not only catching the person who killed him but also finding the evidence to convict them,' Fred told her. 'It's important that we have the full picture.'

'I don't like it.'

'I know, and I'm sorry I have to ask these questions. I wish I didn't. It must be terribly difficult for you. I only want to find who did this to him and why.'

Fred was being clever by only referring to himself rather than to both of us. From the way Moira was looking at him, she trusted him. DS Grace and I should get him to conduct all our interviews with humans; he certainly had the knack for getting them to speak.

'Fine,' she muttered. 'I cooked, I cleaned, I took notes for him. I came to this summit with him so that I could be his assistant. I did lots of things.'

Yeah, yeah. I bet there was a lot more so-called *help* than merely cooking, cleaning, and note-taking. After all, they had been sharing a bed. My stomach turned. I was beginning to think that the Chief could have told Moira that the sky was bright green and she'd have believed him.

I coughed delicately. Moira rolled her eyes, but she did turn to look at me. 'What?'

'I've been speaking to someone else who was part of the Perfect Path.'

Her expression immediately turned wary.

'He's called Jim. Do you know who I'm talking about?'

Something flashed in Moira's eyes. It was too fleeting for me to identify but it made me suspicious. 'You must mean James Kilworth. He's crazy,' she said dismissively. 'You can't listen to anything he says.'

'He's convinced he's a vampire.'

She stared at me.

'He's not a vampire, Moira.'

Her eyes widened. 'Then it worked!' A wide smile spread across her face. 'See? I told you that the Chief was a miracle worker! He cured Jim! That's wonderful news.' She certainly seemed to believe what she was saying.

'Moira, Jim is very ill,' I said.

'I'm so very sorry to hear that. I hope he recovers soon.' She got to her feet. 'Anyway, I have to go to my room. I need to pack.'

'Pack?'

'I'm leaving,' she declared. 'I'm going home to Cumbria.'

Fred gave her a long, sympathetic look. 'I'm afraid we need to ask you to stay here for a while longer. There are a few more questions we need to ask, and we don't know what will come up over the next day or so.'

'You have my phone number,' Moira said. 'You can call me. I need to go home. I can't stay here any longer, not after what's happened.'

I could understand that she wanted to return home and be amongst people who loved her and could support her, but I had the distinct sense there was more to it than needing comfort. 'Until we apprehend the Chief's killer,' I said carefully, 'you could be in real danger.'

'That's ridiculous.' She shook her head. 'I'll be fine. I can look after myself.'

'I'm sure you can,' Fred told her. 'But whoever killed Mr Emerson is strong and powerful, not to mention entirely without conscience. We need you to stay here, Moira.'

'Nathan wouldn't hurt me.' Her words came out in a rush and she avoided looking Fred in the eye.

'Nathan might not be the culprit.'

'He is!'

'All the same,' Fred soothed, 'we have to be careful. I only want to make sure you're safe.'

Moira twitched and I wondered if she was about to rush for the door and sprint away from us, but then she seemed to relax. 'Okay, I'll stay,' she said. 'But I want to go home as soon as I can.'

'Of course you do.' He smiled at her. 'Thank you for helping us look after you.'

'No problem,' she mumbled. 'Can I go now?' She was already moving towards the door.

'Sure. I'll call you later if I have any more questions.'

Moira walked out and Fred turned to me. 'So what do you make of that, boss?'

'Interesting,' I murmured.

Very interesting.

CHAPTER TWENTY-TWO

I CALLED LUKAS AND ASKED HIM TO PUT A VAMP OR TWO IN PLACE to keep an eye on Moira. 'She might try to leave,' I said. 'If she does, ask them to delay her and get hold of me or Fred immediately.'

'Not a problem.'

'Has there been any sign of Nathan Fairfax at Cockpit Steps yet?'

'No.' He sounded grim. 'There's no sign of him anywhere.'

Shit. I needed some good news in my life. I changed the subject in the vain hope that I'd hear something cheerful. 'How are the Rose Room discussions going?'

'Well,' he replied, with considerable frustration in his voice, 'everyone knows what happened to Emerson and it's been the main topic of conversation so far.'

I clenched my fists. We'd fought over and analysed a detailed agenda for weeks. No matter what I did, the summit was going to be derailed by Emerson's murder. 'What about Belly? Has there been much mention of her so far?'

'There was a minute's silence in her memory. But...' he trailed off.

'But what?'

'It doesn't matter.'

'Tell me, Lukas.'

'No, not right now. It's not important and you've got other things to do.'

My eyes narrowed. 'Lukas,' I said. 'Tell me what it is. What's being said?'

'The coffee break is over and the discussions are starting again. I'd better go. Take care, D'Artagnan.'

He hung up and I ground my teeth in frustration. It was starting to feel like I didn't have a fraction of control over anything. I picked up the piece of folded paper that Moira had given us and looked through the descriptions of the supes she'd spoken to with the Chief. There didn't seem much reason to look at the humans she'd listed because everything indicated that we were searching for a supernatural. Unfortunately.

Moira had included names for some people and notes for others. She and Emerson probably hadn't got the names of everyone they spoke to before they were waved away. I thought about the French vamp who'd tried to stuff the leaflet down Emerson's throat. 'Waved away' was a polite way of putting it.

Vampire. Female. Mid-twenties. Brunette. Off the top of my head, I could think of two dozen vamps who fitted that description. We didn't have the manpower or the time to search and interview everyone on the list.

I pressed the base of my palms against my temples. I could feel the approach of a stellar stress headache. 'Did you get anywhere with the hotel staff, Fred?' I asked, without much hope.

'There are a couple I still have to track down, but there are no real suspects and all the keyholders have accounted for their keys. Nothing's been stolen or misplaced. No key is completely foolproof, but the hotel ones have been designed so that they can't be easily duplicated.' He pulled a face. 'Maybe the killer is an expert locksmith.'

Maybe. Or maybe Emerson's murder had been planned from the day he'd signed up to attend the summit. Maybe we'd never know.

'Go further back,' I said. 'Speak to Wilma Kennard and find out which staff members have lost their hotel keys and had to get them replaced during the last twelve months. Setting Belly up for Emerson's murder was opportunistic, but we know that the murder itself was planned – maybe it's been planned for a long time.'

'Okay, boss. I'll go and find her now.'

I watched him leave then glanced at Moira's list again. There had to a way to prioritise the names. 'Are you still looking through the CCTV, Liza?'

'For all the good it's doing me,' she muttered. 'I can't get a clear view of the corridors leading to either the swimming pool or the spa, so I've been trying to scan through the different exit and entrance points in the hotel. The security system is good and it's been ramped up for the summit. I've identified almost everyone who's been coming and going so far. There's no indication that anyone suspicious slipped through unnoticed immediately before or after the murder.'

She shrugged. 'I thought it made sense to focus on the hours after the murder because that footage is easier to narrow down. A small group of protestors tried to sneak in through one of the side doors around midnight, but they were stopped and sent packing before they'd gone five metres down the first hallway. I also found some vampires wandering out in the early hours of the morning. They looked suspicious to begin with, so I tracked them through the hotel.' She pulled a face. 'It turns out they were trying to find somewhere to have a sneaky cigarette without having to go out the front where the protestors could see them.'

I half-smiled. 'You're being very thorough, even if you've not managed to turn up anything.'

'Please. I'm always thorough. I even found a clip of Lord

Horvath talking to someone in the underground car park when he came in this morning. Nobody escapes my notice, not even your boyfriend.'

I laughed, then I thought about Tallulah and how Lukas couldn't open her door. A trickle of unease slid through my veins. 'Could you show me that clip?' I asked.

'Sure.' Liza keyed it up and pressed play. 'I can't tell who he's speaking to. She has her back turned to the camera.'

I leaned it to watch. It was definitely Lukas and he was still wearing his tuxedo, so this was before he'd changed his clothes and we'd gone out to speak to Jim.. He got out of his car and his head jerked up as if someone had called him. A black scowl crossed his face. A figure approached him, a well-dressed woman. I rolled my eyes. Oh.

'You know who she is?' Liza asked.

'Juliet Chambers-May,' I muttered.

'That journalist who wrote that article about you in this morning's paper?'

'The one and the same.' I glared at her on the screen. 'She's hanging around the damned car park like she's Woodward or Bernstein.'

'If she's like the journalists who broke Watergate, does that mean that Lord Horvath is Deep Throat?'

I watched Lukas gesticulate angrily towards Chambers-May before stalking off. 'As if. He was pissed off about the news article and that's probably what he was talking to her about.'

He hadn't mentioned that he'd spoken to her – but there again, I didn't tell him everything. I didn't have to. I reminded myself that he'd earned my trust and gazed at the screen again. It was nothing, only a brief conversation.

'Thanks for that,' I said to Liza. I passed her Moira's list. 'Can you identify some of these people and check whether any of them have records for violence? I'm not expecting miracles, but anything you discover might help.'

'I'll do my best,' she said. 'But…' She grimaced and met my eyes.

I knew what her expression meant. Right now, everything felt like we were clutching at straws.

* * *

I HEARD Barry and Larry before I saw them. 'You have to understand, Baz,' Larry was saying. 'A pretty vamp lady won't look twice at you.'

'What are you saying? I'm a fine figure of a man.'

There was a loud snort. 'You keep telling yourself that, mate.'

'I think I'd look good in a leather catsuit.' There was a louder snort.

I turned the corner and glanced into the massage room. 'Hey.'

The pair of them were on their hands and knees on the floor. They looked up. 'Detective Constable Bellamy!' Barry beamed. 'What do you think? Don't you agree that skin-tight leather would be a good look for me?'

'Barry,' I said, 'you can wear whatever you like.'

Larry looked sceptical. 'You're too easily swayed.' He nudged his partner. 'Suede. Get it?'

Barry laughed heartily. I didn't smile, though I should have because he gave me a concerned look. 'Are you okay, detective?'

'It's been a long night,' I said. 'And an even longer day.' And it was far from over. I managed an awkward smile. 'Have you found anything?'

'We've bagged and tagged a lot of things, but they'll all need further analysis.' Barry held up a sealed plastic bag. 'We did find a few strands of hair and some odd fingerprints. There's no saying who they belong to, but if they are our killer's, they might help confirm an identity.'

'Good work. Is there much more to do?'

'There are a lot of areas we've not covered. We've only

focused on this room, the laundry trolley and around the jacuzzi.' He straightened up, groaning slightly. 'I think the best thing we can do for now is to seal up these rooms to avoid any further contamination and take what we've found back to base to examine in more detail.'

'You've been working for hours. You should give yourselves a break.'

Barry smiled. 'Don't worry about us.'

I folded my arms and looked at him sternly.

'We'll be sure to rest up for a bit,' Larry said. 'How's the summit going?'

'Alright, I think.' Though not great.

'Things will work out,' he continued. 'You've got this. Everyone knows that. Supes don't strike me as the kind of people to roll over and give up.'

'You know that everything indicates it was a supe who killed Lance Emerson?'

'You'll find them.'

I had to; there was no other choice. 'You'll let me know if the lab work reveals anything?'

'We have you on speed dial,' Barry reassured me.

I thanked them and left them to it. I checked my watch as I walked towards the hotel lobby; twenty whole hours had passed since Lance Emerson's body had been discovered, and so far I had many more questions than answers.

I side-stepped a group of gremlins who looked as if they wanted to speak to me, and spotted Juliet Chambers-May. She'd cornered Ochre and appeared to be firing questions at her. Ochre's expression was tight and my stomach dropped. I squared my shoulders and prepared to march over. I didn't get very far.

'Out of the way!' Several of the gremlins were shoved aside. 'Oi! Detective!' Buffy yelled.

I frowned. 'What's up?' Patches of fur had appeared on her cheekbones and her ears were more wolf than human. There was also a wild light to her eyes. I had the sudden horrific thought that another corpse had been discovered.

'I can smell him,' she said. 'He's here. He's really here.'

For a moment I couldn't work who she was talking about, then abruptly I realised. 'Nathan Fairfax? You can smell Nathan Fairfax?' My spine stiffened. 'Where?'

'I went to my room to grab a jumper. The lifts were busy when I came out so I took the stairs. His scent is in the stairwell. It smells fresh.'

There was only one reason that I could think for him to be here. 'Moira Castleman.' Oh God. There wasn't any time to waste. 'The tenth floor.' I ran for the lifts.

'I'll take the stairs!' Buffy called, spinning away.

I elbowed a nervous-looking druid out of the way and dived into the first empty lift. 'Sorry! Take the next one!' I hollered. I pressed the button for the tenth floor half a dozen times, as if my urgency could somehow transfer to the electronics system. 'Come on,' I muttered.

I shook my head as the lift doors finally closed and it started to rise. What the hell was Nathan thinking? He was taking a hell of a risk coming here, even if he hadn't murdered Emerson.

I lifted my head and watched the LED numbers as the lift moved higher and higher through the hotel. With any luck, it wouldn't stop on any other floor. I unstrapped my crossbow and checked it. Relief cascaded through me when the number ten appeared, but it vanished as soon as the lift doors slid open.

Lukas had posted two vampires on the tenth floor to guard Moira Castleman. Both of them were lying prone on the floor only a few metres away from the lift's entrance. I dashed out, praying to whoever might be listening that they weren't dead. I knew Lukas: if Nathan Fairfax had killed two of his own, it wouldn't matter what I said. He wouldn't leave this hotel alive.

I crouched down. The nearest vamp, a blonde woman who was around forty in appearance but could have been far older, moaned slightly. There was blood on her forehead and a purple mark already appearing to indicate what would be a nasty bruise. She was probably concussed – but she was definitely alive. The second vampire, sprawled next to her, was out for the count.

A door thudded open and there was the sound of running footsteps. A moment later Buffy appeared. Despite having sprinted all the way up from the ground floor, she was barely out of breath.

I waved at the vampires. 'Take care of them.'

'Where is he?' she growled. 'Where is the bastard?'

'Deal with the damned vampires,' I repeated. 'I'll sort out Nathan Fairfax.'

She glared at me, about to refuse, then she muttered something and knelt down beside me. I straightened up and started towards Moira Castleman's room. *I hope you've not hurt her, Nathan*, I thought. *For all our sakes.*

Moira's door was closed. I put my ear against it and tried to listen to what was going on inside, then I knocked sharply. 'Moira!' I yelled. 'Moira! It's DC Bellamy!'

There was a sudden muffled shriek. Shit.

I didn't waste any more time. I shoved my shoulder against the door with all my strength. The door frame splintered but didn't give way. I tried again. If Nathan Fairfax could break down a Supe Squad door, I could break down a DeVane Hotel door. All I needed was a little faith.

There was a louder crack as the wood started to break. I heard Nathan's voice. 'Where is it, you bitch? Where have you hidden it?'

'I ... I ... I...' Moira stammered. 'It's in the safe. It's all in the safe.'

'What's the combination?'

I licked my lips and eyed the door. Third time lucky. I heaved in a breath and attacked the door again. It finally yielded and burst open with an ear-piercing crash. Praise be.

Moira Castleman was standing against the far wall, her spine pressed against it and terror etched on her face. She was holding her hands in front of her as if to guard against Nathan Fairfax even though the werewolf wasn't anywhere near her.

He cast a look in my direction before leaping out of the open window, the small hotel safe hugged tightly in his arms. Bloody hell. He was so quick I didn't even have time to raise the crossbow.

I lunged forward to grab him. I grasped at the material of his shirt but he pulled away, then fell twenty feet onto a narrow parapet that jutted out along the side of hotel. I leaned out and watched as he flung the safe at the window nearest to him. There was the sound of shattering glass as it broke into a thousand pieces. A moment later Nathan Fairfax followed the safe inside the room and disappeared.

I cursed. The smart thing would be to take the stairs but I'd lose too much time – and I'm not always known for being smart. I pointed at Moira. 'Stay here,' I snarled. And then I jumped out after Nathan Fairfax, my grip tight around the crossbow's shaft.

The fall was worse than I expected. Air rushed past me and my stomach seemed to leap into my chest. For a horrifying moment I thought I'd misjudged my descent and would miss the narrow stone parapet. I was going to end up flattened on the hard ground below with my intestines splattered in a grim Jackson Pollock-like image. For all that I had considerable experience of death, it could still scare me.

Then my feet smacked onto something solid and, with flailing arms, I managed to stay upright. I gulped air, glad that I was still alive, and dived through the broken window. Nathan wasn't getting away. I wouldn't let him.

Splinters of glass raked my skin and tore my clothes. My sleeve caught on one shard and I had to tug to free it, ripping the material, but within seconds I was up and running again. Nathan had already left the room and he had a good few seconds' lead, but I wasn't worried I'd lose him. The safe he seemed so determined to carry would slow him down and prevent him from transforming into a wolf. I didn't know what was inside that safe, but it would be his downfall.

I hurtled out of the room into the corridor. It was identical to the one above in layout. All the doors were closed and there was no indication that Nathan had tried to break them down so he'd either gone for the stairs or slid into a waiting lift. I headed right, plumping for the more obvious option. When I saw the smear of blood on the banister by the first step, I knew I'd made the right choice.

I moved like the wind and my feet barely touched the steps. There was more blood, some on the floor and some on the banisters. The broken glass had snagged me – but it had snagged Nathan, too.

I was certain that I was closing in on my quarry. Within less than a minute, I'd reached the ground floor and the heavy fire-exit door that led into the lobby. A single bloody handprint marred its glossy white finish. I reached for it, then paused. No; hang on a minute.

Nathan knew I was after him. He also knew that the DeVane Hotel was swarming with supes of all types and he wouldn't make it out of the lobby. The handprint was a red herring – it had to be. He wasn't trying to escape that way, he must be heading for the underground car park. If he could break into a vehicle, he'd have a better chance of escaping.

I spun round, hoping I was right, and continued down the next flight of stairs. Come out, come out wherever you are…

At first glance, the car park seemed to be empty. The cars, including Tallulah, were silent and still and there wasn't a soul to be seen. My tongue darted out, wetting my dry lips. He must have come this way. It was what I'd have done if I'd been trying to escape.

I slowed my steps and started to take my time, my head swivelling from side to side as I tried to pierce the shadows. I couldn't see any more drops of blood and I couldn't hear any breathing or spot any flickering shapes. With slow, deliberate movements, I checked once again that the crossbow was loaded before thumbing off the safety. I wasn't planning to kill Nathan Fairfax but I wasn't beyond maiming him if that's what it would take to stop him.

I took a step and then another. Where was he? I was starting to think that I'd made a mistake and he'd made a dash through the hotel lobby after all. That was when the engine started.

There was a squeal of tyres and I spun round in time to see a large black car bearing down on me. I didn't stop to think before I raised the crossbow, closed one eye and fired. A heartbeat later, I threw myself to the right and rolled away from the heavy wheels.

The car seemed to speed up and its wheels spun as it headed for the ramp leading out of the car park, but my crossbow bolt had done its job. I hadn't aimed for the driver; my bolt had pierced the front tyre. Within seconds, Nathan Fairfax was driving on grinding metal. He tried to keep going, despite the sparks which were flying from the underside of the car, but he couldn't maintain control. Instead of speeding up the ramp and away, he twisted the wheel and smacked straight into a cement pillar.

I smiled as there was a faint whoosh when the airbag exploded, then I picked myself up, walked over and opened the driver door.

'Nathan Fairfax,' I said, whilst he fumbled beneath the airbag in a pointless attempt to free himself. 'You're under arrest.'

CHAPTER TWENTY-THREE

'You're bleeding.' Liza's tone was more one of observation than concern.

'I'm fine.'

'You're dripping onto the pretty carpet.'

I gave her a long look. 'The hotel can bill Supe Squad later.'

She harrumphed. 'I'm quite certain they will. You do realise that we have a strict budget? It's supposed to be for fighting crime and dastardly deeds, not cleaning up your messes.'

I shrugged; at that point, I wasn't sure what the difference was. Anyway, I had more pressing matters to think about than a few bloodstains and a broken window. 'Did you get the over-ride code for the safe from Wilma Kennard?'

'Three-six-four-five B.'

I knelt down and keyed it in. Nathan Fairfax didn't look up. He was handcuffed and sitting in a chair with Buffy and Fred standing over him,.

There was a long beep and the safe door popped open. I peered inside and frowned.

'Is it a smoking gun?' Liza asked.

Nathan jerked but kept his head down.

'Not exactly,' I murmured. With gloved hands, I reached in and pulled out the only thing inside: a transparent baggy filled with little white pills. They looked innocuous enough but I doubted that they were.

'What are these for, Nathan?' I demanded.

He didn't say answer.

'Uppers?' I asked. 'Downers?'

His shoulders slumped still further.

'Are they for you?' I gazed at him. 'Or for Jim?'

Nathan's head finally snapped up and he stared at me. 'Yeah,' I said, keeping my tone friendly and conversational, as if we were just shooting the breeze, 'Jim's with us now. We found him at the old cockpit. If he needs these pills, tell us and we can pass them to the doctor.'

'You can't hold him. He's not done anything wrong.'

'Uh-huh.' I waggled the bag of pills. 'Does he need these?'

A muscle jerked in Nathan's cheek. 'He's addicted to them. I'm trying to wean him off but it's a slow process. If he goes cold turkey, it could be dangerous.'

'What are they?'

'They're not mine.'

I cooled my tone. 'I know that. You took them from Moira. I'm not asking whose they are, Nathan, I'm asking what they are.' I took the chair opposite him so that we were on the same level. 'If we don't find out what they are, we can't help Jim.'

Nathan looked away again. 'Scopolamine,' he said reluctantly. 'A version of it, anyway.'

'What's scopolamine?'

It was Liza who answered. 'In small quantities, it's a motion-sickness drug.'

'And in large quantities?'

'It's also known as Devil's Breath. Taking it can lead to hallucinations, a lack of free will and amnesia.'

'You're a fount of knowledge, Liza.'

She held up her phone. 'Not me, Google.'

Oh. Fair enough. 'It sounds pretty dangerous,' I said. 'Hallucinations? Could someone hallucinate that they're a vampire, maybe? If it causes amnesia, could it also alter someone's memory?' I leaned forward. 'Because these pills pretty much destroy any shred of credibility Jim had as an alibi for you.'

The tiniest crease appeared on Nathan's forehead.

I pressed on. 'Without an alibi, you're the number one suspect for Lance Emerson's murder.'

Nathan's jaw dropped and the colour drained from his face. 'Wh – what?'

I said nothing more but my stomach was sinking. Maybe he *was* completely innocent.

'The Chief's dead?' His eyes darted from side to side. 'When? How?'

News of Emerson's death still hadn't been released. Did he really not know about it? 'Twenty-four hours ago,' I said. 'Give or take. His throat was slit.'

Nathan appeared completely stunned. I could see that he was shocked – but he was certainly not devastated. It was that which made me think he'd played no part in Emerson's death. If he was acting shocked, surely he'd also manage to squeeze out a tear or two. However, I wasn't going to let up on him yet. I needed to know more. 'Where were you yesterday, Nathan?'

'You know where I was!' His confusion and panic were growing. 'I was with Jim, underneath the Cockpit Steps. Oh my God, I didn't know the Chief was dead. How did it happen?' He shook his head. 'This is unbelievable. Who killed him? It couldn't have been Moira. Who did it?'

'I was rather hoping you could tell me.'

He recoiled as realisation dawned. 'You think I murdered him? Is that why I'm here?'

Technically, I'd arrested him for assault on Moira Castleman and burglary. I wouldn't jump the gun on a murder charge, especially when Nathan Fairfax was a werewolf, but I wouldn't give him a free pass either. *'Did* you murder him?'

I knew he would deny it before the word left his mouth. 'No!'

'I can understand why you killed him, Nathan. He wasn't a very nice man. But why did you try and put the blame on the pixie? Was she already dead when you went to murder the Chief? Or did you kill her too, and make it look like an accident?'

'P-p-pixie?' he stammered. 'What pixie?'

'Her name was Belly. She'd had a hard time recently. She came to the summit to prove to everyone that she was stronger than she looked, and now she's as dead as Lance Emerson. So why, Nathan? Why do such a thing to her?'

'I didn't! I didn't do any of this!'

I gazed at him. 'You came to me, remember? You wanted to warn me about Lance Emerson, and now he's dead. I think that you'd better start from the beginning.'

* * *

I LEFT the handcuffs on him; I didn't put it past him to try to break the window and throw himself out. I did give him a cup of coffee, though, which he cradled awkwardly between his hands.

'I've known Emerson for years,' Nathan said. 'I met him not long after I became omega. He knew what I was straight away, and he was fascinated by it. At first I thought he wanted to be turned into a werewolf. It was only when I got to know him better that I realised he had different plans.'

'What was his opinion of werewolves?' I asked. 'Did he think you were a monster because of your wolf?'

Nathan laughed coldly. 'You've been reading the propaganda. No, he didn't think like that. The Chief's motives weren't what they appeared to be on paper.'

He took a slurp of his coffee and sighed. 'You have to understand, detective, that I was a different person back then. I was hurting, and I was angry at the werewolf clans. I'd lost the only family I'd ever known. The Chief took an interest in me – he made me feel special again.' Guilt shrouded his face. 'I want to tell you that the Perfect Path was all his idea but it wasn't. It was mine.'

Bastard. I kept my expression as neutral as possible. 'Go on.'

'It started with a woman, Sarah. I met her in a pub and I liked her.' He sighed. 'A lot. I think she liked me – I *know* she liked me. We had a few dates and we slept together. It was ... good.' He looked away. 'Until the full moon.'

Ah. 'She didn't know you were a wolf.'

Nathan shook his head. 'No. I thought maybe I could control it despite the moon. The first night wasn't too bad – I was a bit shaky but I was okay. But the second night was too much. I couldn't help myself and I changed in front of her. I didn't attack her or anything, but she screamed and I ran away into the woods. Afterwards, when it was over, she made it clear that she was disgusted by what I was. She didn't want anything to do with me.'

'She would have been scared,' Liza said tightly.

Nathan bared his teeth. 'She hated me. It was written all over her face. She spat on me like I was some kind of ... some kind of ... some kind of...'

'Monster?' Fred supplied helpfully.

Nathan sighed and nodded. 'So the Chief and I came up with a plan. I wanted Sarah to feel what I felt when she looked at me like that. The Chief went to her and told her that she would become a werewolf because we'd had sex.'

Jesus. I stared at Nathan. 'She believed him?'

'Oh yeah.' He sniffed. 'He told her that she had a chance to escape her fate before her first full moon. If she paid him five thousand pounds, he'd perform a spell and save her. She gave him the money and he spouted some gibberish, danced around a bit, killed a rat and sprayed her with its blood. I hid in some bushes and howled when it was all over. Then the Chief and I took her money and went on a bender for five days. When we sobered up, we realised we were onto something.'

'Scamming humans into thinking they were supes then taking money from them to cure them, you mean?'

'Yeah.' He met my eyes defiantly. 'I'm not proud of it, alright?'

'So why did you do it?' Fred growled.

'I guess I thought they deserved it.' Nathan's head dropped. 'To be that afraid of becoming a supe? To believe that someone like me is a monster? Just for a little while, I could get those people to see what it was like to feel like me. I was stopping them from hating supes.'

I doubted that very much; his scam probably only made those people hate supes even more.

'Over the years we refined what we did, ' he continued. 'We had a whole act going. I'd prove to potential targets that I was a werewolf, then the Chief would supposedly cure me. We found that the longer we drew things out, the more money we made. A couple of times we snagged some proper rich idiots – we took months with them.'

'Couldn't you have got a job like a normal person?' Fred asked in disgust.

'I'm a wolf,' Nathan shot back. 'I'll never be normal.'

That was hardly an excuse. 'How many people?' Fred asked. 'How many people did you scam over the years?'

'A hundred.' He pursed his lips. 'Maybe more.'

Unbelievable. I folded my arms and did my best to keep my expression neutral but it didn't work. Behind me, I heard Liza snort in disgust.

'You all think I'm a terrible person,' Nathan murmured. 'But it's not my fault those people were so afraid of supes that they'd believe any line we threw at them. Five minutes of research and they'd have known we were feeding them bullshit. That's on them, not me.'

I sensed he was trying to persuade himself, not us, that he

wasn't a bad person. 'So what changed?' I asked. 'Something happened and caused you to walk away from the Chief and the Perfect Path. What was it?'

Nathan drained his cup of coffee and searched for somewhere to put it down. In the end, I took it from him and set it onto the floor by my feet while he gathered his thoughts.

'You have to understand, detective, that at first it felt like we were doing a good thing. You might not see it that way, but the people we targeted were wholeheartedly anti-supe. They'd have lined us all up against a wall and put bullets into our brains if they could have.' He grimaced. 'Despite the protestors outside this hotel, there aren't actually that many people who feel such hatred towards us. Most humans don't give supes a second thought. They don't like us but we don't cross their paths so they don't really care. In some ways,' he said reflectively, 'apathy is worse than hatred.' He shook himself. 'But those sorts of people aren't bad, just ignorant. They have no reason to care about supes so they don't.'

'The Chief started to target people like that?'

He nodded. 'I didn't like it, but I didn't do anything about it. It was easier to go with the flow.'

And to keep getting the money. 'And then?' I questioned.

'It got harder. People became more wary. There was one guy, a businessman, who we met in Carlisle. He realised what we were doing and threatened to expose us. He was going to report us to the police, so the Chief got hold of the scopolamine and spiked his drink. He was easy to manipulate after that so we started using the scopolamine on everyone.'

Nathan twitched and tried to scratch his cheek. The cuffs made it awkward and he raised them with a question in his eyes. I shook my head. No, I wouldn't release him. No chance.

His shoulders drooped. 'Not everyone responded well to the drugs,' he whispered. 'A couple of people ended up in hospital. And you've seen Jim.' His voice was barely audible, 'You've seen what the scopolamine is doing to him.' He shuddered. 'But it didn't matter. The Chief wouldn't stop. He said I was weak for caring about someone like Jim. He said Jim was a liability and we should get rid of him.'

I raised an eyebrow. 'Get rid of him?'

'I think he wanted me to kill Jim,' Nathan said,

'But he didn't actually use those words?'

'He said we could use him as a sacrifice.'

My eyes narrowed. 'What do you mean?'

Nathan seemed to shrink into himself. With a sense of dread, I realised that we were about to hear the worst of what the Perfect Path had done. I steeled myself and remained perfectly still.

'There's not much blood in a rat,' Nathan said. 'It worked a few times, but it's not that impressive. We started to use larger animals. We were in the countryside, so sheep and goats were easy to get hold of. We made a stone altar and the Chief got hold of a special knife and we made a whole show of it.' He jerked his cuffed hands up in a slicing motion, as if to demonstrate. 'But after a while those animals weren't enough. He always wanted to go bigger and bolder.'

Suddenly I felt nauseous. I knew exactly what Nathan was going to say. I wanted to hear him say it aloud, however; I wanted to hear him admit it.

'There are stray supes hiding all over this country. They don't want to put up with laws that make them stay in London. They're easy enough to find, if you look hard enough.' Nathan swallowed. 'The Chief – the Chief said that he could triple his money overnight if we raised the stakes and sacrificed a supe instead of an animal. He called it "a supe for a supe" – kill a monster to destroy a monster.'

Nathan gazed at me with wide, doleful eyes. 'I had to draw the line somewhere and I said no, I wouldn't help him do it. I knew he wouldn't be able to find any stray supes without my help, and

I told him so. He said he'd start with Jim, even though Jim's human. It was too much – I couldn't agree to that.' He drew in a shuddering breath. 'So I took Jim and I ran.'

'When was this?' Fred asked. 'When did you run?'

'About six weeks ago. We hid out in Manchester for a while but by then I already knew the summit was coming up and the Chief planned to attend. He wanted to find more humans to scam and more supes to sacrifice. To *kill*.' He didn't blink. 'I thought that if I told you what was happening, you could stop him. You're a supe like me so I knew you'd be more sympathetic than other police officers. I knew you'd take me seriously.'

He looked at me earnestly, his expression seeming to suggest that he was the hero in this narrative. As if.

'You didn't tell me any of this when you came to find me, Nathan.'

'I was going to. I really was.'

'Why didn't you? Why did you run away from Supe Squad?'

'I made a mistake.' He looked down at the floor. 'I tried to help Moira, to get her away from the Chief. I told her that I was planning to tell you everything but I'd leave her name out of it if she could bring me more scopolamine. I've been trying to wean Jim off it but it's harder than I thought. I was rationing the pills and he was getting better, but then he found my stash and took the lot. It made him crazy, but I still needed to get some more.'

That must have been the night I met Jim when he was dancing on top on the plinth with a bucket of blood.

Nathan read my expression. 'I've tried to tell him he's not a vampire but he won't believe me. He demanded blood so I got some from a butcher – I thought the blood might make him realise he's human and not vamp. It didn't – it made him knock me out and run away. It took days to calm him down so I could leave to find you.'

I stared at him. For whatever reason, Nathan had decided that Jim was his salvation: if he could save Jim, he could save himself.

Unfortunately for Nathan, Jim was too far gone. I changed the subject. 'Let's go back to Moira.'

Nathan's expression tightened. 'I thought I could trust her, that she understood the Chief was dangerous. I didn't realise she was sleeping with him. She'd swallowed all his lies and she betrayed me. I called her and told her I was about to speak to you, but I'd give her an hour to get away from the Chief first if she brought me the scopolamine. She agreed.'

Patches of fur appeared on Nathan's cheeks and his finger-nails turned into angry, curving claws. 'She lied. Instead of coming to me with the drugs, she called the clans and told them where I was. She must have been hiding somewhere close by and watching what happened because she told the Chief when you arrested me. He sent me a text message saying he'd kill Moira if I breathed a word to you, then he'd find Jim and kill him too. He was going to blame me for everything. You can check my phone, it's all on there. I didn't have a choice – I had to run from you to protect Jim and Moira.' He shook his head. 'There was no choice,' he repeated. 'No choice at all.'

There was always a choice.

Nathan seemed to read my expression. 'I scammed people, detective. I did that and I admit it, but I've never ever killed anyone or threatened to kill anyone.' He glanced at Fred and Liza and then met my eyes. 'If I'd murdered the Chief, if I'd known that he was dead, I'd never have come to this hotel. I'm not sorry he's dead, but it wasn't me who killed him.'

CHAPTER TWENTY-FOUR

IN THE END, I CALLED DS GRACE TO COME SO I COULD PASS OVER the custody of Nathan Fairfax to him. Nathan couldn't go to Supe Squad – we already knew it wasn't secure enough to hold him – and there was a pressing need to get hold of more details about the victims of the Perfect Path. They all had to be contacted.

'We'll need to interview Moira Castleman again. She's involved in this, although I'm still not clear whether she's anything more than a victim.' I sighed heavily. 'There's a good chance that she knew Emerson was planning to sacrifice supes as part of his scam. It would explain why she was so terrified of us when we first spoke to her.'

'I'll have Nathan and Castleman taken to Scotland Yard. We can get all the missing information out of them there.' Grace glanced at me. 'You know that Nathan Fairfax will probably end up being passed over to the clans. He's still a supe so he'll be subject to supe justice.'

He deserved nothing less. 'It is what it is,' I said softly.

'What about Lance Emerson? Are you sure neither of them killed him?'

'Nathan Fairfax isn't completely out of the woods, but I don't believe he's responsible,' I replied. 'And there's nothing to suggest it was Moira Castleman. Emerson's murderer is still out there – and there's Belly's death to deal with, too.' It felt as if a heavy weight was pressing down on my shoulders.

'You've done good work here, Emma,' Grace said. Maybe, but nothing had really changed. The only difference was that now we had less time to find the killer.

Grace looked at Liza, who was pointedly staring at her laptop screen and ignoring him. I cleared my throat. 'You know, when all this is over Liza will need a stiff drink somewhere nice.'

Her head jerked up and she gave me a death stare. Fred, who was lying on a sofa with his eyes closed, let out a muffled snort. 'You'll probably need a drink as well, DS Grace,' he said.

DS Grace frowned at us and opened his mouth to snap. I elbowed him sharply in the ribs. He turned to Liza, his cheeks suffused with red. 'Would you like to go for a drink?' he asked. 'With … with me?'

She crossed her arms. 'I suppose I could do that.' She paused. 'Maybe.'

I managed a smile; not everything had to be doom and gloom. 'Perhaps you could wear the green dress you had on at the cocktail party,' I suggested

If looks could kill, I would most definitely have been a dead woman.

'I'll call you,' Grace said. He was still blushing when he walked out of the door.

'I'll murder you,' Liza muttered. It wasn't clear whether she was referring to me, Grace or Fred. Quite possibly it was all three of us.

'Did you get anywhere with Moira's list?' I asked.

'There's not been much time,' Lisa still sounded annoyed at my attempt at matchmaking, 'but I've managed to get names for most of the people she and the Chief approached. I haven't been able to do much about prioritising them as suspects.'

'How many are there?' I wasn't sure I wanted to know.

'Thirty-two.'

I looked at my watch. There wasn't nearly enough time; we had only eleven hours until the investigation was out of our hands. Despite what we'd learned from Nathan, we still weren't close to finding Emerson's murderer.

'Boss,' Fred said softly. When I didn't answer, he spoke again. 'Emma.'

I looked at him. 'What?'

'You look exhausted. Go and lie down again for a bit.'

I shook my head. We were all tired. 'There's too much to do. We have to find the people on Moira's list and speak to them.'

'Hang on,' she said. 'I'll print out everything I've found.'

I nodded my thanks. Now that Nathan Fairfax had gone, the surge of adrenaline I'd experienced when I'd found him had also vanished. In its place was a foggy fugue. I had to focus.

I poured myself a lukewarm cup of coffee and downed it in one, but it didn't seem to help. I was halfway through pouring a second cup when there was a sharp knock at the door. I knew exactly who it was, but that didn't stop me from jerking in surprise and spilling half my drink onto the cream carpet.

'Blood *and* coffee,' Liza murmured from beside the printer. 'A cleaner's delight.'

I pulled a face while Fred walked over to open the door. Lukas appeared, his body filling the door frame. His black eyes immediately found me and within a second he was by my side. 'You look bloody awful,' he said roughly.

At that point, none of us were looking particularly good. 'Thanks,' I said sarcastically.

He touched my face with gentle fingers and I instantly regretted my tone. 'It's not criticism,' Lukas told me. 'It's concern.'

'I know. I'm sorry.' I passed a hand over my face. 'I'm stressed and tired, and we're not getting anywhere.'

'The werewolf isn't the killer?'

'Nathan Fairfax? No. I don't think so. He's flat out denying it, and there's no shred of evidence that he was anywhere near the hotel when Emerson was killed.'

'You're sure?'

'He had the motive, but it doesn't add up. Besides, there's no sign of him on any CCTV footage and nobody saw him.'

'Everyone knows that you caught him here in the hotel. They think he's the one.'

'He's not,' I said flatly. Part of me wished that he were but, no matter what else Nathan Fairfax was guilty of, he wasn't guilty of this.

It didn't help that Lance Emerson had obviously been a bastard of gargantuan proportions. He might not have murdered anyone, but I didn't doubt that he'd been planning to. Despite that, we still had to find his killer even though I'd be more likely to shake their hand than slap them in handcuffs.

'He hurt my vampires.' Lukas's voice was laced with steel.

'I know. I'm sorry. Are they doing alright?'

'They'll live.' He paused and this time his words vibrated with rage. 'He hurt *you.*'

'He didn't,' I said. 'Not really.'

Lukas steered me to the nearest chair. 'You're covered in cuts.'

'I jumped through a window. It was already broken but some of the shards caught me.'

His jaw tightened. 'You're still bleeding in several places.'

'I'll be fine.'

'Stop playing the tough guy,' he muttered. 'Let me fix you.' He dipped his head, his tongue darting out to lick delicately at each small wound. My skin tingled where he touched me and I closed my eyes to submit to his ministrations. There were drawbacks to being a vampire's girlfriend but there were advantages, too.

'How are the summit meetings going?' I asked.

Lukas continued to tend to my cuts and didn't answer.

'Lukas?'

He sighed. 'Not great. It's difficult to focus on anything other than the deaths. There have been a lot of arguments and finger pointing. The trouble is that everyone knows Lance Emerson's death will divert attention from any proposals we come up with. Once news of a human's murder filters out beyond this hotel, nothing else will matter.'

I thought of the harm that Lance Emerson had already done – and the harm he'd been planning. Now he was causing as many problems with his death as he had with his life.

The suite door opened again and Liza muttered a curse. I frowned at the group of supes who marched into the room and pulled away from Lukas. 'You can't storm in here,' I snapped.

'Oh, I see,' sneered Lord McGuigan. He pointed at Lukas. 'You'll let *him* in but not the rest of us. The favouritism displayed by your department is beyond belief, detective.'

'He knocked,' I told him flatly. I stood up and looked at them. Their tension and unhappiness were palpable. Ochre was clenching and unclenching her fists. Albert Finnegan, who'd most likely been asleep for the last ten hours because it was daylight, would have only learned of recent events in the last hour. He looked fresher than the others, but still concerned. Phileas Carmichael was poised with his briefcase, as if ready to defend whoever was about to be accused of murder. The four werewolf alphas – even Lady Sullivan – appeared ready to throw up.

'Where is he?' Lady Fairfax asked. Her voice was quiet and less harsh than I expected.

'You mean Nathan? He's been taken to Scotland Yard.' I realised that she was scared. 'He'll be released into your custody soon but there are questions he needs to answer first.'

'Did he say why he murdered that man? Or the pixie?'

I wet my lips. 'He didn't.'

Lady Fairfax went very still. 'He's not responsible?'

I glanced at the other werewolves; there was no mistaking the relief etched on their faces. Suddenly I understood why: they were afraid of the repercussions they'd face if a werewolf had murdered a human,

'No,' I said. 'He has an alibi. It's shaky, but it'll stand up. There's also no evidence to suggest he was involved in either Belly's or Lance Emerson's deaths. He's far from innocent but he didn't do this.'

Ochre blanched and Phileas Carmichael took a step back so that he was next to her. Finnegan straightened up and all the werewolf alphas turned to look at her. My stomach tightened. I was missing something.

'She won't do it,' Lukas said.

My puzzlement increased.

'You should stay out of this.' Lady Sullivan didn't glance in his direction and her words were without rancour.

My hackles were up. 'What's going on?' I asked.

'You know exactly what's going on,' McGuigan told me.

'No, I don't,' I said through gritted teeth.

Lady Carr sniffed. 'I've always known that girl isn't very bright.'

Finnegan flashed her a warning glance. She shrugged and looked away.

I crossed my arms over my chest. 'Somebody needs to explain what's going on.'

For a long drawn-out moment, nobody said a word, then Ochre lifted her chin. 'I'll say it, shall I? You have a suspect and you have evidence to prove they're guilty.'

I flicked my eyes from her to the others and back again. 'No I don't,' I said slowly. I watched her face and realisation dawned. I turned to Lukas. 'This is what you wouldn't tell me before.'

His expression was blank but I knew him well enough to spot the rage he was trying to conceal. His fingers brushed against the back of my hand. I gave a barely perceptible nod as I recognised that his anger wasn't directed at me, and glared at the other supes. 'No,' I said. 'I will not listen to this.'

'You have to.'

I pointed at the door. 'You can all leave right now.' Nobody moved an inch. I exhaled angrily and glared at them. 'I will not do this.'

'DC Bellamy.' Lady Sullivan actually looked sympathetic. 'This way nobody else gets hurt. She was found next to his bloodied clothes after all. The fact that she was a pixie helps us.'

Ochre flinched.

Lady Sullivan continued. 'Pixies are the least threatening of us all.'

'She's already dead,' Lady Fairfax said. 'That will be an end to the matter. You can tell the world that a human was murdered and the murderer was caught.'

'Belly did not kill Lance Emerson,' I bit out,

'She might have,' Finnegan murmured.

'She didn't.'

'How do you know for sure?' he asked.

The missing notebook for one thing; the fact that the killer was right-handed for another, but I wasn't telling them that. 'I just know,' I growled. 'I am not pinning this murder on someone who is innocent.'

'Belly won't care. She's dead,' Lord McGuigan said.

Anger pulsated through me. I looked at Fred and Liza, who were standing stock-still. They wouldn't say anything, either privately or to an audience, but I knew what they were thinking. Lance Emerson was not a good man and his death was no loss to the world; whoever had killed him had done society a favour. But I still wouldn't do it; I wouldn't blame Belly because I wanted an easy life.

'It helps us,' Carmichael said quietly. 'It helps the summit and it helps supes. Do you think this kind of thing hasn't happened before? You don't need to search very hard through history to find sacrificial lambs who've been offered up to the humans for the greater good. If the pixie did this—'

I glared at him. 'She didn't.'

'If you can't blame Nathan, blaming Belly is our way out,' Lady Fairfax said. 'It solves our problems.'

'No.' I looked at Ochre. 'You don't want this.'

Her body was shaking but she held her emotions together. 'It wouldn't be my choice, but we don't always get what we want.'

I was finding it hard to contain my fury and disbelief. 'You realise this means that the real murderer will walk free?'

'We can find the killer in our own time and without the pressure of the watching world,' McGuigan said. 'They'll face justice in the end.'

Lady Sullivan snorted agreement. 'Have no doubt about that.'

'But this way solves the immediate problem of the humans. It allows us to manage their reaction,' Lady Carr said.

I shook my head. I would never change my mind. 'It's wrong.'

'It's for the greater good.' Carmichael repeated his phrase.

No, it wasn't. It could never be.

Lukas stepped forward. 'You should all go now.'

McGuigan hissed at him, 'If you weren't shagging her, you'd agree with us that this is the best thing to do.'

'Best for whom?' I asked. 'Best for Belly?'

'She's dead,' Ochre mumbled. 'She's already dead.'

'Get out.' My voice shook. 'All of you. Get out.'

'Just think about it,' Lady Sullivan said. 'You don't need to decide straight away.'

I roared at them all. 'Get the fuck out!'

They filed out, leaving Ochre till last. She lingered for a moment, gazing at me with sad, limpid eyes. I thought she was going to say something but, after hovering for a moment or two, she dropped her head and left.

'You should have warned me,' I said to Lukas in a low voice while Liza and Fred hastily moved away to the far corner of the room.

'I didn't think they'd come up here and say what they were thinking out loud,' he replied.

'Don't tell me you think we should pin the blame on an innocent person.'

'I would have once,' he told me, the stark truth reflected in his dark eyes. 'Not because we should let a killer run free, but because it would give us control over what happens next.'

'Why is that different now, Lukas? Is it only because of our relationship?' I stared at him. I needed to know what he was thinking.

'No,' he replied. 'It's because I know you'll catch whoever is responsible. I have absolute faith in you.'

I laughed coldly. 'There's only about ten hours to go before DSI Barnes sends in someone else to deal with this case. I've got no leads.' I lifted my hands in frustration. 'I've got nothing!'

'You can do this, D'Artagnan. I know you can.'

I wished I had his confidence. Yelling at those supe leaders hadn't done me any favours. I didn't believe I'd over-reacted, but I could have handled them better. I cursed to myself. I was tired and overwrought, and caffeine was no longer helping. 'Can you go after them, Lukas? Speak to them? Try and get them to see that making up stories isn't the way forward?'

'If that's what you want, that's what I'll do.'

'I'd appreciate it.'

He gave me a warm smile. 'Don't worry. They'll come around.'

I wasn't so sure. Even Ochre had been prepared to put the blame on Belly. 'Thank you.'

I watched him go, then sighed when my phone started to ring. I slid it out, stared unseeingly at the unknown number and answered. 'This is DC Bellamy.'

'Detective!'

My spine stiffened. I knew that voice. Bloody Juliet Chambers-May was all I needed right now.

'Thank you for picking up. The reason I'm calling is that I'm looking for a comment on a story we're about to run in the online edition of the *Daily Filter*. To be honest, I'm quite shocked that you've not released a statement before now. We know that there's been a tragic murder at the DeVane Hotel and the victim is a human male by the name of Lance Emerson. In fact, I believe I brought him to your attention only yesterday.'

I sat down slowly. Shit. I knew that it was only a matter of time before the press found out what had happened, but I'd been praying that we'd have until tomorrow morning at least.

'I understand that a pixie killed him,' she burbled on. 'Who would have thought such a thing? My source says that the pixie was found dead not far from poor Mr Emerson's corpse and his blood-covered clothing was discovered next to her. I also have it on good authority that this same pixie threatened Mr Emerson with a knife only hours before he was killed with a knife. And I'm told that the knife used to murder him was discovered beneath the pixie's body. Did the pixie kill herself after killing Lance Emerson?'

I didn't say anything. What the actual fuck? Who had spoken to her? Who'd pointed her towards Belly?

'Detective?' The journalist's voice was altogether too bright.

It felt like the words were being dragged out of me. 'No comment.'

'Oh, come now, detective. A human is murdered at a supe conference by a supe? You must have something to say. Can you at least confirm the pixie's name? Or that the murder has been committed?'

'No. Comment.'

'DC Bellamy, I—'

I hung up. Fred and Liza looked at me. 'Well,' I said dully. 'Shit.'

CHAPTER TWENTY-FIVE

'WHO WHISPERED IN HER EAR? WHO TOLD THAT DAMNED WOMAN about Emerson, and why is she so convinced that Belly killed him?'

Fred shook his head. 'I don't know.'

'Sullivan?' I demanded. 'Do you think it was her?'

'I doubt it.'

I glared. 'McGuigan seemed pretty keen to pass the buck. Could it have been him?'

'Maybe it was Lord Horvath,' Liza suggested, 'He was speaking to her in the car park, remember? Did he tell you what about?'

I stiffened. I felt a flicker of doubt creep in then I pushed it away. No, it wouldn't have been Lukas. I could trust him. It had been too hard a road to get to that point and I wouldn't start questioning him now. Besides, he'd just proved that he was on my side and didn't want Belly to be blamed. 'It wasn't him.'

Fred and Liza exchanged looks.

'Boss,' Fred began hesitantly.

I narrowed my eyes. 'No. Don't say it.' I turned to Liza. 'Do you have that printout of the supes that Emerson approached?'

She reached across and passed it to me. 'Here. The top five have all spent time in the Clink for various infractions including assault, so I prioritised them. But—'

My phone rang again, interrupting her. I answered it without checking the screen. Bloody Chambers-May. She should have got the message the first time around. 'No. Fucking. Comment.'

'Good evening to you too, Emma.'

I winced. 'Sorry, Laura. I thought you were someone else.'

'I get that all time,' she said warmly.

'Really?'

'No.'

I scratched awkwardly at a non-existent itch. 'We've been having a few problems,' I muttered. 'I am sorry.'

'No problem. Maybe I can brighten things up a bit for you.' She paused. 'Or not. It depends how you look at it.'

I ran my tongue over my dry lips. 'Go on,' I said. 'What do you have?'

'I've completed the initial post-mortem on Lance Emerson. It's taken me longer to get back to you than it should have because I was waiting on a couple of confirmations from the lab. I wanted to be sure of my findings before I spoke to you.'

'Okay.' My fingers tightened around the sheet of paper that Liza had handed to me. 'Is there good news?'

'Well,' she hedged, 'my initial assessment of Mr Emerson's death appears accurate. His throat was cut from behind by someone who possesses considerable strength and is right-handed. The wound matches the blade that was found beside Belly in the jacuzzi. I've done numerous tests and there's little doubt that Mr Emerson was anything other than one hundred percent human.'

That was hardly a shock, though it wasn't what I wanted to hear. I sighed. 'Alright.'

'The exciting part,' Laura continued in the same tone of voice, 'is that I found a single strand of foreign hair.'

I immediately straightened up. 'From the murderer? We have their DNA?'

'Hold your horses. I can't tell you whether the hair is from the killer or someone Emerson came into contact with earlier in the day. What I can tell you is that it was caught in his scalp, suggesting that it came from someone who was either much taller than him or was leaning over him while he was either sitting or lying down. I found it on the back of Emerson's head, though it may have been dislodged.'

'As if he was lying face down,' I said. 'As if he was on the massage table.'

'Don't get too thrilled. I didn't find the strand of hair until after he'd been moved to the morgue. It could easily have shifted from the top of his head or from elsewhere.'

I felt a renewed surge of optimism. 'But it might not have been. It might be from the killer.'

'Yep,' Laura conceded the point.

'Have you tested it? Did you get any DNA from it?'

'Those lab results will take longer but there's a good chance that we'll get a clear DNA reading because we have the hair root.'

I thought of Belly's bright-blue hair. 'What colour is it?'

'Light brown. That's not the interesting part, though. Although it's too early for DNA, I was able to conduct an initial assessment and the lab has confirmed it. The hair is from a vampire.'

I stared down at the list of names in my hand. There were four vampires in Liza's top ten, and one of them had done time. 'You're sure?'

'Positive.'

* * *

FRED and I marched through the hotel lobby. Everywhere I looked, supes were milling around and almost all of them glanced in our direction. From their expressions, I knew that Juliet Chambers-May had already published her 'revelations' online. I couldn't worry about what she'd written right now; I had more fanged fish to fry.

'There are twilight workshops going on,' I murmured to Fred. 'And the steering committee should be sitting again in the Rose Room. We don't want to alert the vamps to what we're doing. If someone on this list murdered Emerson, the last thing we want is to let them know that we're onto them. We have to be swift and stealthy.'

Fred nodded sombrely. 'Like a fart.'

My steps faltered for a moment and I stared at him. He had the grace to look abashed. 'Sorry,' he said, 'that slipped out. I didn't mean to say it aloud.'

I made a face at him.

'Detective! DC Bellamy!'

I turned and spotted Flax, Belly's pink-haired friend. She was holding up her phone and waving it at me. 'Have you seen this?' she demanded. 'Have you seen what this fucking woman has written?'

I exhaled. 'I haven't seen the article, but I know what she was planning to write.'

'And you couldn't do anything about it?' Her voice was rising. 'You couldn't stop this?'

'Flax—'

'She can't get away with this! This woman cannot make these sorts of allegations and get away with it! Belly can't defend herself! Why didn't you stop her?' She dropped her phone and reached out to grab my shoulders. Like most pixies, she was a good foot shorter than I was but her grip was surprisingly strong.

Fred stepped forward to make her back off but I waved him away. She had the right to be angry. She stared at me, fury and pain in her face, and her fingers tightened. I winced involuntarily and the movement seemed to make Flax realise what she was doing. She released her hold and dropped her arms to her sides, though she didn't take her eyes off me.

'Wait,' she said slowly. 'Is this what you wanted?'

'No,' I said firmly. 'It is not.'

Flax didn't seem to hear me. 'It solves all your problems, doesn't it? If you can say that Belly was the murderer then everything is done and dusted. She got her comeuppance because she's already dead and you don't need to look for anyone else. The summit continues without any problems and everybody's happy.' Her expression turned icy cold. 'Except for Belly.'

'Belly didn't kill Lance Emerson,' I said. 'She's not being blamed for anything.'

'That's not what that news article says!'

To call it 'news' was stretching the truth somewhat. 'The journalist is wrong. Belly didn't do this. And, as long as I am here, she will not be blamed,' I added with every ounce of feeling I possessed

'But she's already been blamed!' Flax was growing angrier rather than calmer. 'How could you let that woman print those lies?' She threw her hands out towards two passing vampires. 'How could any of you let her do this?'

The vamps hurried away. I kept my expression bland. 'You have to trust me. We're going to—'

'Trust you? Trust *you*?'

She lunged for me again, but this time it wasn't Fred who tried to stop her. Ochre appeared and stepped between us. 'Flax,' she said, 'you need to come with me. We can talk about this somewhere else.'

'What are you going to do?' she sneered. 'Lock me up for speaking the truth?'

'Flax,' she repeated. 'Nobody will lock you up.' She started to steer her away. 'Come with me. We'll sit over there and we'll talk about this.' Ochre glanced over her shoulder at me. 'Don't worry, detective. You get on with your job.'

'She's not doing her job!' Flax yelled.

I flinched.

'Boss,' Fred said softly.

I nodded. 'Let's go.' We walked away without looking back but I could feel a hundred pairs of eyes boring into my back – Flax's included.

* * *

THE HIGHEST NAME on the list was a male vamp called Dregs. It wasn't a moniker that inspired confidence. He was signed up to attend a workshop entitled 'How to talk to humans' in the west wing of the hotel. Given that he'd spent three years in the Clink for breaking both legs of a human male who'd approached him in a bar, I guessed it was a workshop that he was sorely in need of. Unless he actually had killed Emerson. If that was so, he probably ought to be attending 'How not to cut the throats of humans who talk to you when they want to use you as a sacrifice in a fake ceremony 101'.

My fingers itched, desperate to curl round my crossbow with a loaded bolt that I could wave in Dregs' face. Instead I left it on my back and told Fred to check the workshop and bring the vamp out if he was there. Fred would cause less of a scene and arouse much less suspicion than I would.

I didn't have long to wait. In less than a minute Fred led Dregs out, chatting to him with an easy manner that I wished I possessed. 'Sorry to drag you out of there,' he said.

'S'alright mate,' Dregs shrugged. 'It was a bit dull anyway. I only signed up for this workshop because Lord Horvath told me to. If you ask me, he's got soft since he started going out with that stupid mate of yours. She's not even that pret—' Dregs swallowed the word when he caught sight of me and paled so dramatically that I'd have laughed if the situation had been any different.

'Hi Dregs,' I said.

'Uh … er … uh … shit.' He ran a hand through his hair. 'I was only joking about that. Sorry. I … shit. Sorry.'

One thing was for certain – we'd certainly caught him unexpectedly. I pointed to the empty room behind us. 'Can we have a quiet chat?'

'Uh … sure.'

I directed Dregs to a chair. Fred checked the corridor to make sure that nobody else was there then closed the door.

'We have a few questions, Dregs,' I said conversationally. 'We're speaking to everyone who came into contact with the human who died, Lance Emerson.'

Comprehension dawned on his face. 'Oh,' he muttered, 'I should have known this would happen.' He crossed his arms. 'You want to know if I had something to do with it. You want to know if I killed him.'

At least we weren't going to beat around the bush. 'Why would I think you might have done that?' I enquired.

He rolled his eyes. 'I got history, ain't I? I did my time for that. I said I was sorry.'

I didn't say anything and my silence encouraged him to keep talking.

'I only broke his legs. I didn't kill him. Besides, he deserved it. He was goading me for a good hour before I made my move. The man didn't know when to shut up. I know I'm supposed to take the higher ground, but there's only so many times you can be told you're a disgusting monster before you snap. It was a long time ago. I wouldn't do it again.'

'Did Lance Emerson call you a dirty monster?'

'No.' Dregs glared at me. 'For what it's worth, Lance Emerson was nice to me. He told me he could see I was in pain and he could help. He said he had this retreat up near Scotland and I could join him there if I wanted to. He gave me his card. I kept it because it seemed like maybe it would be a good idea. I like the countryside. I could do with some fresh air for a change.'

Not that sort of fresh air. 'Where were you yesterday between the hours of five and seven?' I asked.

Resignation lit his shadowed brown eyes. 'In my room on my own,' he muttered. He lifted his chin. 'I was watching *Pointless* on TV, and then I took a shower.' His words had an edge of hurt defiance. 'But just because I don't have someone who can alibi me doesn't mean I killed anyone.'

'Do you still have Emerson's card?' Fred asked.

Dregs looked at him suspiciously. 'Yeah.' He took his wallet from his back pocket and flipped it open; sure enough, Lance Emerson's business card was nestled inside it, the same version as the one that had been found on his corpse.

'Okay,' I said. 'Thanks for your time.'

He frowned. 'That's it?'

'For now. We might need to talk to you again later.' I flashed him a business-like smile which only seemed to confuse him even more.

'I can go?' He looked at Fred.

'Yes. Thank you.' When Dregs didn't move, Fred repeated, 'Thank you.'

The vampire scratched his head, shrugged and left. Fred and I glanced at each other. 'He's not the one,' Fred said.

'It doesn't seem likely. Who's next on the list?'

He checked the sheet of paper. 'Tinkerbell. Female vamp around fifty years old.'

I raised an eyebrow. 'Tinkerbell?'

Fred grinned. 'She's not signed up for any workshops, but she might be in the bar or the restaurant.'

I nodded. 'Then let's move.'

CHAPTER TWENTY-SIX

IT TOOK LONGER TO FIND TINKERBELL THAN IT DID TO SPEAK TO her. She was sitting alone in a dark corner of the outdoor courtyard with a serious-looking book. No wonder Emerson had approached her; although she wasn't delicate or fairy-like, she had an air of fragility and vulnerability.

It was hard to believe that she'd been sanctioned for assaulting a human until she explained that she'd only bitten him after he'd grabbed her arse for the second time. Her fangs had barely scraped his arm but they'd drawn blood, and for that reason her name had ended up high on my list. She'd been fined a lot of money and spent twenty-eight days in the Clink. Alas, self-defence wasn't considered a reasonable excuse where supes were concerned. No wonder there were so many problems.

'Yeah,' she sniffed. 'Emerson talked to me. But he talked to a lot of people.'

'What did he want?'

'Who the fuck knows? I cut him off before he could finish his first sentence, so I don't know why my name is on that list.'

Probably because Lance Emerson had decided that Tinkerbell was vulnerable enough to warrant a second attempt at luring her up north. The situation beggared belief. If Lukas or any of the senior vamps had worked out what the Chief was up to, they'd have... I swallowed the thought. For now.

'Why did you stop Emerson so quickly?' I asked. 'Why not hear him out first?'

Her lip curled. 'I'd watched him do the rounds. He was slimy. My instincts told me to keep away.'

'Those are good instincts,' I told her.

Tinkerbell smirked. 'Yeah, I know.'

'Where were you yesterday evening? Before the champagne reception started?' Fred asked.

'I didn't go to the reception. I went for a walk and didn't get back till late.' She smiled slightly. 'I wasn't alone, if it's an alibi you're looking for. I got chatting to a druid who'd come from Cornwall and I was showing him the sights. I'm sure he'll vouch for me.' She held my gaze.

I took down the druid's details, although I was sure he'd confirm what Tinkerbell had told us, then I thanked her. Fred and I turned to leave.

'You can't tell me that you're sad Emerson is dead, detective,' she called after us.

I paused. No, I wasn't sad, but I wished I'd had the chance to deal with Emerson my way. Due process exists for a reason, and it would have allowed the world at large to see what sort of shit supes were up against.

It was easy to say, but it felt like death was the easy way out for someone like the Chief.

* * *

DESPITE OUR FAILURES SO FAR, my renewed sense of optimism wasn't fading. After thirty-six hours of running around like headless chickens, it felt like we were getting somewhere – even though the next vampire on our list wasn't in the bar, the restaurant or any of the twilight workshops.

'He's probably in his room,' I said.

Fred consulted the paper. 'Six-oh-four.'

I nodded at the lifts. 'Let's go.' We stepped inside and I pressed the button for the sixth floor. Before the doors closed completely, a hand appeared and forced them to re-open.

'D'Artagnan,' Lukas drawled. He wasn't smiling. 'May I have a word?'

'Can we take a rain check?' I replied. 'I'm a bit busy right now.'

A muscle ticked in his cheek. 'It's important.'

I sighed. 'Five minutes.'

Lukas looked at Fred. Fred offered him a smile. 'Leave,' Lukas said.

Fred blinked. 'Oh.' He glanced at me and I nodded. 'Okay.' He walked out of the lift and Lukas walked in.

As it started to rise, Lukas reached across me and pressed the emergency stop button. The lift came to an abrupt halt. 'Is that really necessary?' I asked.

He didn't answer my question. Instead he turned to me, his black eyes glittering.

'Did something happen with the other supe leaders?' I demanded.

Lukas folded his arms across his chest. 'I did as you asked. They'll hold back on Belly. They're not happy about it, but once I'd politely explained matters to them, they agreed that blaming her wasn't the best way to go.'

An awful lot in that answer was left unsaid. It was best not to ask what Lukas's polite explanation had involved. 'So what's the problem?'

'I want to know,' he bit out, 'why you're suddenly interrogating my vampires. If one of my people is a suspect, I need to know about it.'

Oh. I wondered how he'd found out. Dregs, probably. 'I'm handling it, Lukas.'

'D'Artagnan.' His voice was silky smooth. 'These are my people.'

I drew in a breath. 'This is one of those many occasions, Lord Horvath, when you need to step back and let me do my job.'

'I've been trying my best to do that since this shitstorm started. But, *Emma*,' he said, 'you have to remember that I've got a job to do as well. And my job involves making sure my vampires toe the line. If you suspect one of them, I need to know,' he repeated.

I shook my head. 'Not yet, you don't. Once I have a definite answer – if I *get* a definite answer – I'll tell you. Until then, it doesn't concern you.'

'Of course it concerns me,' he growled.

'This isn't about our personal relationship, Lukas. This is wholly professional.'

'If it was wholly professional, I'd have done a lot more to ensure I had a greater involvement from the start. I held back because of our personal relationship, not in spite of it.' His jaw tightened. 'Do you have evidence that a vampire is the murderer?'

I sighed. 'There's enough to suggest that it's a strong likelihood.'

Lukas's expression closed off. 'Who?'

'I don't know yet. If you hadn't interrupted me, I might already have the answer.' As I gazed at him, the shadows of doubt that I'd put to one side flickered again. 'What else do you know?' I asked. 'Have you also found out why Lance Emerson was really attending this conference?'

'Are you interrogating me now?'

'It's only a question.'

His black eyes narrowed. 'Why do I get the feeling there's more to this? Do you still not trust me completely?'

I looked away. 'There are things you've not told me, Lukas.'

'There are obviously things you've not told me, too. I'm not the one who's been keeping secrets.'

'I'm not keeping secrets, I'm doing my damned job. Besides, you've kept quiet about plenty of things. What about Juliet Chambers-May? You had a chat with her in the car park. I saw it on CCTV. You didn't mention it to me.'

'I didn't realise that I have to tell you about every conversation I have.'

'You should have told me about that one and you know it,' I snapped.

'It was nothing,' he said dismissively. 'I was warning her off, that's all. She was causing problems and she knows better than that. I told her to back off.'

'She didn't listen.'

He grimaced. 'I saw the news article. But this isn't about her. If you genuinely believe that a vampire murdered Emerson, I have to be involved. You can't shut me out. I don't want to fight with you, I want to help you. I'm responsible for my vampires.'

'And that's exactly why you shouldn't be involved. Not yet. You're responsible for your vampires and that means you want to protect them.'

'Not if one of them is a murderer!'

'As soon as I get any real answers, I'll come and find you,' I said levelly. 'But right now, let me do my job. I need a bit of time, Lukas. That's all.'

He cursed. When he spoke again, his voice was quieter. 'This is a balancing act for me as well as you. I love you and I want to be with you, but I can't forget that I'm Lord Horvath.' There was a sudden painful honesty in his eyes.

'I love you too,' I said simply. 'But it's clear that we still need to work out some problems between us in a way that's not just fair for both of us, but fair for everyone else too.'

'If you're suggesting we sit down and write up some kind of contract...'

It wouldn't be the worst idea in the world. 'We've not had to deal with a situation like this before,' I said quietly. 'I've not had to investigate your vampires before.'

'So you *do* believe that a vampire did this?' His eyes flashed again. 'Who?'

'Lukas—'

He held up his hands. 'Alright.'

'I've got this,' I said. 'I'll find you when I need to. I promise.'

He ran a hand through his hair. 'Fine.' He pressed the emergency stop button again and the lift creaked into action.

I pressed for the ground floor. 'I have to go and pick up Fred.'

Lukas nodded. 'I wasn't trying to pick a fight, Emma. I wasn't trying to cause problems.'

'I know.' I managed a smile. 'I'll involve you as soon as I need to.'

'Okay.' He exhaled. 'Okay.'

The lift doors opened again. Fred, who'd been wringing his hands anxiously, looked up. Lukas inclined his head towards him in brief apology and moved out of the lift.

'I'll wait here in the lobby,' Lukas said. 'You—'

'I'll find you as soon as I have something,' I replied.

The lift doors started to close again. 'Everything alright, boss?' Fred asked.

I nodded distractedly – then my foot shot out to prevent the lift doors from closing. I forced them open and looked at Lukas. 'What did you mean?' I asked suddenly. 'You said that Juliet Chambers-May knew better than that. What did you mean?'

He looked puzzled. 'I meant exactly that. No matter how she chooses to live her life, as a supe she knows better than to go around causing problems for the rest of us.'

My heart chilled. 'As a supe? That journalist is a supe?'

He blinked. 'I didn't tell you. I didn't think it mattered.' His body went rigid and his eyes met mine. His words were barely audible. 'Juliet Chambers-May is a vampire.'

CHAPTER TWENTY-SEVEN

'She doesn't look anything like a vampire,' I said when we were back in the Supe Squad suite.

Fred's eyes were wide. 'She doesn't even have fangs.'

'She files down her teeth,' Lukas said. 'She's had surgery to make her appear less attractive. Less *vamp*.'

I'd realised she'd had work done to her face the first time we met, but it hadn't occurred to me that she'd had plastic surgery to make herself look less appealing. I shook my head. 'I don't get it.'

'It doesn't happen very often, but it does happen,' Lukas told us. 'She was turned about sixty years ago during the Swinging Sixties. At the time, a lot of people saw vampirism as a sort of liberation. After a decade or so, she started to hate what she'd become. She had counselling and we did our best to help her, but she started to despise herself. In the end it was easier all round when she left.'

'And decided to pretend she was human?' I was unable to keep the disbelief from my tone. It was hard to wrap my head around the way she acted towards supes, given that she was one.

'What else could we do? She wanted a clean break from supe life and the only way out is to behave as if you're not a supe. Over the years, she's perfected her act. The older vampires know what she is and some of the other supes do, too—'

'I didn't,' I growled.

'I can only apologise for that. It didn't occur to me to bring it up.' He looked guilty. 'Not until now.'

I passed a hand over my eyes. All the signs had been there: I'd seen other vamps glaring at her; she'd known things that few humans would have been aware of; she'd known the significance of the Tears of Blood necklace that Lukas had given me. I'd assumed that I could spot a vamp by their appearance alone, but it turned out I was wrong. 'Are there many others like her?'

'You know there are but they tend not to stay in London. Most of them find it easier to leave the city. But I don't know any who've gone to the lengths that she has to conceal the way she looks.'

'Doesn't she still have to drink blood?' Fred asked, his bafflement mirroring my own.

'Yes, but as long as her efforts to get human blood don't cause harm or disruption, it's not an issue.' Lukas pulled a face. 'I think she bribes a local hospital. I truly am sorry – I'd have told you about her if I thought I had to.'

Chambers-May had taken a hell of a risk coming to the supe summit to complain publicly about supes. Maybe she found it easier to hide in plain sight, or maybe she wanted to confirm to herself that she'd done the right thing by abandoning her true self. And maybe, just maybe, she'd been sent into a murderous panic when Lance Emerson had approached her. Like me, he would have believed she was human. If he'd spoken to her, it would have been part of his scam to beat the fake supe of a human being. Except it wasn't a fake supe inside Chambers-May; her supe was real.

'We have her on CCTV,' I said. 'Juliet Chambers-May was talking to Lance Emerson moments before Belly attacked him.'

Lukas was very still. 'Did she murder him?'

'At the moment, there's no real evidence that she did,' Fred said.

I pulled back my shoulders. 'Moira's list, her original list. Where is it?'

Liza went to her desk. 'Here.'

'We didn't spend any time looking at the human names because we knew we were looking for a supe. But Lance Emerson spoke to her – we have it on CCTV. Is she on the original list?'

Liza scanned it. 'Her name is here,' she said quietly.

I thought about the news article Chambers-May had published. 'She wants us to blame Belly. It would be pretty damned convenient for her if we did.'

'Why did she wait so long to write the article?' Fred asked.

'She was waiting. She wanted *us* to accuse Belly. When we didn't do that straight away, she took matters into her own hands.'

'It still doesn't prove she killed Lance Emerson, Emma,' Lucas said. 'I'm not defending her, but you still don't have any real proof.'

He was right. My eyes widened. I reached for the phone and dialled Wilma Kennard's direct number. 'It's me,' I said. 'I have one quick question.'

She sounded wary. 'Go on.'

'You told me that you'd had problems with the press in the past. Something about guests' privacy being invaded?'

'Not recently. It was a couple of years ago.'

'What happened?'

'We had a minor celebrity couple from the States staying here. A bitch of a journalist stalked them round the hotel and published several salacious stories about what they were supposedly up to. She followed them around the bar, tried to get into their room, that kind of thing. We closed off the swimming pool for a few hours one evening so the guests could get some privacy but the damned journalist somehow managed to get in and sit beside them in the bloody sauna. We'd posted a security guard at the entrance to the pool so the only way the journalist could have got through was via the spa and—'

Kennard halted abruptly and cursed under her breath. 'Shit. At the time, the spa staff swore blind that they hadn't let her through the connecting door. I assumed one of them was lying, but I couldn't prove anything.'

'Has the security system changed since then? If someone had managed to get hold of a master keycard that would gain access to either the pool or the spa area two years ago, would it still work?'

'They couldn't get into any of the hotel rooms,' Kennard said. 'That system is refreshed regularly and those keycards are time-coded.'

'That's not what I asked.' Besides, no system was ever completely secure. As the old saying goes, locks are only for honest people.

She sighed. 'I know.' Her voice was heavy. 'And yes, a master keycard for the pool and spa would probably still work. Because guests don't have keys for those areas, we don't update them in the same way.'

I bet they would from now on. Although I already knew the answer, I asked the question anyway. 'Who was the journalist?'

'I wanted to ban her from the hotel but I was over-ruled.' Kennard was doing her best to explain and offer excuses. 'Hell hath no fury like a scorned tabloid newspaper. The hotel manager at the time put in a complaint and threatened to report the paper to the police, and the editor told us it wouldn't happen again. The hotel received several positive stories as a pay-off. It's not how I'd have done things but I wasn't in charge then,' she hissed.

'Wilma,' I said softly, 'who was the journalist?'

'Her name was Juliet Chambers-May.'

I closed my eyes. Juliet had had access to the spa for the last two fucking years. She could have bribed a member of staff back then to give her a master keycard, or maybe she had managed to clone one of the cards. We might never know.

I thanked Kennard and put down the phone. Fred and Liza were staring at me. Lukas was pale, a muscle in his cheek ticking furiously. I looked at them all. 'It's still not evidence that she's the murderer.'

'But we have motive,' Liza said.

'And opportunity,' Fred added.

'Not to mention the feeling in my damned gut,' I agreed.

Lukas shook his head. 'If she did this —' His voice faltered. 'I should have told you about her before.'

'It wouldn't have changed anything. And she might be innocent.'

'Except I trust your gut in the same way that I trust your heart, D'Artagnan,' he murmured. 'And mine, too.'

For a long moment we fell silent as we considered the implications. The atmosphere in the room felt heavy and oppressive.

Fred cleared his throat. 'We have to speak to her, but we don't know where she is. Hauling a journalist off for questioning when they might have done nothing wrong could cause more problems than it solves.'

I shook my head. 'We don't need to haul her anywhere and we don't need to go to her. She'll come to us.'

* * *

'I HAVE TO ADMIT, I'm surprised you offered an interview now, detective.' Juliet crossed her legs and gave me what was meant to be a disarming smile.

Now that I knew what she was, it was hard to see anything else. It irritated me beyond belief that I'd missed her vampirism. She was still wearing a lot of make-up, which had clearly been applied with a confident hand. Her face looked slightly bloated, suggesting she'd had filler inserted in all the wrong places, and her canines were slightly odd looking yet identical in appearance. She'd been hiding her true self away for decades now, and become incredibly adept at using every possible tool at her disposal, but I was still annoyed with myself.

I smiled politely, playing the role of weary detective who'd been forced into this position. 'Well, I did promise you an interview.'

'On Tuesday. After the summit.'

'You didn't give me a whole lot of choice, given the news article you published. I had to … clear some space.'

There was a triumphant light in Juliet's eyes. 'You mean your superiors made you do this.' She was really enjoying having the upper hand.

'My boss suggested it would be a good idea,' I murmured.

She snorted. 'I bet he did.'

I unstrapped my crossbow from my back and laid it carefully against my chair. Juliet's clever gaze watched my every move. 'Is it normal for you to walk around with a lethal weapon?' she enquired.

'It's permitted for Supe Squad detectives,' I explained, telling her nothing she didn't already know. 'But it would be against the law for me to use it against a human, so there's no need for you to worry. We're alone in this meeting room and the hotel staff know not to interrupt us. And I've made sure that no supes will drop by unannounced.'

Juliet betrayed herself with the faintest satisfied twitch of her mouth. She must have been concerned that Lukas had told me what she was. Of course, until now I'd given her no hint that I was aware of her true nature because I simply hadn't known. Perhaps she thought that Lukas's allegiance lay with her as a vampire, rather than with me as his girlfriend. Fortunately she was wrong – although if she wasn't now a prime suspect in Lance

Emerson's murder, I might have remained completely in the dark.

'Are you expecting to have to use the crossbow?' she asked.

'Off the record?' I asked.

Juliet waved a hand. 'Sure.'

'I always have to be prepared,' I told her. 'There's no telling what might happen with this many supes in attendance.'

'Indeed,' she said. 'Indeed.' She reached into her bag, drew out her phone and switched it on to record. I kept my expression blank; she wasn't the only one taping this conversation. And she'd also just proved that she was right-handed. It wasn't much, but it was a start.

'Let's begin with Lance Emerson, shall we? What do you know about him?' she asked.

'You probably know as much as I do,' I said. 'After all, you brought him to my attention.'

She looked pleased with herself. 'Yes, I did. I gave you enough information to remove him from the summit. You didn't do that, and he ended up dead. Do you regret not listening to me now that he's a corpse?'

So that was why she'd told me about him during our first meeting; she'd been hoping that I'd get rid of him so that she didn't have to. 'It was my decision to let Emerson stay. Although this is the Supernatural Summit, humans are still welcome. The purpose of the summit is to improve relations between humans and supes and we can't very well do that if we forbid humans from attending.'

'He ran a dodgy cult called the Perfect Path to Power and Redemption. He claimed that he could remove the supernatural element from any supe. Is that true? Is it possible?'

She knew that it wasn't. 'We're investigating his organisation,' I said blandly. 'But, no, I don't believe it's possible.' I leaned forward, my expression and my voice growing more earnest. 'You see, Ms Chambers-May, no supe can escape what they truly are. Whether you're a phoenix like me, or a werewolf, or a pixie, or a vampire, you are supernatural. You can dye your hair blonde but you'll still be a brunette. Don't get me wrong – being a supe isn't a superficial thing, it's an inherent part of you. It is power and beauty and strength and so much more that a human could never understand.'

She was no longer smiling. 'So you believe that supes are superior to humans?'

'I didn't say that.'

'You implied it.'

I shrugged. 'What do you think, Ms Chambers-May? Do you think that supes are superior?'

She snorted loudly. 'Obviously not.'

Uh-huh.

'Let's move on,' she said. 'Tell me about Lance Emerson's death. How did he die?'

'He was murdered. His throat was slit from ear to ear by someone who cold-bloodedly lured him out of his room. Whoever murdered him is callous and unfeeling.' I met her eyes. 'I'd go so far as to say that they're pure evil.'

Her body tensed. 'Even though Lance Emerson was a con artist who damaged dozens – if not hundreds – of lives?'

'That doesn't mean he deserved to be murdered.'

'Does every supe in this hotel agree with that, detective?'

'I don't know,' I answered calmly. 'You'd have to ask them.'

Juliet sniffed. 'So the pixie who killed him, she was pure evil? Is that what you're saying?'

'I didn't say that Lance Emerson was killed by a pixie.'

She chuckled. 'Come, detective. You read my article and you know that I'm aware of the truth. The pixie was found drowned with the knife that was used to murder Lance Emerson. His bloody clothes were next to her. She killed him and then either killed herself or drowned by accident. You can't escape the facts.'

'That part is true.' I nodded. 'You can't escape the facts. How did you find all this out?'

'I have my sources but I'm certainly not going to reveal them, detective. And you can't make me.' She uncrossed her legs. 'Isn't it also true that this same pixie was seen assaulting Mr Emerson earlier in the day?'

'That is still to be confirmed.'

'I saw her with my own eyes. She looked as if she was about to slit his throat in the middle of the hotel lobby! And then his throat was actually cut! That's a smoking gun if ever I saw one.'

'There was no gun involved in the murder,' I said expressionlessly.

She rolled her eyes. 'Don't be obtuse, detective.'

There was a loud knock on the door. Juliet started and glared at me. 'I thought you said we wouldn't be interrupted.'

I looked concerned. 'Not unless it's urgent.' I picked up my crossbow, got to my feet and opened the door. Barry and Larry, wearing identical expressions of excitement, were waiting on the other side. Barry was jigging from side to side.

'We've found a fingerprint on the knife!' Larry burst out. 'It's not Belly's. The pixie didn't kill him and this proves it. If you can find a match for the print, it'll be more than enough to convict Emerson's killer.'

Barry held up a kit. 'We know everyone who was inside the DeVane Hotel at the time of his murder. If we fingerprint them all, we'll find the murderer.'

'Great!' I said with slightly overblown enthusiasm. 'You already have my prints on record but I'm here with one of the journalists who's covering the summit. You can take her prints and clear her while you're here.' I glanced round.

Juliet was already on her feet. 'You're obviously very busy,' she said. She was moving towards the door. 'Let's finish this interview another time.'

'You should stay. If you hang around long enough, you might

witness us catching a murderer first hand. That would be quite the scoop.'

She shook her head. 'You have the murderer. It was the pixie.'

'No, Juliet. It wasn't.' I stepped in front of the door in case she decided to take a leaf out of Nathan Fairfax's book and make a run for it. I also adjusted my grip on the loaded crossbow.

Juliet's eyes flicked down towards it then up again. 'Oh,' she murmured.

In that instant, I knew we had the right person. I hadn't been convinced that the fingerprint act would work, but apparently it was enough.

'Belly the pixie was left-handed, but the killer was right-handed, ' I said. 'There's also a missing notebook that contained details of everyone Lance Emerson spoke to. It should have been with his other belongings but it was missing. Fortunately his assistant has an excellent memory and she wrote down their names for us.' I didn't say that those names had included Juliet's. I didn't have to.

She started to shake her head from side to side. 'That means nothing. None of that means a fucking thing.'

'Not on its own,' I agreed. 'But we found a single strand of hair on Emerson's scalp that didn't belong there. We believe it's the killer's.'

For the first time I registered panic in her eyes.

'We don't need to do a full DNA check to know that the hair belongs to a vampire,' I said softly.

'Well, it's obviously not mine,' she spluttered. 'I'm human.'

From beyond the corridor, Lukas stepped into view. 'You're not human, Juliet.'

Her face contorted. 'You bastard. I'm one of yours. You're supposed to protect me!'

'I don't protect murderers. And you're not one of mine.'

'He deserved to die,' she snarled.

'That wasn't your decision to make.'

Juliet took a step backwards and her eyes narrowed as she looked at me. 'You bitch. This is all your fault. I gave you everything you needed and I tried to get you to throw Emerson out of the summit, but you didn't. Then I gave you the prime suspect and you could have closed the case within an hour. But you were too fucking stupid to do that.'

'Yeah,' I said. 'Let's talk about that. Let's talk about how you tried to set up Belly.'

'I didn't kill her,' Juliet spat. 'You can't pin that on me. She sneaked into the pool after I did, and she was already dead by the time I'd dealt with Emerson. It's not my fault she died. I only used the pool entrance because a bunch of damned wolves were hanging around near the spa door and I didn't want them to see me.'

She didn't think she'd done anything wrong; as far as Juliet was concerned, she truly believed she was one of the righteous. 'You could have pulled her out of the jacuzzi and started CPR. Instead you took full advantage of the situation and decided to pin Lance Emerson's murder on her. She was already dead, so what it did matter?'

'Exactly,' she spat. 'And I did the world a favour by getting rid of that bastard! If I hadn't stopped him, who's to say what he'd have got away with!'

Not much, because Nathan Fairfax and Jim had already tipped me onto the Chief. 'He deserved to be brought to justice,' I said. 'Real justice, where the world knew what he'd done. And Belly deserved to be treated with as much respect in death as she should have had in life. You acted as judge, jury and executioner, Juliet.' I paused. 'And don't give me that nonsense about how you gave me a chance to boot Emerson from the conference. You knew I wouldn't do that. You'd already prepared the fake spa invitation and sent it to him. You'd bought the candles that would mask your scent should any werewolves get involved. All you wanted was an excuse to deal with him yourself. You were always going to kill him.'

'Sucks to be you,' Barry said solemnly.

Juliet let out an inarticulate yell and ran at him. I tried to bar her way, but she shoved me aside. She hauled Barry towards herself, her mouth open next to his jugular. 'I might not have fangs like you, Lord Horvath, but I can still do plenty of damage,' she screamed.

Barry stared at me, wide-eyed. 'When I said I was looking for a vamp lady friend,' he muttered, 'this was not what I meant.'

I held up the tip of my crossbow and sighted down it. 'I will shoot you, Juliet. You'll be dead before you can do him any damage. Don't be stupid.' I let compulsion thrum my voice. 'Release him.'

Juliet started to shake.

I repeated my words. 'Release him now.'

Beads of sweat appeared on her forehead. She was fighting it, but she'd give in sooner or later. We all knew it.

Lukas moved up beside me. 'If you kill Barry or even hurt him like that, all you're doing is giving into your vampirism.'

'I'm not a vampire! Not inside! Not in my heart!' Juliet glared. 'Deep down, I'm not a fucking supe! I'm not going to the Clink. I won't be treated like that. I refuse to be!'

'Then we'll treat you like a human,' I said. 'You'll be charged like a human and you'll go to prison like a human. You can live out your days as a damned human. Let Barry go, give a statement admitting to everything you did, and we'll all pretend that you're not one of us. If that's what you really want.'

'Fine,' she snapped. She let Barry go and he staggered forward. 'As long as everyone knows I'm not a monster, I don't care what else they find out.'

'Juliet,' I said, 'you're far more of a monster than anyone else in this hotel.' I shrugged. 'But so be it.'

CHAPTER TWENTY-EIGHT

'HAVE YOU SEEN THE HEADLINE IN TODAY'S *DAILY FILTER*?' LIZA held up the newspaper.

SUPES, WE'RE SORRY. I blinked and peered more closely at the strapline underneath: *DAILY FILTER COLUMNIST'S EVIL PREJUDICE LED TO MURDER.* And then: *SHE USED US TO STIR UP HATRED AND BLAME AN INNOCENT*

I rocked back on my heels. 'That's ... nice.'

'To be fair,' Liza said, 'the paper didn't have much choice. It'd be difficult to defend someone who used their platform not only to get away with murder but also to set up an innocent pixie to take the fall.' She smiled with satisfaction. 'There's more inside, including that Lance Emerson wanted to kill supes as sacrifices. They've made it clear that the supes are the victims here, not the villains.'

'There are hardly any protestors outside this morning.' Fred beamed. 'Juliet Chambers-May did such a sterling job that nobody wants to be associated openly with either her or her beliefs. All those humans who think they hate supes are finally being confronted with the consequences of their actions.'

For the moment. Anti-supe sentiment wouldn't disappear

overnight; the world didn't work that way. It felt like a step in the right direction, even if it had happened for all the wrong reasons, but nobody should have died for us to get to this point.

'Did Emerson's notebook ever turn up?' Liza asked.

'Juliet admitted that she burned it. We've got her confession and the DNA from the hair strand found on Emerson's body. It's more than enough.'

'And she's still demanding to be convicted as a human?'

I nodded. 'She truly despises what she is. Her hatred of herself destroyed her. We need to make sure that supes are proud of what and who they are. Nobody should be ashamed to be themselves, not ever.'

'Amen,' Fred murmured.

The door to the suite opened and DSI Barnes strode in, followed by Grace. 'Well,' she said, clapping her hands, 'Supe Squad wins the day. Congratulations.'

I guessed that my employment wasn't about to be terminated. 'Thank you.'

'We should look into getting you a promotion, DC Bellamy.' Barnes glanced at Liza and Fred. 'And the two of you as well. You're to be commended for your work.' She checked her watch. 'Turn on the television. There's something you'll want to see.'

Fred did as she asked. The screen opened onto the news channel and the familiar face of the Home Secretary in front of Downing Street.

'Good morning. The shocking events over the last few days at the DeVane Hotel have proved a stark reminder that there are elements in our society who seek to cause discord and disharmony. The supernatural community is *our* community, and we need to remember that. I supported the Supernatural Summit from the outset, because it aimed to promote cohesion and tolerance within our community. It is due to the hard work and continuing efforts of this government that the summit went ahead in the first place. The tragic situation that occurred there has proved how right we were to give it our full backing.'

DS Grace went to Fred, gently took the remote control and turned off the television. 'I don't think we need to watch that.' He tossed down the remote as we gazed at him in surprise. Liza went over and kissed his cheek. 'Well,' he said. He coughed. 'Well.'

I smiled and walked to the door. 'I'm heading downstairs. We still have a summit to get on with. It's not over yet and I think we all deserve a happy ending.'

* * *

THE DEVANE HOTEL lobby was buzzing. There were pockets of supes all over the place, chatting and smiling at each other. I glanced round, aware that it wasn't celebration that had caused the bubbly atmosphere but relief.

'Well done, detective,' a voice murmured in my ear.

I glanced at Buffy. 'Thank you.'

She curtsied and offered a girlish giggle. 'You're a real hero.'

'Uh-huh.'

'I wish I could be more like you.'

'Uh-huh.'

'Maybe one day I could join the police. I think the uniform would suit me. Especially the hat. I do enjoy a helmet.'

I gave her a long look and Buffy grinned. 'For what it's worth,' I told her honestly, 'your help was invaluable.'

'Does this mean that you owe me? Are you in my debt, detective?'

I rolled my eyes. 'No, it means that I'm thanking you for your help. Nothing more.'

She shrugged. 'It was worth a shot.'

I tilted my head. 'Did you know that Juliet Chambers-May was a vampire when you saw her taking my photograph?'

Buffy snorted. 'Of course. You don't really think I'd have attacked a human, do you?' She winked and sauntered away.

Hmm. Hindsight was most definitely twenty-twenty.

I caught Kennedy's eye across the lobby. He raised a silver hip flask in my direction and winked, and I smiled in return. Then I spotted Lady Sullivan, seated on the same sofa where Belly had attacked Lance Emerson. I went over to her.

'Emma, darling!' The werewolf alpha smiled at me. 'Isn't it wonderful that you found our killer? And isn't it wonderful that she turned out to be a vampire who hates herself and not,' she added pointedly, 'a werewolf?'

'All's well that ends well,' I murmured non-committally.

She patted the cushion next to her. 'Do sit down, dear.'

I shook my head. 'I only wanted to let you know that I appreciate your concern for me.'

'Whatever do you mean?'

I smiled at her. 'Lukas and I are fine. We will always be fine. We can have our differences in terms of opinion and professional priorities, but in the end those differences won't affect us. I love him,' I told her, without a trace of self-consciousness, 'and he loves me. That's more than enough to get us through whatever lies ahead. We won't always agree with each other but we'll work it out.'

'You say that now.'

I leant down and spoke in her ear. 'I say it now and I'll say it forty years from now. In fact, I'll look forward to our disagreements. You know why?' I pulled back. 'Because the make-up sex is mind-blowing.' My smile broadened. 'Enjoy the rest of the summit, my lady.'

I stepped away and looked round. There was one more person I needed to talk to. Flax was in the bar, sitting with several friends in the same spot where I'd first spoken to her. There was an empty chair where Belly should have been. I inclined my head towards the space and cleared my throat. 'Hi, there.'

Flax dropped her eyes. 'Hi, detective.'

'Do you have a moment?'

She coughed and nodded. 'If this is about what I said to you before, then I'm sorry. I shouldn't have yelled at you. I shouldn't have jumped to conclusions. I just—' She ran a frustrated hand through her cloud of pink hair. 'It hurts. I wish she was still here.'

'So do I,' I said. 'What happened to Belly wasn't fair. She deserved better. Things should have turned out differently for her.'

Flax nodded miserably. 'Yeah.'

I drew in a breath. 'I'm not here because of what you said to me. I understand why you did that. I have a couple of questions, that's all. I'm hoping you can help to answer them.'

She raised her eyes. 'I'll do my best, DC Bellamy.'

I smiled. 'That's all I can ask for.'

* * *

THE GRUBBY CAFÉ didn't look like much. The tables were lined with worn Formica that was chipped in several places, and the tinny music was a loop of ten cheesy pop songs that was recycled over and over again. I'd been there long enough to know. The tea, however, was strong and tasty, and the fried egg sandwich I'd eaten earlier had been cooked to perfection.

The woman behind the counter had given me a suspicious look when I entered, but she'd left me in peace. Maybe she recognised me from the news, or maybe I was obviously with the police. Either way, it didn't matter; I wasn't there for her.

It was ten to five, minutes away from closing time, when the three men entered. They were wearing almost identical suits. Perhaps the office where they worked demanded that everyone wore tight, shiny, grey trousers.

I eyed them as they strolled up to the counter and requested 'the usual'. So this was their regular haunt; that was good to know.

The shortest one paused long enough to turn and sweep his eyes around the café. I felt his gaze rest on me, as if assessing me for a moment, but his eyes didn't linger. Maybe I wasn't as obvious a target as a petite pixie would have been. I sipped my tea and waited, biding my time. I wasn't in any particular hurry.

They paid for their food and walked out. I placed my mug onto the table and followed. The woman behind the counter watched me. I wasn't sure, but I thought I saw an approving glint in her eyes.

It was cold outside, with a steady drizzle that could snake its way past anything but the best waterproof clothing. Several drops trickled down my collar, making me shiver. The weather didn't appear to be dampening the spirits of the men, though; they were talking loudly and jostling each other for attention.

A car appeared next to them and one man shoved another towards it in some sort of mean-spirited joke. He staggered slightly, narrowing avoiding being clipped by the bumper. The car honked and the man swung a half-hearted fist at his friend. There was a roar of laughter from all three of them when it failed to connect.

I picked up my pace until I was less than a metre away from them. When we drew level with the narrow alleyway into which Belly had been dragged less than a month earlier, I veered round the three of them and turned, blocking their path.

Flax had only known what Belly had told her, that one of her attackers had sported a beard and his breath stank like rotting meat. Another of the men had been wearing a heavy watch, which had clipped Belly on the cheek and drawn blood when he'd struck her. The third man had giggled like a hyena all the way through the attack.

I gazed at the three men in front of me and smiled. Beard:

check. Over-sized watch: check. Two out of three wasn't bad. Then the third man started to laugh. 'Out of the way,' he sneered. His high-pitched chuckle really did sound like a hyena on one of those nature programmes.

'Good evening, gentlemen,' I said politely.

The man with the beard stepped forward. 'You're in our way.' A cloud of rancid breath hit my face.

'The three of you work nearby. Am I right?'

'What's it to you?' Beardy Man snarled.

'You walk this way every evening?'

'Fuck off, lady.' He tried to move past me but I moved with him.

'About a month ago, you assaulted a pixie on this street.' I pointed to the alleyway. 'You tried to drag her in there.'

'Don't be ridiculous.'

'There's a little shop across the road,' I said conversationally. 'They've had several break-ins recently so they've taken the sensible step of installing a camera directly outside. It films everyone who walks past.'

The man with the watch rolled his eyes. 'Piss off.'

I reached into my pocket and took out my warrant card. 'I'm Detective Constable Emma Bellamy and—'

I didn't get the chance to finish my sentence before the hyena made a run for it. He twisted, trying to cross the road and sprint away. I stuck out one foot and he fell forward into a puddle.

Beardy Man raised his fist and swung. I dodged and tutted. 'Violence is never the answer.'

'We didn't hurt that blue-haired bitch!' he spat.

I raised an eyebrow. 'I didn't say she had blue hair.'

'You did! You did! You...'

I raised my hand in the air. There was a whirl of sirens and, within seconds, two police cars squealed up beside us. Several uniformed officers jumped out and grabbed hold of the men.

I stepped back and folded my arms, watching as their rights

were read to them and they were bundled away. That was easier than I'd expected. They certainly weren't the brightest trio of losers in London.

'Nice.'

I turned to see Lukas leaning against a lamp post. 'Where did you spring from?' I asked. He hadn't been there a minute ago.

'I didn't want to get in your way.' He gave a lazy shrug. 'I thought I'd come and watch you in action. You're pretty good at your job, you know.'

'There's always more to learn,' I said. 'But I'm getting there.'

Lukas put an arm round my waist and pulled me close. 'And us?' he asked. 'Are we getting there?'

I smiled at him. We would argue sometimes, and we would disagree. Sometimes I'd make mistakes and sometimes Lukas would. A cold raindrop found its way down the front of my top and past my collarbone and I shivered involuntarily. Life wasn't always sunshine and hearts and flowers, but in the end it was how you dealt with the storms that made you what you were.

I leaned my head against his shoulder. 'We've been there,' I told him, 'for quite some time.'

ABOUT THE AUTHOR

After teaching English literature in the UK, Japan and Malaysia, Helen Harper left behind the world of education following the worldwide success of her Blood Destiny series of books. She is a professional member of the Alliance of Independent Authors and writes full time, thanking her lucky stars every day that's she lucky enough to do so!

Helen has always been a book lover, devouring science fiction and fantasy tales when she was a child growing up in Scotland.

She currently lives in Devon in the UK with far too many cats – not to mention the dragons, fairies, demons, wizards and vampires that seem to keep appearing from nowhere.

ALSO BY HELEN HARPER

The *WolfBrand* series

Devereau Webb is in uncharted territory. He thought he knew what he was doing when he chose to enter London's supernatural society but he's quickly discovering that his new status isn't welcome to everyone.

He's lived through hard times before and he's no stranger to the murky underworld of city life. But when he comes across a young werewolf girl who's not only been illegally turned but who has also committed two brutal murders, he will discover just how difficult life can be for supernaturals - and also how far his own predatory powers extend.

Book One – The Noose Of A New Moon

Book Two – Licence To Howl

The complete *Blood Destiny* series

"A spectacular and addictive series."

Mackenzie Smith has always known that she was different. Growing up as the only human in a pack of rural shapeshifters will do that to you, but then couple it with some mean fighting skills and a fiery temper and you end up with a woman that few will dare to cross. However, when the only father figure in her life is brutally murdered, and the dangerous Brethren with their predatory Lord Alpha come to investigate, Mack has to not only ensure the physical safety of her adopted family by hiding her apparent humanity, she also has to seek the blood-soaked vengeance that she craves.

Book One - Bloodfire

Book Two - Bloodmagic

Book Three - Bloodrage

Book Four - Blood Politics

Book Five - Bloodlust

Also

Corrigan Fire

Corrigan Magic

Corrigan Rage

Corrigan Politics

Corrigan Lust

The complete *Bo Blackman* series

A half-dead daemon, a massacre at her London based PI firm and evidence that suggests she's the main suspect for both ... Bo Blackman is having a very bad week.

She might be naive and inexperienced but she's determined to get to the bottom of the crimes, even if it means involving herself with one of London's most powerful vampire Families and their enigmatic leader.

It's pretty much going to be impossible for Bo to ever escape unscathed.

Book One - Dire Straits

Book Two - New Order

Book Three - High Stakes

Book Four - Red Angel

Book Five - Vigilante Vampire

Book Six - Dark Tomorrow

The complete *Highland Magic* series

Integrity Taylor walked away from the Sidhe when she was a child. Orphaned and bullied, she simply had no reason to stay, especially not when the sins of her father were going to remain on her shoulders. She found a new family - a group of thieves who proved that blood was less important than loyalty and love.

But the Sidhe aren't going to let Integrity stay away forever. They need her more than anyone realises - besides, there are prophecies to be fulfilled, people to be saved and hearts to be won over. If anyone can do it, Integrity can.

Book One - Gifted Thief

Book Two - Honour Bound

Book Three - Veiled Threat

Book Four - Last Wish

The complete *Dreamweaver* series

"I have special coping mechanisms for the times I need to open the front door. They're even often successful..."

Zoe Lydon knows there's often nothing logical or rational about fear. It doesn't change the fact that she's too terrified to step outside her own house, however.

What Zoe doesn't realise is that she's also a dreamweaver - able to access other people's subconscious minds. When she finds herself in the Dreamlands and up against its sinister Mayor, she'll need to use all of her wits - and overcome all of her fears - if she's ever going to come out alive.

Book One - Night Shade

Book Two - Night Terrors

Book Three - Night Lights

Stand alone novels

Eros

William Shakespeare once wrote that, "Cupid is a knavish lad, thus to make poor females mad." The trouble is that Cupid himself would probably agree…

As probably the last person in the world who'd appreciate hearts, flowers and romance, Coop is convinced that true love doesn't exist – which is rather unfortunate considering he's also known as Cupid, the God of Love. He'd rather spend his days drinking, womanising and generally having as much fun as he possible can. As far as he's concerned, shooting people with bolts of pure love is a waste of his time…but then his path crosses with that of shy and retiring Skye Sawyer and nothing will ever be quite the same again.

Wraith

Magic. Shadows. Adventure. Romance.

Saiya Buchanan is a wraith, able to detach her shadow from her body and send it off to do her bidding. But, unlike most of her kin, Saiya doesn't deal in death. Instead, she trades secrets - and in the goblin besieged city of Stirling in Scotland, they're a highly prized commodity. It might just be, however, that the goblins have been hiding the greatest secret of them all. When Gabriel de Florinville, a Dark Elf, is sent as royal envoy into Stirling and takes her prisoner, Saiya is not only going to uncover the sinister truth. She's also going to realise that sometimes the deepest secrets are the ones locked within your own heart.

The complete *Lazy Girl's Guide To Magic* series

Hard Work Will Pay Off Later. Laziness Pays Off Now.

Let's get one thing straight - Ivy Wilde is not a heroine. In fact, she's probably the last witch in the world who you'd call if you needed a magical helping hand. If it were down to Ivy, she'd spend all day every day on her sofa where she could watch TV, munch junk food and talk to her feline familiar to her heart's content.

However, when a bureaucratic disaster ends up with Ivy as the victim of a case of mistaken identity, she's yanked very unwillingly into Arcane Branch, the investigative department of the Hallowed Order of Magical Enlightenment. Her problems are quadrupled when a valuable object is stolen right from under the Order's noses.

It doesn't exactly help that she's been magically bound to Adeptus Exemptus Raphael Winter. He might have piercing sapphire eyes and a body which a cover model would be proud of but, as far as Ivy's concerned, he's a walking advertisement for the joyless perils of too much witch-work.

And if he makes her go to the gym again, she's definitely going to turn him into a frog.

Book One - Slouch Witch

Book Two - Star Witch

Book Three - Spirit Witch

Sparkle Witch (Christmas short story)

The complete *Fractured Faery* series

One corpse. Several bizarre looking attackers. Some very strange magical powers. And a severe bout of amnesia.

It's one thing to wake up outside in the middle of the night with a decapitated man for company. It's another to have no memory of how you got there - or who you are.

She might not know her own name but she knows that several people are out to get her. It could be because she has strange magical powers seemingly at her fingertips and is some kind of fabulous hero. But then why does she appear to inspire fear in so many? And who on earth is the sexy, green-eyed barman who apparently despises her? So many questions ... and so few answers.

At least one thing is for sure - the streets of Manchester have never met someone quite as mad as Madrona...

Book One - Box of Frogs

SHORTLISTED FOR THE KINDLE STORYTELLER AWARD 2018

Book Two - Quiver of Cobras

Book Three - Skulk of Foxes

The complete *City Of Magic* series

Charley is a cleaner by day and a professional gambler by night. She might be haunted by her tragic past but she's never thought of herself as anything or anyone special. Until, that is, things start to go terribly wrong all across the city of Manchester. Between plagues of rats, firestorms and the gleaming blue eyes of a sexy Scottish werewolf, she might just have landed herself in the middle of a magical apocalypse. She might also be the only person who has the ability to bring order to an utterly chaotic new world.

Book One - Shrill Dusk

Book Two - Brittle Midnight

Book Three - Furtive Dawn

9 781913 116378